PRAISE FOR

Paper Airplanes

"With depth and empathy, Tabitha Forney navigates the emotional wreckage left by tragedy, exploring questions of fate, self-destruction, and ultimately hope. *Paper Airplanes* is a lovely and moving novel."

—MARK HABER, author of *Reinhardt's Garden*

"This haunting novel captivated me from the beginning. Forney pulled me in with her gorgeous prose and a heroine who made my heart ache. I rarely cry when I read, but *Paper Airplanes* had me sobbing. This is the kind of book that comes around only once in a lifetime."

—LAURA HEFFERNAN, internationally best-selling author of *Finding Tranquility* and *Anna's Guide to Getting Even*

"As the Twin Towers fall on September 11th, Erin struggles through a world she neither recognizes nor understands. She begins a journey to find her missing husband and comes to realize that she has lost not only him but also herself. This is a compelling story of destr[illegible] and the slow process of self-discovery a[illegible]lly written debut novel that [illegible]orst nightmare imaginable: the [illegible]

—K. BLANTON BRENNER, [illegible] *Sky*

PAPER AIRPLANES

PAPER AIRPLANES

A Novel

TABITHA FORNEY

SHE WRITES PRESS

Published 2021
Printed in the United States of America
Print ISBN: 978-1-64742-177-9
E-ISBN: 978-1-64742-178-6
Library of Congress Control Number: 2021907085

For information, address:
She Writes Press
1569 Solano Ave #546
Berkeley, CA 94707

She Writes Press is a division of SparkPoint Studio, LLC.

Book design by Stacey Aaronson

"Don't Save Me" on page 116 is published with permission of poet Outspoken Bean.

To all the victims of 9/11, and to those they left behind.

May we never forget.

WARNING:

Content in the following prologue may be traumatic for some people.

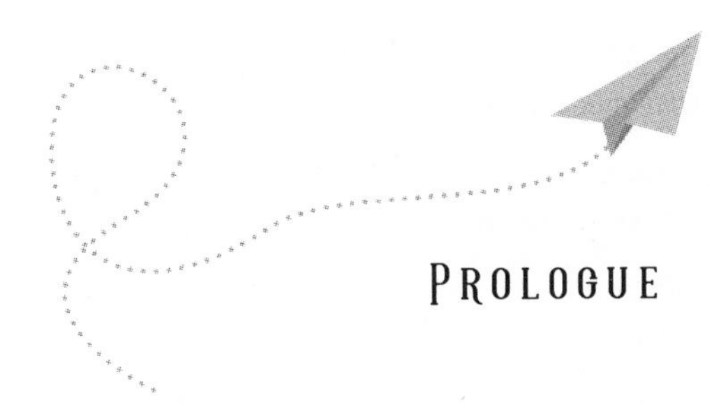

Prologue

A silver bullet with red, white, and blue stripes shone in the morning sun. Probably another plane taking off from LaGuardia, but it was flying low.

He ran a hand through still-wet hair, drank warm coffee, and flipped through the report on his desk. A trading software company going public. It'd be a huge coup, his first significant deal. There'd been conference calls and meetings. This call could seal it. He stood and paced, practicing his pitch, calming his nerves. He had space: people wearing headsets were trading on the far side of the floor but nobody near him, the rest of the team in a morning meeting he had to miss for the call.

He jotted a few notes, then checked the horizon. The plane was closer now. Too close.

A lot of things happened up here—lightning storms, bird flybys, hovering helicopters. But never planes at eye level.

Coming so fast.

Flying too low. It wouldn't clear the building.

Adrenaline rushed his veins and took his breath. Time slowed. In that space where an entire life should flash by, just one moment, frozen in time. Her skin soft and sweet. Half-lidded eyes, contented smile. Making love in the innocent slant of morning sun. He felt it viscerally, this ephemeral life. Moments slipping past and evaporating like raindrops.

The plane banked up. His eyes widened as the adrenaline hit. A swatch of dark in the cockpit—the pilot's hair?—coming for him.

He dove under a desk and curled into a fetal position. The building exploded.

Full-bodied maelstrom.

Skin, bones, skull reverberated under a shock wave of pressure.

Metal screeched on metal ripping into concrete.

The heavy tang of jet fuel and burning steel throttled his senses.

The building lurched, a roller coaster going over the precipice. The desk pitched over him. Keyboards, monitors, and chairs flew past. Blows to his shins, back, head. The floor buckled. Debris rained down.

He curled up tighter. Eyes pinned shut, jaw clenched.

He waited to die.

But the building didn't capsize. Instead it came back the other direction, like a boat in a raging storm. He curled around something heavy, what felt like a file drawer, metal and solid.

After an eternity the swaying stopped, noise abated. Everything went quiet.

He unfurled, heart pounding. Blinked and dug knuckles into eyes. The atmosphere was punctured and tainted, kerosene and metal and burning plastic. A quick patdown—no blood, no broken bones.

Lights were out, nothing in its place. Shattered computer

monitors, desks upended, wheels up on black office chairs. Paper floated in strangely silent air. The building's metal skeleton showed through broken layers of drywall on exterior walls. On the other side of the floor, a few hundred feet away where the traders had been, was a gaping chasm. Bundles of wire dangled from ceiling and busted from walls.

The faint whine of sirens in the distance.

Heat radiated from beneath. He climbed onto a desk and yelled for help, but nobody was there. Just an abyss, black with a faint orange glow.

He screamed again, louder. "Hey! Hello?"

Smoky, crackling silence.

Within moments, the heat intensified. He jumped down and leapt his way over debris, across the floor toward the exit signs, still backlit even though the power was out. Backup batteries, he remembered from a safety talk his first day. Also, there were stairwells. Three, maybe, in the core of the building.

The door of the first stairwell, the one he used to go up and down to the other floors when the elevators were too slow, was pinned shut, wouldn't budge. The second opened, but the stairs were impassable. A smoking, dimly lit scree field of drywall, wires, and debris. He couldn't find the third stairwell, on the side of the building where the floor was gone, caved in.

Stomach twisting, panic rising, he made his way back to the desk.

An office phone, not his, lay upside down on the floor. He put it right and yanked the handset, expecting nothing. But by some small miracle, there was a dial tone. The dull hum of normalcy comforted him. If only he could crawl through the line and escape.

He dialed, hard plastic buttons burning his fingers.

A woman answered. "911, this is Rosie. What's your emergency?"

"I'm in the World Trade Center. I think a plane hit us."

"What's your name, sir?"

"Daniel O'Connor."

"What floor are you on, and which tower?"

"One World Trade, the 101st floor."

"OK, sir. Units are coming. They're on their way up."

"The stairwells are blocked. Do you know if there's a way out?"

"Just sit tight. Help is coming."

"It's really hot. And there's a lot of smoke."

"Can you get on the floor? And put a wet towel over your mouth?"

"The floor is too hot. The room's filling with smoke. There's so much smoke."

"OK, sir. Help is on the way. I have to go now; we're getting a lot of calls. Stay down, breathe through a towel, and do whatever you have to do to stay alive. God be with you."

He nodded, confused. He hung up and dialed Erin. Incessant fast beep of a busy system. Again and again. Once, a distant, flat ring and then a woman's recorded voice, in Spanish, telling him his call could not be completed at this time.

Floor too hot to stand. Heat an entity, compressing him. Thick, acrid smoke burned his eyes. He dropped the phone.

Focus, stay calm.

He scanned again, looking for a way out. Twisted steel protruded twenty feet in front of him, like a broken bone. It seemed impossible for metal to bend like that. Along the side, white markings: A343-99-102. Decades ago someone knew what that number meant, where that beam would go.

His ears still rang from the cacophony—exploding concrete, shrieking metal, glass shattering.

Where the fuck did the plane come from? What did I do wrong? And what do I do now?

He crouched on the desk. Dialed Erin again. He'd be OK if he could hear her voice. They were in the middle of a stupid fight. He had to tell her he loved her. He hit redial again, again, again. The line beeped fast, overloaded circuits. His kingdom for a ring, her voice.

It was useless; he couldn't get through. He hurled the headset away. He yanked his shirttail over his face, breathing in scalding air. Heat curled into his head, brain, soul. Thoughts sizzled, broke apart, floated away like smoke.

Dry, incinerated ash around him, inside him. The building was a fucking furnace.

There had to be a way out.

The air smelled of jet fuel burning, rancid concrete.

Parachutes? Air packs?

The floor was a hot skillet, searing into his soles.

He shoved chairs, high-stepped around desks, over wires and smashed computers and chunks of debris.

Smoke writhed around him, obscuring his vision. The floor buckled and groaned under his feet.

Hail Mary, full of grace.

Flames licked at the carpet.

The Lord is with thee.

Black smoke squeezed his lungs. A chunk of floor collapsed in front of him, an inferno blasting from it.

Dizzy. Need oxygen.

He retreated to his desk. Hurled a computer monitor through the narrow window. Burning gray soot blew past and out. He jumped up, braced himself between concrete on either side, shoved his head and torso through the gap.

In front of him, glimpses of freedom. Buildings not burning, roads intact, cars driven by people not trapped. He tried to suck in fresh air from outside. Smoke rushed over, thick black coils taking escape. If only he could follow, float like a feather on wind.

He couldn't. But paper could.

Paper flotsam all around him. He grabbed the biggest piece he could find, flipped it over. Yanked open a drawer, grabbed a pen. Scribbled letters that formed words as fast as he could. Folded the best paper airplane of his life and sailed it out the broken glass, watched as it was swept away by smoke spiraling with sweet morning air. He watched it glide down until it was out of sight and prayed for a soft landing in the city streets. His words, at least, would be safe.

Units are coming. On their way up.

Sirens whined. Tiny red and blue lights flashed. The blades of a helicopter swooshed somewhere above. He waved his arms. Ripped off his white button-down shirt, yanked it side to side.

The sound retreated. His skin felt like it was melting.

Please, God. Not like this.

He tried to cough but couldn't get air.

Framed by jagged shards, blue sky peeked through shifting black haze.

Holy Mary, Mother of God.

His lungs were sandpaper, voice gone.

Pray for us sinners.

Thick, stifling soot rasped in and out of his chest, his lungs in a vice.

A fire-breathing demon behind him, fresh air and redemption before him.

Now and at the hour of our death.

Chapter One

November 27, 1999

A paper airplane hung in the afternoon air and glided to a landing in front of the park bench where Erin sat reading. It was a design she recognized, angles sharp and intentional. Daniel's paper airplanes were works of art, sleek and aerodynamic. She smiled, standing up and searching among the people walking, jogging, standing nearby, but couldn't find him. As it sank, the sun painted streaks of gold across the Hudson. Peals of laughter rang out from a knot of children playing a few hundred yards away. It could have been child's play, but something told her it was him.

In the years to come Erin would think back on this moment often, as we do later in life about the moments that define us. Dissecting why we make the decisions we make, choose the people we choose when, on paper, other people would do just as well. On paper, Daniel and Erin weren't necessarily suited—a girl from Texas and a boy from the Bronx—except, of course, that paper started it all. But how can one ever identify or sort out what makes one person attracted to another? It's chemistry or kismet or pheromones or the subtleties of facial structure, or some combination of it all. It's genetics and upbringing, nature and nurture and timing and choices made by you and the other person and a million other people before you that lead you to that one moment when you make your decision.

She said yes.

But what if she hadn't? What if, instead of her heart thrilling at the sight of a paper airplane flying toward her out of nowhere, she'd been scared, or hesitant, or impressed with his intrepidness but not at all ready? After all, before Daniel, she'd never imagined this moment. Never wondered what her new last name would be, never folded up those paper fortune-tellers in middle school to divine the number of kids she'd have and all their names. Never dreamed of planning her wedding or what her dress would look like. She might have said no, or not yet, or *Can I take a rain check?* Or what if she'd said yes but then dreamt dreams where her subconscious brought out her fears—dreams about sitting at a table with impossibly tall stacks of invitations to address, being chased into corners, wanting to flee but feeling weighted down, limbs mired in molasses? Maybe things would have turned out differently.

Then again, maybe they wouldn't have. We can't rewind. Fate is hard to challenge since we never know its contenders.

She reached for the airplane, breathless, and unfolded it. Pressed out the paper's creases. It said, in Daniel's handwriting: *I wish Erin James would marry me.*

She turned circles, laughing, searching for him. "Daniel!" People in the park walked dogs and rollerbladed past. Diners at the outdoor café across the sidewalk sat under green umbrellas eating farm-fresh salads and sipping white wine. "Dan-IEL!"

He emerged from bushes behind a fence separating the

sidewalk from the café. Catapulted over the fence with one arm and strode toward her. Crooked smile, five o'clock shadow, red roses in hand.

Grinning, she launched herself into him. "Yes!" she squealed. He was warm and smelled of leather and fresh air and aftershave. She could've melted into him forever.

"Yes?" he teased, eyes twinkling. "I haven't asked a question yet." He pushed her away, dropped to one knee, pulled a small blue box from the pocket of his leather jacket. People slowed down, heads turned in their direction. Earnest green eyes looked up at Erin, hands outstretched with a diamond. "Erin James, will you marry me?"

The world crawled in slow motion. Her heart was floating, buoyed by helium. She grabbed his hand with hers and nodded like a bobblehead doll. "Yes!"

He smiled and popped to his feet, leaning in. The kiss was slow and deep. Around them, people squealed and clapped, cheered and whistled. Daniel pulled Erin in close, burying her face in his neck. Peeking out from over his shoulder, she blinked through happy tears, smiling at the crowd and feeling more content than she could remember.

Above them, the contrail of a real airplane cut a hazy line across a cloudless sky.

It's how they met. A paper airplane.

April, sophomore year. She was sitting cross-legged on a blanket under a pink magnolia planted on a slow rise. Her back was propped against the trunk and she was studying. Wearing a white sleeveless T-shirt and jeans. She'd seen him before, in Econ

101 the previous year. Tuesdays and Thursdays at 9:00 a.m. He was the one who came in late and sat in the back, a ball cap hiding most of his face. She was the one on time who sat in front, glancing his way as he walked in and took his seat. There was always a moment when their eyes met, and she was always the one who blinked first. He was not like the Ken doll boys from Dallas. He seemed gritty and real, rough around the edges.

Later, he told Erin she was different from the pale, soft Irish girls he knew from the Bronx. For one, she wore lipstick.

Daniel sat about thirty yards away from her, under another tree. It was the first time she'd seen him outside of Econ. She was trying to study for finals, but her eyes moved like magnets toward him. A few times he was looking at her at the same time and she turned away quickly, as if he were a hot fire. Meeting his eyes would burn.

After a while, she lay back on the blanket, pages covering her chest, and closed her eyes. She tried to fall asleep, but all she could think about was whether he was still there and how she was going to meet him. She wanted him to come over and talk to her, but she didn't know how to make it happen. Eyes closed, she focused all her mental energy on him. Trying to communicate telepathically.

From a reclined position, she cracked an eye at him. Rummaging around in his backpack, he pulled out a piece of paper and a pen. Jotted something down. Then he pulled out a book, laid the paper on top, and began to fold it. In half, then on the sides, turning the paper this way and that. He pressed creases with his thumbnail, meticulously making each edge sharp and smooth. It took several minutes. When he was done, the paper airplane in his hand was angular and streamlined.

He dug something else out of his backpack, then glanced around as if to make sure nobody was watching. His eyes landed on her. She closed her eyes, pretending to be asleep. When she glanced at him sideways again, he was popping a lighter. He set the paper aflame and sent it sailing into the air in the same practiced motion. The aerodynamics were good. It sailed away from him, higher than she would have thought.

A gust snuffed out the fire and sent the smoking airplane even farther away, toward Erin.

He dashed in pursuit of his missive, eyes wide open. The same wind whipped her organic chemistry handouts into the air. She jumped up, stomped on them, and tucked them under her books. Took a few steps toward the boy and the paper and held out her palm. His plane was about to crash. She leaned out a little more and caught it just in time.

She opened her palm to look at it, and for a moment, they both looked down at it. Then heat seared her skin and she dropped it, still smoldering. He put it out with the toe of his sneaker.

He lunged toward her to grab her hand and with it, her heart. "Are you OK?"

Her hand in his, she looked down at a small red spot on her palm. She nodded. "Fine."

She pulled her hand back and wrapped her jacket tighter, shivering. The wind had settled, leaving behind an awkward silence. They stared at each other. Erin looked down at the half-burned paper airplane on the ground and picked it up. "What is it?" she asked.

"It was a paper airplane."

"I know. But why did you light it on fire?"

His face reddened, soft green eyes crinkling with embarrassment.

"It was a burning wish," he said with a shrug and a confident smile. Erin's heart skipped a beat as he looked into her eyes. "Usually my burning wishes don't go so far. I'll admit, I was trying to get your attention. Looks like I did that and more." He glanced down at her hand, holding the crumpled plane.

She laughed. "You could've just said hi."

The airplane was singed on the sides, but the paper was still intact. She wanted to unfold it and read what he wrote. Instead, she handed the crumpled airplane back to him, lingering a moment as their hands touched.

She narrowed her eyes and smiled at him. "What does it say?" she asked.

He shook his head and smiled as he ripped apart what was left of the paper airplane, but his eyes stayed with her. "Maybe I'll tell you one day."

One day. As though they had a future.

Erin giggled, and that was that. They became inseparable. There was something about the two of them that fit. It was easy, comfortable. No need to pretend or posture or compete. They studied together on blankets on the lawn, ate their meals together, went to parties hand in hand. Erin thought Daniel could do anything. Work a room, fix what was broken, melt a glacier with his smile. He played for the Princeton baseball team, and she went to all of his games. On the field, he was intense, authoritative, powerful. She'd never known anyone from the Bronx before. She always thought it was a scary place, somewhere you went if you wanted to get shot. It gave him a tough-guy aura.

Before Erin met Daniel, it seemed like she had everything, even to her. The pampered only child of a successful businessman and his model-perfect wife. But in reality, she'd been miserable. Anxious and stressed most of the time, as if life were an obstacle course—a series of hoops to jump through in order to receive the carrot at the end, only to start over again the next day. Erin grew up with certain implied expectations. She was expected to be beautiful, ambitious, and accomplished. She was expected to be smart and athletic. Where some families have multiple children to spread the expectations around—the smart one, the athletic one, the beautiful one—Erin had to be all of it wrapped up in one. No opportunity to consider what she thought, how she felt, or what she wanted out of life. The blueprint was drawn up for her at birth.

The first Thanksgiving after they started dating, Daniel went to Dallas with Erin over the Thanksgiving break. They spent four days with her parents, Fitz and Eleanor James. It was Daniel's first trip to Texas, and he experienced what could only be described as culture shock. He took in the wide, manicured lawns with seasonally planted color, stately mansions, big hair and rhinestones, and the occasional bullhorn hood ornament and told Erin he felt like he was in a foreign country. Summoning a tidbit from her fourth-grade field trip to Austin, Erin told Daniel that Texas had indeed been a sovereign nation for a decade in the 1800s, called the Republic of Texas, so he wasn't far off.

On the Wednesday before Thanksgiving, the day after they flew into DFW from LaGuardia, they woke up, had breakfast and coffee, and drove to Valley View mall to get out of Eleanor's way. It wasn't that she was cooking. Eleanor didn't cook much. Instead she'd buy a Greenberg smoked turkey and order the traditional sides like cornbread stuffing, mashed potatoes, green bean casserole, and rolls from the Junior League. Her culinary contributions were limited to boiling cranberries for the sauce and making two pies—one pumpkin, and one chocolate cream —which, of course, she wouldn't eat. But all that had been done before Erin and Daniel got there. On the Wednesday before Thanksgiving, Eleanor busied herself with polishing silver, setting the table, and making sure the decorations were in place and on trend. Spode Woodland china with matching brown rattan chargers, sterling silver cutlery, crystal wine glasses, engraved napkin rings, calligraphed place cards. She had a housekeeper, Liza, to help her of course, but overseeing everything was a job in itself.

Watching everything, Daniel said to Erin, "But there are only four of us."

Erin laughed. "It doesn't matter. She'd do this if we were twenty or three. She has nothing else to do." Rather than focusing on what really mattered, which might cause the pain of introspection, Eleanor was a master at making the surface appear perfect.

When they got to the mall and parked in the wide-open lot, Daniel emerged from the car and gazed up at the glowing orb in the sky. It was sunny and clear and the sky was a bowl of golden light. He took off his jacket and tilted his face upward, closed his eyes and spread out his arms.

"This is amazing," he said, soaking it in.

Erin smiled, viewing the flat asphalt mall parking lot with

renewed appreciation. She knew what he meant. In New York in the winter, people were starved for sunlight. As the days got shorter, sunlight became a rare commodity, each building-flanked street getting only a small ration of the sun's energy before it moved on to the next. Erin was struck in that moment by Daniel's ability to stop and enjoy the things that most people took for granted. The sun. The sky. Warmth. Life with Daniel was like viewing the world through the lens of a child, wowed by the smallest miracles.

On Thanksgiving Day, after they ate and Fitz had fallen asleep in his recliner while the Cowboys battled the Dolphins, Daniel came into the kitchen, where Erin was helping her mother put away the last of the Spode Woodland china. He was wearing a Princeton T-shirt and black basketball shorts, and he was holding a football.

"Let's go," he said to Erin, flipping the football up into the air and catching it again, over and over, as Eleanor winced and glanced around, presumably to gauge how much breakable china was in harm's way.

"Where?" Erin asked.

"I saw a park a few blocks away," he said. "Let's go toss the pigskin around."

Erin's first instinct was to tell Daniel she didn't know how to toss a pigskin around, but her next thought was *How hard could it be?*

Eleanor looked at Daniel and frowned. "We don't play football ourselves," she said. "We just watch it on television."

"Come on," Daniel said, grabbing a roll from the basket as

Eleanor transferred them into Tupperware. "You too," he said, waving toward Eleanor, his voice muffled with bread. "It'll be fun."

Erin looked at her mother, taking in her beige cashmere sweater, pressed wool slacks, Gucci flats, gelled fingernails. And then she laughed. "Daniel, Eleanor James will not be playing football in the park down the street."

He was undaunted. "Come on, Eleanor, it'll be fun. We'll get Fitz to come too." He turned to yell over his shoulder, "Fitz! Are you ready for some football?" but the only reply from the family room was a light snore.

There were so many things technically wrong with this. Cajoling Eleanor after she'd said no. Imagining Fitz might go outside and play football when the Cowboys were on. Calling Fitz and Eleanor by their first names. Even though Erin did it, she was their daughter. They'd never told Daniel he could call them by their first names. If he were following the rules of a good southern boy, he'd call them Mr. and Mrs. James until well after he married their daughter, and he would call them by their first names only after they said to him at least three times, preferably more and not while drinking, "Oh, Daniel. Call me Eleanor," or "Son, it's about time you called me Fitz." But Daniel wasn't a southern boy, and he didn't know the rules. Or maybe he didn't care.

Judging by the scowl on Eleanor's face, she didn't approve. But it only made Erin like him more. She never would've dreamed of explaining to him the rules of a good southern boy.

Eleanor looked at Erin like she'd lost her mind, even though it was Daniel pushing the football, not Erin. Erin grinned and kept her eyes on Daniel as she said, "Come on, Eleanor. It'll be fun."

"Erin Elizabeth James!" Eleanor said, sounding actually offended. "You cannot seriously tell me you're going to play football outside in some pickup game? It's cold and dirty out there. What will the neighbors think?"

Daniel grinned back at Erin. "They'll think we're having a great time."

"What about your nails?" Eleanor asked, taking Erin's hand in hers and rubbing the smooth surfaces. They'd gone to get gel tips on Tuesday after they arrived, Eleanor having been horrified at the rough, natured state of Erin's hands. Since Erin had started dating Daniel, she'd let her nails go, preferring short, filed nails instead of the unwieldy thick gels. But Erin had acquiesced and had been regretting it ever since.

"Who cares?" Erin said, walking toward her bedroom to change out of her sweater into a T-shirt and shorts. "They only get in my way anyway."

In that moment, Erin knew that while this house may have been where she grew up, Daniel was home to her.

Instead of focusing on the cover, as most people in her life did, Daniel focused on the girl inside. He made her see there could be joy in living itself, not just in accomplishing things. He cared about her not only for what she looked like or how smart she was but also for who she was. To Erin, there was something familiar and comforting about Daniel. Genuine husband material, her friends called him. Solid and dependable, as grounded as she was volatile. The yang to her yin. He could always make her laugh.

Once they became a couple, they had plans for their life together. Manhattan was the here and now, but what they really wanted was a house in the country with horses and chickens and a garden and a picket fence. A tire swing and baby goats. Erin had an irrational Hallmark vision of her future, and now the man to go with it. She didn't know what she'd do for a living, maybe have an organic farm, or teach aerobics in town, or own a bakery where she created photo-worthy confections. Maybe all three. It didn't matter. What mattered was that it would be as far from her childhood as she could get, physically and symbolically. Daniel was on board, but he wanted to make enough money first to pay for the house and the kids' college funds so that they didn't have to worry about making enough to live on in the country. Their plan was to buckle down for ten or twenty years and make enough to retire early and live happily ever after.

They graduated from Princeton and spent most of the summer traveling. That fall, Erin went to law school at Harvard while Daniel stayed in New York to work for an investment bank. It was dicey, being apart. There were ups and downs. But the night before her graduation, she skipped the parties to spend the evening with Daniel, and they both knew they'd survived.

When he asked her to marry him, it reflected how they met. That paper airplane he sent burning, flying into the April afternoon, seared into her palm. He never told her what was written inside, but she liked to think it was a burning wish for her.

Chapter Two

September 3, 2001

"I'm sorry, Jess. I can't."

This was the second time Erin had said these words during this conversation. She was trying to hang up, because she had a client on the other line and a meeting with a partner in three minutes. She squirmed in her chair. She'd needed a bathroom break for the past thirty minutes. The red light on line one blinked at her steadily, implying with each pulse that she was a bad lawyer. She stared out the window of her Times Square office toward the southern tip of the island. Afternoon sun bounced off the World Trade Center and shone off a row of windows, about where Daniel's floor was. He worked at Schaeffer McKesson, an investment bank.

He told her once, when she was visiting his office one wintery Saturday afternoon, that he could see her south-facing Times Square office from where he worked. That he'd be watching over her. She'd never forget that view. Manhattan looking tiny and insignificant, the Bronx to the north, Queens stretching across the East River, Brooklyn below Queens. New Jersey on the other side with its smokestacks and warehouses. The Hudson cut a border from sleepy towns north, under the George Washington Bridge and west of the World Trade Center on its way to the bay. Daniel said Earth's curve was just visible from that far up, but Erin couldn't see it. The twins flung shadows across Manhattan, across the East River and into Queens, claiming dominion like giants in the sky. She didn't know how people went to work every day that far up in the clouds.

"You have to. I'm desperate. I can't go alone, and the trip is already paid for."

"Can't we switch it to next weekend? It's Daniel's mom's sixtieth birthday party on Sunday. I can't miss it."

"It'd cost way too much to switch." Jess huffed. "Let me get this straight. You're going to attend your mother-in-law's birthday party at her cramped trilevel in the Bronx, where his family who doesn't like you is going to serve cake and tea and no wine, rather than go on an all-expense-paid trip to Mallorca—which is in Spain, by the way, which, in case you don't know, is in Europe—with me, your best friend, who's currently suffering from a desperate case of post-breakup depression?" Jess paused for effect.

The red light continued to blink at Erin accusingly.

"I thought about slitting my wrists or drowning myself when I was taking a bath last night. Did I tell you that?"

Erin laughed. She couldn't hang up on Jess now she'd mentioned suicide. "Jess, come on. Marc's not worth killing yourself."

Jess could be overly dramatic, but the thought had probably crossed her mind. Until two days ago, she'd thought Marc was The One, but on Saturday night he dumped her for a Giants cheerleader he met on the Jersey Shore over the summer. Twenty-two years old and fake everything—boobs, teeth, tan. Poor Jess couldn't compete. Yesterday, one of Marc's friends told Jess he'd been paying thousands of dollars for hookers in Vegas when he was supposed to be on business trips. Insult to injury. The trip to Mallorca was supposed to be a romantic getaway for their one-year anniversary. She was hoping he'd propose. Instead, he told her to take a friend. Consolation prize.

"I wonder how one would kill one's self in Spain?"

"Jess, stop!"

"Probably by leaping off the balcony. It's a five-story hotel, I think."

"OK, come on. Don't do this. I have to go. I have a client waiting and a meeting. Can we talk about this later?"

"Fine. But I mentioned it's paid for, right?"

"Yeah, you mentioned that." A pause while Erin considered. Honestly, it was a no-brainer. Five days and four nights in Mallorca with Jess sounded fabulous. Erin had never been to Spain. But Daniel was going to be upset about it. "It's not that I want to be at my mother-in-law's party, but Daniel wants me there."

"You're not newlyweds anymore. It's been over a year."

"Barely."

"How long does the honeymoon last?"

"Daniel and his siblings have been planning this for a few months. He'll be so upset. Can we please go next weekend?"

Jess's sigh was audible. "The change fees would be way too much. I've checked. Plus, we can't get the same type of room. I'll call somebody else if you can't do it. Maybe Joni can go. But I'd rather it be you."

Erin chewed on her bottom lip and stood up, leaning over the phone's cradle. Ready to hang up. One minute to her meeting. Red light still blinking. She was going to be late for all of it.

She really wanted to go to Mallorca. She glared at Daniel's building, considering. Surely he'd get over it. It was just his mother's birthday. Jess was right, it was going to be a miserable afternoon. None of his family liked her very much. No matter what she did, it was never right or good enough. Daniel was the O'Connor golden boy. Nobody would have been good enough for him.

Erin shook the black liquid in the fortune-teller on her desk, a gag gift from some girlfriends that she used when she couldn't make decisions. She didn't like to admit how much stock she put in the opinions of this randomized trinket.

All signs point to yes.

Except.

Why did she feel guilty? Getting married didn't involve putting on handcuffs, for most people. It didn't mean she couldn't travel without him. Just last month, they'd gone to Napa for their first anniversary and had a wonderful time. It was her turn to go somewhere with friends. And Jess needed her. Daniel's mother wouldn't miss her. To the contrary, Helen would be thrilled to have her favorite son all to herself. Erin would be doing her a favor.

The red light of her waiting client blinked at her, about the same rate as her heartbeat. Her meeting was starting. And she still had to pee, bad.

"OK."

"OK? OK what?"

"OK, I'll go."

"Really? You need to talk to Daniel?"

"No. I mean, I'll tell him. But I don't need his permission."

Jess squealed. "Yes! I'll email you the itinerary. We leave Saturday night on the red-eye."

Erin's cabbie wound his way up the West Side Highway, careening in and out of lanes, honking at bikers and pedestrians. The energy of this place—so alive. Three million people moved in and out of Manhattan every single day with all of their agendas and needs. Water, food, transportation, toilets. From the layers in the bedrock that supported human life to the tip of the tallest building—the World Trade Center—and every layer in between. Erin saw a diagram once of what lay beneath the city—it went eight hundred feet down. Deep water tunnels at the bottom, topped by sewers, subways, underground shopping, gas and steam lines, water, cable, electrical. And then the street layer where it was all happening—from the pedestrians to the delivery trucks, cabs and private cars, motorcycles, harried businesspeople, messengers on bikes, tourists and moms with baby carriages. At any given intersection they were all streaming through, constantly, perpetually, with apparent chaos, but underlying it was some invisible system keeping everything in check. Like a symphony with no conductor, playing the melody of New York City.

Erin could do anything, be anyone, go anywhere in this city. She loved the exhilaration, the pace, the challenge of it. Walking out her door in the morning, feeling the crisp, cool air, seeing everyone on the move constantly. Desiderata for a good life sold at every corner—Starbucks and a nail salon and a sushi place next door to a doctor's office and a museum and a theater. She described it to her baffled Texan friends as Life: Concentrated.

Better than a jolt of caffeine. She breathed it in, felt it seep into her marrow.

The car pulled up to her apartment building at 79th and Columbus, across from the Museum of Natural History. A thirty-one-story apartment complex built in 1986. Living on the Upper West Side was her idea. If Daniel had his way, they'd have lived in the Bronx, Woodlawn Heights. More room, less money. But if she was going to be a New Yorker, she was going to live in Manhattan.

Orlando, the doorman, stood on the sidewalk in front of the propped-open door. When he saw her, he hurried to open the cab door.

"Evening, Mrs. O'Connor. Welcome home."

"Thanks, Orlando." He followed her into the building, where an elevator waited. She stepped on and pushed the button.

"You have a good evening, Mrs. O'Connor."

"You too, Orlando."

At the twenty-second floor she got off and walked to their apartment, number 2201. She dug through her purse for a key and realized she didn't have one. She must have forgotten it when she rushed out that morning. She knocked on her own door, hoping Daniel was home.

Within a few seconds, he threw open the door. "Hi, hot stuff." He wore a T-shirt and running shorts, a can of Budweiser in his left hand. In the living room, another crushed can lay on the coffee table next to a bag of tortilla chips and a jar of salsa, along with a few crumpled tissues. The room smelled like someone had diced a raw onion in a locker room. The television blared commercials.

"Home early?"

"Yeah, work was slow today." He gave her a kiss then walked back to the couch and fell into it, flipping channels.

"What time'd you get home?"

"Couple hours ago."

"What've you been doing?"

He paused the TiVo. "Caught the end of the game."

"Mets?"

"Yep."

"Did they win?"

"Yep."

He lay back on the couch, still flipping channels. She couldn't help herself. "I don't get how you can just sit here watching TV when all the city is happening around you."

He paused the television, jumped up, grabbed her by the waist, and nuzzled her neck. She fought the impulse to pull away. It was his love language. But sometimes she just wanted to talk.

He kissed her neck again, then looked at her, green eyes mischievous. "I'm so glad I have you to save me from my idle ways."

She laughed, as she always did when he looked at her that way, then cleared the chips and salsa from the coffee table. "Just turn off the TV and open some wine. I'm making dinner."

"Got it." Daniel walked over to the stereo and put in a CD. Alabama—*Feels So Right*. It was ironic that she tried her hardest to get away from Texas, then managed to find the only man at Princeton who loved country music. As she was picking up empty beer cans, he grabbed her and pulled her in close, cans clattering to the floor as they two-stepped across the wood parquet. Through the south-facing windows Manhattan gleamed, dusky and beginning to sparkle with lights. Streaks of orange and pink slashed through low clouds in the glimpses of horizon visible from their apartment.

She squeezed his left hand with her right and laid her right ear on his chest. He smelled like Daniel—eau de cedar and cotton and beer. When the song was over, he twirled her around a few times. She curtsied and he bowed. "Love in the First Degree" began to play, and Daniel disappeared into the bedroom. Erin took it as an opportunity to take out Alabama and put in Soundgarden—Alabama was the only country band she liked, but even they had their limits. Then she went into the kitchen, opened a bottle of cab and poured a glass, and started pulling things out of the refrigerator.

As she sliced and pounded chicken breasts, raw and slimy with streaks of red, she considered how to tell Daniel about the trip. When he came back to the kitchen, he opened the refrigerator and grabbed another beer, this time a Negra Modelo. He popped off the cap with a bottle opener and shot the cap into the trash can like he was shooting a free throw, then hopped up on the counter and watched Erin prep dinner.

She tossed the chicken breasts into the hot skillet and washed her hands. As hot water and bubbles ran into the drain, she steeled herself. "Hey, I told you Marc dumped Jess a few days ago, right?"

"Can't say I'm surprised. Never liked him much."

"They had planned a trip to Mallorca. Jess thought he was going to propose."

Daniel took a swig of beer. "Obviously that's not gonna happen."

Erin pulled vegetables out of the refrigerator and rinsed them. "Yeah, no. Poor Jess. But the trip to Mallorca is paid for, and Marc's letting Jess have it. So she invited me. Isn't that great? I won't have to pay for anything but meals."

"That's fantastic. When are you going?"

She chopped off zucchini ends and cleared her throat. "We leave Saturday night on the red-eye."

Daniel set his beer bottle down on the counter. "Saturday? But my mom's birthday party is Sunday."

"Nobody will miss me. Your family barely tolerates me."

"That's not true."

Erin pushed the zucchini into another skillet, grabbed an onion and chopped its ends off with a couple good whacks. "Yes, it is. You know it is." As she sliced and diced, she squinched her eyes against the sting. She didn't blame his family. They were a big, raucous Catholic family from the Bronx, and she was the only child of southern, self-absorbed WASPs. They couldn't have been more different. While opposites attract in romance, that didn't hold with in-laws.

"Fine, I won't try to convince you. But I love you. And I want you there."

"I'll get her a really nice present. And write her a card."

"My sister's been planning this party for months. A lot of people I want you to meet will be there."

"Like who?"

"Well, family and friends. Close family friends."

"I've met all your family and most of their friends."

"They'll think there's something wrong with our marriage if you don't come."

She turned to look at him. "I'll think there's something wrong with our marriage if you force me to stay."

Daniel squared his jaw and looked up at the ceiling. It was a thing he did when he was angry. It made all of the muscles in his neck tense and thicken. It also made him look sexy, which was counterproductive for him and his anger, but Erin had never told him that.

She paused and sifted through her thoughts, knife aloft and pointed at Daniel. After a pause and a deep breath, she decided to go for humor. "Are you really asking me to pass up a free trip to Spain with my best friend so that I can hang out in the Bronx with Helen O'Connor?"

It was the wrong thing to say. A bolt of hurt shot through his eyes. He didn't have to say it. She knew what he was thinking. *You think you're too good for my family*. It was a little bit true. Though she fought it, she couldn't completely shed her upbringing. Fitz and Eleanor James had laid the circuitry of her brain, and no matter how hard she tried to rewire, the infrastructure was already in place.

Erin put down the knife. "I'm sorry. It's not that I don't want to go with you. It's just that I can't believe you'd ask me to stay here for that when I could go to Spain. That's all."

He avoided her eyes. "I thought marriage meant not being lonely anymore. And besides, I thought we decided to start trying."

Erin backed away from him. "Oh, so that's what this is all about? We agreed to have children, so I can never travel without you again?"

"That's not what I said."

"I have a life, Daniel. It didn't end when I got married, and it won't end when I have kids." Erin grabbed the cutting board and tossed it into the sink, onions and all. Pulled the skillet off the stove and threw that in the sink on top of the cutting board, where it sizzled as cold water droplets met hot metal. She wiped her hands of the mess and smiled at him. "You can make your own dinner," she said, walking away. "I'm out."

In hindsight, Daniel had been more certain about marriage than Erin had been. From what she saw, marriage was a convenient arrangement between a woman and a man where the woman received a home and the bills paid while the man got to have a life outside the home, including but not limited to a career, regular golf outings, and other women in discreet doses. It went mostly unacknowledged, but Erin had been eleven when one of Fitz's women showed up at the house and knocked on the door. Erin had answered. The woman, who was tall and dark haired, smiled a fake smile and asked, while looking past Erin, if her mama was home. Erin knew from the moment she saw the woman's thick makeup, unnaturally white teeth, cleavage, and high heels, as well as the nervous way she gazed over Erin's head into the house beyond, that this wasn't one of her mother's friends or a package delivery or someone whose car had broken down and who needed to use the phone.

It was a Saturday afternoon. Erin went to get her mother, who'd been lying in her bedroom, drapes drawn and white-noise maker on, clutching her head and claiming a migraine. Fitz was away on a hunting trip with business associates in south Texas. Eleanor had protested but Erin persisted, rocking her by her shoulder, until her mother got up and emerged from her cave. When Eleanor peeked out the side window and saw the woman outside, she gasped and told Erin to go to her room. But Erin wasn't about to miss what the woman had to say. She obediently walked away but then quietly doubled back, tiptoeing until she was just outside the foyer.

She'd never forget the conversation that followed. The woman, who said her name was Brenda, proceeded to tell a stunned Eleanor that Fitz was a cheating bastard who'd told Brenda he was divorced and his name was Frank when he met her on a Southwest flight from Dallas to Chicago. She was the flight attendant. Their affair lasted six months. He told her he was from Houston and came to Dallas often for business, about every two weeks. Brenda said she found out the truth when she waited and followed him after one of their hotel rendezvous, watching as he drove his Mercedes to a sprawling mansion in Highland Village and parked in the three-car garage. It took her a few months to confirm he was married and had a child. Brenda said she decided to tell Eleanor out of concern for her and her daughter, unable to remain silent any longer. She apologized profusely while claiming it wasn't her fault.

Eleanor, silent and reserved while Brenda went through her lengthy recitation, waited until she was done.

"Are you finished?" she asked.

Brenda nodded. "Yes," she said.

"Well, thank you for your time," Eleanor said, just before she slammed the heavy wooden door in Brenda's face and locked all the locks and set the alarm. She took a deep breath and pushed her palms down her sides to smooth her blouse, then turned and walked back into her cold, dark room, closing the door and locking it too.

When Fitz came back from his hunting trip late the next afternoon, a dinner of roasted chicken and potatoes was waiting in the oven, table set, wine glasses already filled. Erin had never seen her mother as engaged in the table conversation as she was that night, as Fitz told stories about the quail hunt, how he'd shot the most quail and also bagged the three-year contract from the client he'd been entertaining. Erin had sat quiet the entire meal, listening and watching her mother's face, but there was no sign of the trauma she expected to see there.

With her parents as her model, Erin didn't know what a healthy relationship looked like. When she looked at the future, she wasn't married with children. But when Daniel asked, she'd have regretted saying no. That felt like enough of a sacrifice for now.

Erin knew that Daniel wanted kids. Four or five of them. A big family like his, bursting at the seams with chaos and noise. She thought it was just talk though, that eventually he'd see reason. Change his mind, or give her time to establish her career first. She was only twenty-seven, and in New York that was way too young to start a family. But last month in Napa on their one-year anniversary, Daniel had pushed the issue. Erin demurred, tried to change the subject, because having a baby wasn't yet on her radar. The thought of it made her hyperventilate. Erin was afraid of being a mother. She didn't know how to do it right.

They had fought. And in the end she agreed, grudgingly, to get off the pill. But it was just to end the argument because she hated arguing with him. She didn't really mean it. And now it felt a little like someone took a lasso and threw it loosely around her neck, with a smile and an *attagirl.*

✧

Against the advice of all marital experts, Erin and Daniel went to bed angry Monday night. All week things between them were tense, neither willing to apologize.

Saturday came, and they still hadn't hashed it out. Daniel woke up before Erin did and snuck out early to run in the park. She left before he came home. In the spot on the table by the door where they left notes for each other, she left a yellow Post-it.

D — Went to the gym. E

Paper notes, old school. Even with email and cell phones, it was still the way they liked to communicate. Daniel's were always folded like tiny yellow paper airplanes, while Erin's were flat and plain. They only ever used their first initials. But usually, they signed off with *Love.* This time, she didn't.

When she got back, there was a little airplane next to her note. She unfolded it.

E — Gone to work. D

After the gym, Erin cleaned the apartment and packed for her trip. She was leaving for the airport at 5:00 p.m. to catch the red-eye to Madrid out of JFK. She couldn't believe Daniel was working all day on the day she was supposed to leave. It wasn't unusual for him to work on Saturdays, but still. She thought he would want to see her off.

When her bags were packed and it was time to go, she took one last look around the apartment, spotless and clean as it always was when she left for a trip, and closed and locked the door.

Out on the street, cloudy and dull air gave the day a lifeless, failure-to-launch quality. As she followed Orlando and her suitcase to the intersection of 72nd and Columbus, she looked around, half expecting to see Daniel's long stride coming toward her. She could've called him, but stubborn pride prevented it. He could've called her too.

Orlando stood halfway into the first lane, looking to his left for a cab. On the wide sidewalk across the street, a man working a food cart hawked hot dogs and roasted nuts. People jogged, biked, walked their dogs. A group of tourists emerged from the museum grounds looking tired and disheveled, holding maps and pointing in various directions. Cars streamed by, finally one of them a cab with its numbers lit. Orlando, fingers in mouth, let out an earsplitting whistle. The tourists across the street had their hands up, waving, but the cab crossed four lanes of traffic and screeched to a halt in front of Orlando instead.

Erin dug into her purse, searching for singles to give Orlando. When she pulled out the wad of cash, a gold tube of lipstick clattered to the sidewalk. Estée Lauder Rich Red. She had that particular brand of lipstick with her always, always the same shade of red. Daniel told her it was one of the first things he noticed about her. Tall girl, blond hair, red lips. She never left her dorm room without it, which made her a bit of a novelty at Princeton. One of her freshman-year suite mates, a crunchy girl from New Hampshire named Connie, made a snide remark while watching Erin apply lipstick one night before a party. Something about how trying to take Texas out of the girl was like trying to take chewing gum out of big hair. After that, Erin made it a point never to be without it, and to apply it slowly and carefully in front of Connie.

Erin reached down to the sidewalk to pick up the lipstick, but someone else got there first.

"I got it," he said.

Their eyes met, and she realized it was him. Daniel. Her

heart beat overtime. He still took her breath away. She smiled at him.

Orlando was loading her suitcase into the trunk. It was almost time to go.

Erin reached her hand out for the lipstick. Daniel flipped it into the air and caught it with a swipe, out of her reach. "Think I'll hold on to this," he taunted with a grin. "Put it on a blow-up doll and take her to the party. Nobody'll notice it's not you."

She tilted her head at him and shrugged. Tried not to laugh. "Whatever floats your boat. Maybe the blow-up doll will keep you warm at night."

Erin was sure she had another tube packed, since she tucked them everywhere. Every purse she owned, random drawers in the apartment, in the console of the red Mercedes parked in a garage five blocks from the apartment for $476 a month, which they hadn't used in three months but she insisted on keeping just in case. A girl from Texas needed independence, the possibility of open road before her and no one to stop her.

Suitcase loaded, Orlando stood next to the waiting cab, back door open. Through his rearview mirror, the cabbie looked at Erin impatiently. The tourists across the street waved at cabs with fares and lights out, exasperated when they didn't stop.

"Just one second!" Erin said to the cabbie, then turned back to Daniel.

Daniel slid Erin's lipstick into his front jeans pocket and leaned in. Amid the stench of the subway that passed beneath them, rumbling hot and grimy under their feet, she caught a whiff of his aftershave. He was wearing his Grateful Dead T-shirt and jeans. God, how she wanted to kiss him. Tell Orlando she'd forgotten something and drag Daniel upstairs for fifteen minutes. But no time to spare. She hugged him and offered her cheek instead.

He took a step back. “What, no kiss?”

Erin smiled and pointed at her red lips. “This has to last the whole trip.”

She ducked into the cab, closed the door, and put up a hand to wave goodbye as the cab pulled away from the curb. Daniel stood watching as the cab headed south on Columbus. Erin stared back at him until he disappeared behind a stream of cars and buses and she couldn’t see him anymore.

As she rolled into JFK, she dug into her purse to freshen her lipstick but couldn’t find a tube. After the taxi peeled away, she opened her suitcase on the sidewalk, pulled out her makeup bag, and dug through that too. With a sinking feeling, she realized the lipstick now in Daniel’s pocket had been her only one. And she was pretty sure the airport didn’t carry Estée Lauder.

Chapter Three

September 11, 2001

Erin dug her toes in warm sand and swirled the last of her margarita. The straw roof of the palapa shading her beach chair rustled in the wind, carrying an earthy wheat aroma. Gentle waves of turquoise licked the white sand in front of her. A seagull cried over the faint sound of the surf. In the distance where sea met sky, the world appeared all blue. The weather was breezy and balmy, and by all appearances, her cares should've been far away.

But they weren't. She was still unsettled over the fight with Daniel. And she missed him. Vacations without Daniel weren't the same now they were married.

In the warm sun, tequila and salt made her fingers swell. Her wedding rings dug into her flesh, as if punishing her for being there. She pulled them off and slipped them into her bag.

The Gipsy Kings crooned from unseen speakers. Jess swayed in her lounge chair. "I love Mexican music!"

Erin grimaced. "It's Spanish, not Mexican. We're in Spain. And the Gipsy Kings are French."

"Whatever!" Jess was on her third margarita, maybe fourth.

She was slurring her words, the letters running together like cursive.

The music stopped for an extended pause just as the woman serving beach drinks walked by. Jess swept her arm up. "*Más música, por favor! Y más margaritas!*"

The woman nodded and smiled, then turned to Erin. "*¿Y para tí?*"

She shrugged. "*¿Por qué no?*"

"*Muy bien.*" The waitress hurried off, scratching notes on a pad. Erin savored the last of her margarita, licking a bit of salt. She'd pay later, with a terrible headache. Tequila was the first liquor to get her drunk, at a party freshman year of college. Body shots. Kryptonite, her strength and her undoing. It made happy shoot from her pores.

Jess sighed. "This is heaven. I'm so glad you came." She peeked from under her hat. "How did Daniel take it, by the way?"

Erin shook her head, surprised it took Jess this long to ask. Her friend had been absorbed in her own troubles. "Not that great. If you'd seen the look on his face, you'd have thought I was leaving him for good."

"He was that upset you were missing his mom's birthday?"

"I don't know. I think he also misses me. He's ready for the whole thing. Kids, family, all of it. But sometimes I still feel single. It is weird though, going on vacation without him."

Jess pushed her sunglasses to the top of her head and frowned at Erin. "I'm sorry. Now I feel bad."

"No, I'm sorry. I didn't mean that. I don't know how to explain it. It's like I'm still getting used to being married. I don't know how to do it."

A breath from the sea rustled past, the smell of salt water

tinged with decay. "What is it really like, having a husband?" Jess asked. She seemed so sad, so wistful.

Erin smiled at the word *husband.* "It is great," she said, "when you're married to the right person."

Jess settled back into her beach chair and pushed her hat down. "I'll never get married."

"Yes, you will. Marc wasn't the one. You dodged a bullet."

"Then why do I feel like I want to be hit by one?"

"Stop. Your life is perfect." Erin smacked dry lips together and dug around for lipstick, then remembered, again, that it wasn't in her bag. A grimace at the memory of how she left things with Daniel. Their first significant fight, and neither had apologized yet.

After twenty-four hours, she'd begun to ache for him. His lopsided grin, his comfortable warmth, his Daniel scent. In the past year since their wedding, she felt like two different people, wanting to be married but still needing to be independent. It wasn't wrong to want to have your own life, so why did she feel so bad?

The waitress returned, margaritas in plastic cups crowned with salt and lime wedges. Jess raised her cup.

"To Erin. The kind of friend who will come halfway around the world to help her best friend get over a breakup. You're my Slim Shady, all those other Slim Shadys are just imitating."

"To Slim Shady!" Erin gulped her margarita as the music started up again, much louder.

She checked her phone again, but Daniel hadn't called. Buried it deep in her beach bag. Jess gave her a sideways glance. "Stop checking your phone."

"I'm just looking for lipstick. I am not checking my phone."

"Good, because whatever it is can wait. Nobody needs you right now."

An hour later Erin's phone, still buried in her beach bag, pealed, waking her from a tequila-induced nap.

The line was crackly, his voice splintered into cuts and jolts. She jumped up to find a better signal, holding the phone with her left hand, plugging her other ear.

"Dad, I can't hear you."

Jess leaned over and grabbed Erin's margarita, mouthing, *Take this!* Erin took it and walked along the beach toward the hotel, hunting a signal. The sun beamed on her shoulders, still burned from yesterday's beach outing. "Dad? Can you hear me?" In between crackles and silence, his voice was a jumble of words —*plane, center, Daniel.* Frustration knotted in her forehead. "It's a bad connection. Can you call me back?"

No response.

"Dad?" The line went dead. Blank screen. Why would her dad be calling about Daniel? She couldn't think of a good reason, unless something was wrong.

Barefoot, she darted across the sand toward the resort. Still one fat little signal bar, the rest stubborn ghosts. Up the stairs, over the beach scrub, and under the pavilion. At the top of the stairs, *hallelujah!* A second bar. She dialed Daniel's cell phone. A fast busy signal, jammed network. She tried again and again, same result.

Nerves fraying, she descended toward the pool and resort, walking past half-naked people lounging around the pool. The phone buzzed in her hand. She looked down, eager, but it was just a voice mail. Heart pounding irrationally, she dialed and hit speaker.

Her dad's voice sounded very serious. "Erin, I'm just watching the news. Something's happened in New York. A plane hit the World Trade Center tower. I think that's where Daniel works, but I don't know which one. Call me, please."

Cold needles pricked her spine. She dialed Daniel again, office number this time. *Two-one-two-three-two-three-two-four-oh-eight.* Fast busy signal again. She hit redial repeatedly, finally got through. Her heart soared. Nobody answered. She froze, waited, conjured his voice. *Hello, Daniel O'Connor here. Hi, babe. Of course I'm fine.*

Of course everything was fine.

Someone jumped into the pool cannonball-style, splashing pool water on Erin's legs. Vacationers lounged, sipping drinks and reading books. Hotel staff strolled by, checking on guests. Everything looked as normal as before, when she was one of them relaxing at the beach.

She tossed her half-empty margarita cup into the nearest trash bin.

Daniel told her she tended to overreact. When he didn't come home at the time he was supposed to and didn't answer his cell phone, her imagination took hold, diving to worst-case scenario—mugged, bleeding, facedown in an alley. She closed her eyes, willing it away.

Her dad said something about a plane. Could a plane have hit Daniel's building? An unspoken fear, those buildings jutting into sky—what if a pilot flew too close? She imagined a toy plane sticking out of the World Trade Center at an odd angle, nose crumpled on steel.

Daniel was the closest thing to Superman she knew, but he couldn't fly. How long would it take to walk down 101 flights of stairs?

Erin stood paralyzed to the cement, cell phone in hand, while holiday happened around her. There was a hand on her shoulder, then an accented voice. "Excuse me, miss, are you OK?"

She turned and looked into the kind blue eyes of a stranger, worry creased onto his forehead. "No. I need a phone. A land-line."

The man nodded. "Right then, do you know where the lob-by is?"

"No. I mean, yes, but . . ." Her voice cracked. She looked around helplessly, unable to remember where her room or the lobby was. As if her brain had turned off all but essential functions. Fear settled into her bones like an ice-cold bath.

"Let me take you there." The man, who sounded English and looked like he was in his early thirties, grabbed something from the chair he'd been sitting in, slipped on a pair of flip-flops, and guided Erin toward a set of glass doors at the opposite end of the pool.

They passed diners at café tables, sunbaked concrete searing Erin's bare feet. Forks danced on plates, the low hum of conversation. Waiters wended around tables bearing platters. She imagined sitting at a table with Daniel, eating, sipping drinks, laughing. Debating how to while away the evening ahead: a walk along the beach maybe, or champagne and early bedtime. Why had she come without him? But she did, and now she was stranded on the other side of the world when he needed her.

The man led her through the doors of the hotel. Inside to the right was a fully stocked bar, more vacation revelers drinking and eating. Smoke infused the air.

The man she was following kept going past the bar toward the front doors that led into the lobby. Erin gravitated instead toward the bar, where a row of televisions showed men in shorts sprinting on soccer fields and beautiful people acting devastated on a Spanish soap. The bartender, white cup towel over shoulder, stared at the television on the far right.

It was a helicopter view of the twin towers. Blackness slashed through one, fire and smoke spewing out like an erupting volcano.

Chapter Four

September 11, 2001

The bar air was heavy and dense, distorting sounds of conversation and consumption. Coils of cigarette smoke snaked through the air and into Erin's lungs. She coughed, jolting her feet into motion. She darted past diners. At the bar, a man exhaled a cloud of smoke as she approached. She blinked her eyes and called to the bartender, "S'cuse me!"

The bartender, tall and tan with a pockmarked face, pulled his eyes from the screen and glared at her. Light hazel, piercing. He growled, "*¿En qué puedo servirle?*"

"What happened?"

The man squinted his eyes at her, not following her English. She pointed at the screen and summoned memories from tenth-grade Spanish. "*¿Que pasó?*"

"Ah." He shrugged and wiped the glass he was holding with a cup towel, then set the glass down. "A plane," he said, and with one hand, he mimed a plane crashing by jabbing it into the other hand, his English halting and rolling, "*beats* the building." Then he grabbed the cup towel from his shoulder and flicked it toward the television. "*Es loco. Idiota.*"

Around her people talked, laughed, and ate despite the burning images. "*¡Más!* I need . . . *más información*." She pointed at the other screens.

The bartender reached up and pushed buttons on the TVs. Soccer and soap operas morphed into different angles of Daniel's building on fire.

At least Erin thought it was his building. Maybe his building was the other one, the one that wasn't burning.

From behind her came an English-accented voice. "There you are. Still need a telephone?" The man from the pool followed her gaze. "Oh my God. What happened?"

She pointed at the television, voice calm as a sociopath's. "My husband works there."

Blue eyes bulged. "Fucking hell. Which floor?"

Saying it would make it real. A tear fell. "One hundred and one."

"Bloody hell." He rubbed at his scruff and narrowed his eyes. "Is he there?"

She nodded. "I think so."

"And you're sure he works in the building that was hit, not the other one?"

She wasn't sure. "The one with the cell tower on top. I think."

The man shook his head. "I'm so sorry. Here, let's sit you down." He pulled out a barstool and motioned for her to sit, but she couldn't. Sitting was too passive. He perched on the edge of another chair. "Do you want me to call someone?"

She glanced at her phone. "I've tried calling him. I can't get through."

"Did you try email?"

Email. She hadn't thought of that. She pulled out her BlackBerry and thumb-tapped a quick message: *Are you OK? Please respond ASAP. Or call me! Please. Now!* She hit send and held her breath.

A phone rang. Hope surged. But it was his, the guy next to her. He turned away to speak, as if she couldn't still hear. "Hey, mate. Did you see what happened? I know, it's nuts."

Erin thought of Jess, on the beach drinking margaritas with no idea what happened. Erin's stuff was there too, her beach bag. But she couldn't walk away from the televisions, her lifeline.

People started to notice what was happening. Conversations quieted, but forks still tinkled on plates, people still ordered drinks, waiters still circled tables. Lit cigarettes suffused air, smoke billowing as it did on screen.

The volume on a Spanish channel was turned up, reporters speaking too fast for Erin to translate. The one on the right was CNN, tickers at the bottom in English. She wanted to ask the bartender to turn up that channel, but she couldn't recall the right Spanish words. She turned to the man next to her. "Can you ask him to turn up the one in English? And turn the rest of them down?"

English guy got the bartender's attention and pointed to the TV. "*Inglés, por favor.*" The bartender shook his head, and the man got mad. He pointed at Erin and yelled, "*¡Su esposo está allí! ¡En el edificio! ¡Inglés, por favor!*"

The whole bar must have heard. Around her, people half-whispered, "Her husband is in the building." The surprised bartender pointed the remote at the row of televisions. The Spanish faded away, the bar became quiet, CNN got louder.

Reporters talked about a plane hitting the building. They

interviewed witnesses. *How big was the plane? It was big*, people said. *A passenger plane.* Reporters asked if the plane was still in the building; people said yes. Witnesses said things like:

"There was a big boom. A gigantic sonic boom."

"There are a lot of fire engines."

"People are waving shirts."

"It's the north tower, not the south tower, and there's fire all around the building, on all sides."

"Paper is raining down like leaflets. The uppermost floors are definitely on fire."

A woman on the street pegged the impact zone at eighty to maybe eighty-five. Daniel was sixteen floors above that. So he was OK, the phone lines probably busted out. The TV said cell phones weren't working and maybe it was because the cell tower was on top of the building.

But then the reporter said people were trapped on the upper floors, no way out.

Erin planted her hands on the barstool next to English guy. "But they can do something, right? They'll get helicopters or something?" He was silent, gape-mouthed. Blond hair, sunburned skin. Not clean-shaven but not bearded either. Four-day scruff. His nostrils flared as the tower burned on the televisions above them.

He noticed her scrutinizing him, offered his hand. "I'm Alec, by the way."

She nodded, shook. Civilities seemed out of place. "Erin."

They turned toward the televisions as the commentator spoke again: "Our eyewitness says that it was a plane, a big plane. Possibly a 737."

A black dot flew onto the screen and disappeared. Suddenly

a big, fiery explosion farther down the building. Or maybe the next building. Orange flames and smoke exploded. Reporters wondered if it was the fuselage exploding. But Erin had seen another plane disappear.

On CNN, an eyewitness started yelling. "And there's more explosions right now. People are running. Hold on. The building's exploding!"

The building *was* exploding. The other building. People screamed and cried. The witness said people were panicking. The call got dropped. Commentators tried to make sense out of chaos. "It seems clear now that this was a deliberate act of terrorism."

Terrorism. The word lodged in Erin's head, foreign and misplaced. Somebody did this on purpose. Set out to kill people like Daniel, just for going to work.

Jess showed up a few minutes later in a rainbow sarong, straw hat, and Jackie O sunglasses. She was lugging both beach bags with an unsteady gait. She saw Erin, glanced at Alec, and did a double take, a question mark on her face. "Why didn't you come back? I was worried." She sat down next to Erin and held her hand out to Alec. "Hi, I'm Jess. Erin's friend." They shook, and Jess looked at Erin. "Drinking without me?"

Erin pointed to the television.

Jess pushed her sunglasses onto her head and gazed at the screen. After a few moments, recognition dawned. "Oh my God, is that . . . ?"

Erin gulped. "The World Trade Center."

"Oh my God oh my God oh my God." Jess's mouth gaped. Her head whipped toward Erin. "And Daniel?"

Erin shrugged her shoulders to hold her body together, her skeleton flailing in cheap padding.

Jess threw arms around her. "Oh, honey!"

Jess took the barstool on Erin's left, and the three stared at the televisions, listening to the commentators. The bartender asked if they wanted a drink, on the house. Alec ordered a beer and Jess, a scotch. Erin couldn't remember how to swallow. She felt numb, a blank slate, waiting for information. The bar quiet now, all eyes on the burning buildings. Cigarette smoke and sour hops hung in the air. Erin felt like when she'd smoked her first cigarette—greenish and nauseated.

Every few minutes she checked email, dialed Daniel's numbers, hopelessly put phone to ear. The results always the same—no response, no answer.

Constant calculations in her head—which floors the plane hit, how many floors total. Where would Daniel be? Was there a clear way down? The camera was too far away to see detail. But the tops of both buildings were intact. No orange flames, just thick, black smoke.

No helpful facts were offered. Professional news jockeys silent and stunned, working it out along with the viewers. Erin wanted to scream, *Was the building evacuated? How many people are still there? What floors are burning? Did everyone get out? How are they rescuing people? Where are the helicopters?*

Then, something happened in DC. CNN shifted from twin towers to a smoldering Pentagon. The other stations still showed the twin towers. The second tower, the one behind Daniel's, looked worse than his. Smoke poured from the gash and streamed up, obscuring the top. Chunks of debris tumbled from the impact zone, chased by a bright orange trail of sparks. As the commentator on CNN talked about the Pentagon, the top tilted to the left, buckled, collapsed. Over a hundred stories went down in less than ten seconds.

In the bar, a collective gasp. Stars sparkled in the dark periphery of Erin's vision.

How many people were in that building? How many people just died?

The guy on CNN still talked about the Pentagon.

"The whole fucking thing just collapsed." Alec sounded dumbstruck.

Jess grabbed Erin's hand, her face contorted. Erin gave her a steely gaze. "Daniel's building is still standing. It wasn't his building."

Finally the commentator on CNN noticed something amiss and interrupted his witness. The camera went back to New York, but smoke obscured the new gap in the landscape.

Jess yelled at him, "The building went down, you idiot!"

Finally, the reporter caught on. "We are getting reports that the south tower has collapsed."

Daniel's tower was still standing. He could be alive, on the street, walking home. Erin closed her eyes and imagined Daniel striding down frenzied Manhattan streets. Dipping head to cellphone to call her, not getting a signal.

She grabbed her phone and left, through the lobby to the front of the hotel and out big wooden doors. Taxis and town cars sat in the circle drive. People packed suitcases and kids into taxis and drove away. Others emerged sporting big hats and sunglasses, fresh and ready to start vacations. Erin tried to breathe.

A batch of unread emails from friends and coworkers, but nothing from Daniel. She dialed again, with the same result. She hit redial, pacing from valet station to trash can and back again. On a wooden bench next to the trash can, an old man smoked. In Spain, someone was always smoking.

She dialed her father. He picked up first ring. Maybe only New York phone lines were jammed.

"Daddy! Has anyone heard from Daniel?"

He was silent at first, a habit engendered from years of business calls, as if making his response weightier to ensure attention.

"Daddy!"

"I'm here, baby." His words slow and measured. "No, I haven't heard from Daniel. I've called several people, including Helen. Nobody has heard from him. But that doesn't mean anything—the phone lines are all jammed."

"I don't know what to do, Daddy. I'm stuck here on an island in Spain."

"Who's with you?"

"Just Jess. And some English guy we met at the bar."

"Erin, you need to start thinking about how you're going to get home."

"They said all the flights are grounded."

"Yeah, but that won't last long. When they start again, you want to be somewhere with an international airport. Can you get to London?"

"Why London? What about Madrid?"

"That would be OK. But in London you can speak the language. It'll be easier there."

He was probably right. "OK, I'll work on it. Call me if you hear from Daniel?"

"It'll be the first thing I do."

Next, her office. Judy answered, "Erin O'Connor's office" in that pure Long Island accent. Erin could picture her: gray cubicle, frizzy dark hair, red fingernails. She usually sounded bored. But today, Judy's voice was shaky and high-pitched.

"Judy, it's Erin."

"Erin, are you OK?"

"I'm OK. You heard about the towers being hit?"

"Oh yeah, of course. Everyone's in Mr. Strauss's office. He's got the TV, you know. We're all trying to figure out what to do."

"Has Daniel called?"

"No. Why?"

"You know where he works, right?"

"No, where?"

"Daniel—" Erin's voice cracked. She couldn't show weakness. She'd worked hard to build authority, not easy as a young lawyer with a middle-aged secretary. "Daniel works in that building."

A gasp. "Oh my God, Erin. No. I didn't know that."

"Just call me if you hear from him, OK?" Erin hung up before Judy could ask more questions like *What floor does he work on?*

Back at the bar, Alec and Jess hadn't moved, Erin's empty chair between them. She stood, too anxious to sit. "What's the latest?"

Jess turned to Erin, eyes squinty and unfocused.

Best friend drunk, husband missing in a burning building, all swirling and rotating and fomenting until Erin erupted. "You're drunk? My husband may be dying, and you're fucking drunk?"

Jess's eyes went wide; her lip quivered.

A collective gasp. Heads whipped toward the televisions.

The second building folded, floor by floor by floor. A violent plume of gray-black dust swallowed concrete and steel and straight edges.

Both buildings gone. Nothing but smoke and ash where they once stood as sentries, guarding the Manhattan skyline.

Chapter Five

September 11, 2001

Outside the oval window was nothing but white wingtip and dark blue sea, somewhere between Mallorca and mainland Spain. Each time Erin closed her eyes, a video played in the darkness—Daniel's building, cascading into a billowing mass of smoke and fire. She opened her eyes, gripping the armrests, staring at the water, repeating a mantra.

Daniel will be OK, and I will get home.

But another thought kept creeping in. *Daniel could be dead.*

Daniel was, without a doubt, the love of her life. She knew it from the moment the paper airplane landed in her palm, a homing pigeon delivering its message. And now he could be dead.

Regrets threatened to choke her. From not kissing him when she left to not telling him enough how much she loved him. Leaving on this trip without his support. Fights over money. Not wanting to go to Mets games with him. She knew now she wanted children, desperately. Daniel's children. Why was she being so stubborn?

She held it all back because regrets would mean that he was gone.

She remembered only snippets from the moments after the building fell, like old movie reels where the image flashes for a split second. The world going black, pinpricks of light dancing around the edges. Clammy and cold skin, but feeling hot and dizzy. Alec leading her away from the bar. In the suite, an open balcony door and the sea breeze. The crash of the surf and the cry of seagulls. Slamming the doors so hard the panes shook. Jess opening the safe and handing passports to Alec. Smashing clothes into suitcases. A waiting taxi—white hatchback with a yellow stripe. Graffitied stucco buildings, people sitting on chairs and smoking. A mostly empty airport, a plane waiting for them.

They were in business class, Alec in the aisle seat and Erin by the window, Jess behind her. There were more empty seats than filled. Erin had been staring out the window since takeoff, keeping her mind blank. Holding it together one pixelated breath at a time. Like a star in the night sky, if she looked too closely at the situation, she'd lose it altogether.

Alec was a calming presence. Authoritative, resourceful, confident. Erin realized that she knew nothing about him, what he was doing in Mallorca, or who he'd been there with. She asked him what he did, and he told her he was an international banker with Barclays in London.

"That sounds stressful. I'm sorry you had to cut your vacation short," she said. It suddenly seemed strange that he was flying back with them, alone.

He shook his head. "The vacation was over."

"Were you with someone?"

He nodded. “My brother.”

“A guys’ trip?”

Alec paused, pursed his lips. “That’s right. But also a bit of a soul-searching trip.”

“Midlife crisis?”

His lip curled. “Not quite yet. Just trying to decide whether to go through with something.”

“You’re engaged,” Erin blurted out.

He tilted his head at her. “That’s right. Are you a psychic then?” His two front teeth crossed slightly.

“So have you made a decision?”

“I don’t know.” He looked at her, sadness and pain in his eyes. “In the midst of all this, it seems I’m more muddled than ever.”

Erin looked down at the water beneath them, and her hands began to shake. She turned back to Alec. “Wait, is your brother still in Mallorca?”

“That’s right. Seemed safer to him than a big city.”

“I’m so sorry. You didn’t have to come with us.” This stranger had cut his vacation short to escort them to London. She felt like a selfish American. At the same time, this wasn’t a typical day. It was one of those emergency situations you never think will happen, where societal norms fall away and you find yourself traveling with strangers. “You don’t even know us.”

There was kindness in his eyes. “You need help. Your friend’s in no condition to give it.” He gestured at Jess behind them, passed out, mouth wide open. Snoring off the tequila. “Plus, I want to be home. On a day like today, there’s no other place to be.”

Erin had to whisper so she wouldn’t cry. “I want to be home so badly.”

Alec looked chagrined. "I'm so sorry. That was rude of me. Of course you do." He pulled out the *SkyMall* magazine and flipped to the middle. Then looked at her again. "Don't worry. We'll get you there."

Erin wished she were as confident as he. Right now, she felt a million miles from home.

Chapter Six

September 12, 2001

She stands at the edge of a vast chasm, wide as the Grand Canyon, wearing her bathrobe. The wind whips her hair and the robe writhes, a banshee trying to fly away. She has to use both hands to hold it down. At her feet, a few scrubby bushes spring from dead soil. Past them, sharp rocks populate a steep cliff, meshing into the hazy wall of red rock on the other side. Standing at the edge of an outcropping across the chasm is a small figure. He tries to tell her something. But he's too far away. He tries harder, lifting his face up and screaming into the wind. What? *she yells, cupping her mouth, throwing her body into the effort. No sound comes out. The robe billows. He puts his hand up to say wait, then backs up a few paces, halts, takes a running start, and leaps toward her, arms spread as though he can fly. He becomes a floating light, a tiny firefly. The light hovers, so close. Then dips toward earth.*

Erin bolted up in bed, sweating, heart hammering, breathing as if she'd had the wind knocked out of her. For one fleeting hair of a second, the whole thing could have been a dream. She reached for Daniel instinctively, her arm crashing across his pillow, but his side of the bed was cold and smooth.

The hum of an air-conditioning unit rattled her ears. The air was musty and cold. She felt like she was floating free of her body, slightly detached. Like a shadow or an electron, hovering somewhere in the vicinity but embodying only slight mass.

She lay back down in the bed, skull throbbing. Sunlight pierced through the tall window behind her, sending light and shadows over the beige comforter.

The weight of reality hit like a bullet to the gut. The impossibly high building collapsing on itself, the slow-motion replay. She groaned as she sat up in bed, nausea cresting over her.

She was in a hotel room in London. Her head was clouded and her limbs felt thick, as though she'd been drugged. And then she remembered taking the sleeping pill Jess offered her last night. She fought the overwhelming urge to cry, to shove her head under the pillow and pretend it was all a dream.

Instead she grabbed her phone, relieved that she'd had the presence of mind to unpack her charger and plug it in before she fell asleep. She dialed Daniel's cell, jammed the phone to her ear, held her breath. It rang and rang, distant and trill. Each ring rended her heart, dashed her hope. Then a click and her heart surged.

"Daniel!" But it was just his voice greeting. *Hey, it's Daniel. You know what to do, so do it at the beep.* His voice, confident treble with a Bronx accent, melted her. His voice still existed, at least on voice mail, and that gave her a small amount of peace.

Erin's yell woke Jess. She sat up in bed, disoriented. Her curly brown hair was matted and frizzed, her eyes red and crusty.

She dug at them with her knuckles and then, with a groan, fell back down onto her pillow.

The sleeping pill was wearing off, a headache settling into its place. But Erin didn't have the luxury of going back to sleep. She tried the other numbers, home and office, with no luck. Panic rising, she called Daniel's older brother, Aidan. She'd made so many calls with no answer in the past twenty-four hours that it was almost a shock when he picked up. His *hello* was hushed and weary, then she remembered it was the middle of the night in New York.

"Aidan, it's Erin."

There was a hesitation. Across thousands of miles, she heard him swallow. "Erin, I've been trying to call. Are you OK?"

"I'm fine. I'm at a hotel in London. I'm worried about Daniel. Have you heard from him?"

Deep pause. "No. We haven't. Have you?"

It was not a hopeful question. Erin clapped her hand over her mouth and sucked in air. Jess heard her and sat up in bed. "But there's still a chance he got out, right?"

"I've been hoping the same thing. When did you last speak to him?"

Erin choked up, remembering their last conversation. "Sunday morning." It sounded like such a long time ago. They'd gone a whole day without talking, probably the first time that had happened since they started dating.

Aidan sighed. She pictured him rubbing his dimpled chin, looking like an older, more worn version of Daniel.

"I tried him Tuesday morning, but I couldn't get through. Did anyone talk to him?"

"I tried him too. And Mom and Robert and Cathleen. We all tried. Nobody got through."

Of course they were looking for him too. Why hadn't she called them before? She felt all alone in this ordeal, but she wasn't. "He could've been in the stairwell, right? Where the phones don't work."

"Yeah, that's right. He could have been in the stairwell." Aidan cleared his throat and then gulped as if he were drinking water. "Listen, we're doing everything we can. Schaeffer and his friends are too. We're looking for him, OK? In fact, that's all we're doing."

"Aidan, I need to know where he is. What—" The sob came out of nowhere. Jess got out of bed and sat next to Erin, grasping her free hand.

Aidan's voice took on a paternal tone Erin had never heard from him. She'd never shown weakness around Daniel's family before. His words were slow and measured, as if she were hard of hearing. "Erin, right now you need to focus on getting home. Call the airlines, see what you can do. We're doing everything we can do here. There are rescue operations looking for survivors. There's nothing you could do anyway. For now just get yourself home safely, OK?"

"Aidan, can you go to our apartment? See if he's there? The doorman can let you in. He might be there, worried about me. He doesn't know where I am—"

"Erin, I've been to the apartment—"

"—so you need to tell him I'm stuck here in London, but I'm coming home. I'll be home as soon as I can. And tell him I love him. He'll be OK, right?" She knew she sounded crazy. But if she said it, she might believe it, and it might be possible.

The sound of Aidan's breath was heavy, close to the mouthpiece. When he spoke, it was with a throaty voice. "I'll tell him,

Erin. I'll call you if I have any information. And take care of yourself."

Erin somehow managed to brush her teeth, get dressed, and pack her suitcase, each action wedged between another attempt to get in touch with Daniel. She must have called ten times, leaving him a voice mail each time, telling him how much she loved him and to please call immediately. Jess went downstairs to the hotel buffet and came back up with coffee and toast.

Together, they called all the airlines they could think of—American, United, British Airways, Virgin Atlantic, Delta. Each call took at least half an hour and ended with the same result—there were no scheduled flights to the US, and the airlines were not allowed to book tickets for passengers to US or Canadian destinations until the airspace reopened.

One by one, they checked the airlines off the list. When it became clear that they were all dead ends, they moved on to travel agents. They were no help either—none of them had any idea when flights would resume. They could only advise them to pack up, get to the airport, and wait.

At noon, Erin called her father, even though in Dallas it was six in the morning. She expected him to be awake and ready to help, and he was.

"Erin, any news?"

"Nothing."

"What can I do?"

"Send a boat?" Erin was only half joking.

Jess covered the mouthpiece and turned to Erin. "This person is saying we might be able to get to Canada sooner than the states. Toronto or Montreal."

"How far is the drive from there?"

"Eight or nine hours. And there's no guarantee we'll get a rental car. But it might get us there a day or two earlier."

"Dad, did you hear that? Jess says they're telling her we should try Canada and drive."

"Erin?"

"Yeah?"

"What about Mexico? I think its airspace is open. You could fly in there and I could pick you up. Then we could figure out what to do from here."

"I don't want to go to Dallas, Dad. I need to be at home, with Daniel. What if he's hurt? He's going to need me."

Her father took his time responding. "Yeah, yeah. I suppose so. OK, well if you change your mind, let me know. You could probably get there today or tomorrow."

"Dad, why would I go to Mexico? It's a three-day drive from there to New York." Silence, and then she got it. "You think he's dead, don't you?"

"I didn't say that, pumpkin." He always used pet names when he was asserting his fatherhood, patronizing her.

"You didn't have to."

At the hotel checkout desk, Jess told the receptionist that they might be back and asked if she could hold a room for them. In a clipped British voice, the woman told her she couldn't guarantee a room when they returned unless they paid for the night, which would be nonrefundable.

Jess tilted her head to the left and narrowed her eyes. "Are you aware of what's happening in New York?"

The woman gave her a dispassionate look. "Yes, of course I am."

Jess pointed to Erin. "And are you aware that my friend's husband is missing from the World Trade Center?"

Jess's words unhinged Erin, and she began to cry for the first time. It was true, but she couldn't bear to hear it.

The woman at the registration desk looked aghast, her facade crumbling. "Well, no. I was not aware of that."

Jess pushed her next words through gritted teeth. "Given our situation, do you think it would be too much trouble to hold a room for us? We promise we will call should it turn out, God willing, that we don't need it."

The woman looked down at the keyboard and typed for what seemed like an eternity. Jess looped her arm in Erin's and they waited, silent tears dripping down Erin's cheeks. Finally, the woman looked up. "All right then, I've got a room held for you. Please do let me know if you will not be needing it." Then she turned to Erin, awkwardly. "And good luck . . . I mean, I do hope you find him."

They walked the five minutes to the tube station, which was a few stops from Heathrow. In newsstands on the street, the headlines starkly declared the attacks: "War on America," "Suicide Hijackers Blitz America," "The Day that Changed the World." Erin forced her eyes away.

On the train, Erin stared at the blue cloth seat underneath her legs, the jostling making her regret the toast and coffee.

Along with the nausea, an escalating panic. She tried to breathe through it, but without an activity to keep her mind occupied, it bore down like a boa constrictor.

She looked at Jess, chest heaving, breath forced. "What if he's dead?"

"Stop that, now." She turned and grabbed Erin's shoulders. Since recovering from her hangover, Jess was focused and competent. "You can't think that way."

A knife plunged into Erin's lungs. She dropped her head to her knees, hyperventilating. The world spun, needles poked at her arms and legs, covered by a sheen of cold sweat.

The subway lurched to a halt, doors opened, people scurried off. *Mind the gap, please.* Erin stamped her feet on the floor and waved her tingling arms back and forth.

Jess pressed something small into her right palm. "Erin, take this. Now." Her voice brooked no opposition.

"What is it?"

"It'll take the edge off."

When she looked up, Erin realized everyone in the car was staring at her. The pill felt small and powerful in her palm. She thought of the pill bottles in her mother's closet, tucked next to the vodka in the Ferragamo shoebox hidden on the top shelf. The mood swings, the drawn curtains. Spending all day in her room one day, the life of the party the next. There were different pills for headaches, for depression, and for the debilitating panic attacks brought on by the neighbor's invitation to a holiday party. Growing up, Erin told herself she'd never be that way.

"Give me two."

Jess twisted the cap off and handed Erin another small white pill and a water bottle. Together with the water, the pills glided down on a slippery slope of surrender.

There were no flights to the United States or Canada on Wednesday. And so it became their routine. They woke each morning in a different room of the same hotel, drank black coffee and ate dry toast, repacked their suitcases, and went to the airport to wait all day. Checked in with each of the airlines, sat in navy blue vinyl seats avoiding televisions and eating wilted airport food. Mushy egg burritos and soggy Caesar wraps and stale pretzels. The food was simple sustenance, prevention against stomach growls. Erin called Daniel constantly, incessantly. Sometimes just to hear his voice. Always hoping and praying that this time he would answer, *Hey, babe*, just like he used to. But the only bit of Daniel Erin could find was his voice mail in the ether.

She began to hate his greeting, even as her heart lifted when she heard his Bronx accent.

Her hope evaporated a little more with each passing hour, as her need to get to New York became more desperate and her mind more muddled. Jess took care of everything. She found them seats far away from the television screens, where they could spread out and create a working base. She walked away at regular intervals to get updates from airline agents, check the status of flights, and call other airlines. She disappeared for a few minutes each hour, and Erin knew she was finding televisions at a bar or restaurant, maybe having a drink, and watching the news that Erin couldn't watch, being one disturbing image away from a breakdown.

Erin ate little and cared nothing for her appearance. She showered using the stock shampoo and bar of soap the hotel provided, but that was the extent of her beauty routine. Her thoughts were dysfunctional and irrational. She thought she'd never get back to New York. That the whole world was conspiring against her. She imagined that Daniel was punishing her, avoiding her calls, because of the fight. Because she wasn't there for his mother's birthday, because she didn't want a baby yet. Maybe everyone was in on it, Aidan and his mom too. Like that fucked-up movie *The Game*, where Michael Douglas thought it was real but instead it was an elaborate hoax planned by his brother to make him appreciate life more.

After labeling those thoughts as the ridiculous wanderings of a sleep-deprived mind, she thought she hadn't tried hard enough, didn't want it bad enough. She'd try harder. But what else could she do? There was an ocean between her and where she needed to be, and no way to cross it.

For the first time in her life, Erin didn't know what to do.

Alec called Jess a few times each day to check on them. He asked how they were getting on with the airlines, whether they needed anything. He asked if he could bring them dinner, told them they were invited to his home anytime. *Thank you*, Jess told him, *but we have to get back home*. He had some banker connections with the airlines and called all of them, but even that wasn't enough to get the planes flying again.

Daniel would have found a way to get home by now. Daniel would have found her and saved her if the tables were turned.

Instead, Daniel could be buried alive under rubble, calling out for help that hadn't come.

During the day, Erin focused on all the ways he might still

be alive. But at night, it was all the ways he could have died that kept her gasping for breath, pinned under the weight of a thousand tons of steel and concrete. So when Jess gave her pills, she gulped them down, inviting the medication to flow across the synapses of her brain, smoothing out the snarls.

Even with the pills, by Friday afternoon she was starting to lose it. The airlines told them that flights to Canada would resume that day if all went according to plan. They'd been sitting at the Air Canada gates since early morning, Jess getting up frequently to check on the status and remind gate agents they were there, waiting.

After one of her checks, she came back with a hopeful look on her face. "Air Canada is resuming flights to Toronto. The first one is reserved for all the people who've been waiting since Tuesday. But the agent took pity on us, and we have two seats in first class. It leaves at 3:12."

The tears began in Erin's belly and moved up through her chest, contorting her face and emerging from her eyes. "I can't believe it."

"I know. But it's happening. Gate seventeen. Let's go."

Nine hours later, the wheels on an Air Canada plane touched down on North American soil, and passengers broke into applause. After visiting five different car rental kiosks, Jess and Erin ended up with a blue Dodge Neon and a map to New York City. They went through a McDonald's drive-through. Jess ordered a burger, and Erin had a coke and two white pills. The customs officer at the border thought Jess was crazy when she said they were driving to New York City. Jess handled it with calm diplomacy. If Erin had been able to speak, she'd have told him to fuck off and mind his own business.

Erin managed to fall asleep at some point after the sun went down, her head resting awkwardly against the window. When she woke, they were in the dead of night and the middle of nowhere. She turned to Jess, a silhouette in the dark. Her curly hair was matted and tangled, mouth set in a hard line. Her eyes were slits, focused on the road. Erin's heart surged for her friend. "Do you want me to drive?"

Jess shook her head no. "Thanks, but you're on a double dose of Xanax. I'm fine."

"Where are we?"

"Binghamton." Jess inhaled deeply. "About three hours away."

Erin glanced at the clock on the dashboard, glowing at 1:01 a.m. Six in the morning in London. Jess had been awake for twenty-four hours. "So we'll get there at 4:00 a.m."

Jess nodded her head. "Just about."

Erin took in the desolate landscape. She and Daniel had gone to Binghamton once, for a powerboat racing competition at Whitney Point Lake. He met some of his friends from the Bronx—tough, blue-collar types. Mud, mud, mud. That's all she remembered—the mud-brown lake, mud up to their ankles. And not a Starbucks anywhere. At the time, she vowed never to go back to Binghamton.

A few hours and two more Xanax later, Jess nudged Erin awake. She didn't say anything, but she didn't have to. They were on the

New Jersey Turnpike, approaching the city from the top, at the George Washington Bridge. It was bathed in white light, two glowing pillars connected by strings of light. Far in the distance, the bright lights of the city rose above the darkness. Downtown wasn't visible from there, but Erin looked anyway, straining to catch a glimpse of what wasn't there.

The West Side Highway was like a ghost town compared to normal. Just a handful of private cars, a few taxis and black Suburbans. Two police cars passed, lights and sirens blaring. When the noise receded, it was eerily quiet.

They passed a hundred blocks in no time, approaching the exit for West 79th Street. Jess took it and turned left, past four avenues, to Columbus and 79th. The Park Belvedere.

Jess didn't even bother to pull up the right way. She just cut across the street and screeched to a halt in front of the building, blocking the cars parallel parked on the street. Erin jumped out and pushed into the brass-edged revolving glass door. It didn't budge. "Shit!" she yelled, and then yanked on the side door. Locked tight. She pounded on the glass, and Orlando's head appeared from a door behind the doorman's desk. His red-rimmed eyes went wide when he saw her. He rushed to the door, fumbling with the huge key ring at his belt. He unlocked the door, and Erin tumbled in.

"Mrs. O'Connor! So good to see you home safe."

"Where's Daniel? Have you seen him?" Erin's voice pitched and cracked.

Orlando looked stunned. There was an awkward pause. "No, Mrs. O'Connor, I haven't seen him. I was hoping he would be with you?" It was hollow, insincere. Orlando knew everything that went on in the building. He knew where Daniel worked. He knew Erin had been on a trip and that Daniel didn't go with her.

She shook her head defiantly at him. "No, I was on a girls' trip. Remember? Anyway, I'm home now, and I'm going to find him." Avoiding his eyes, she gestured toward Jess, still outside, arms laden with luggage. "Can you help her?"

He lunged for the door and held it open for Jess. "Right away, Mrs. O'Connor. Right away."

Erin jumped on the elevator, letting it close without waiting. On the twenty-second floor, she rushed down the hallway, jammed the key into the lock, and threw it open. "Daniel!" she screamed.

She flipped on all the light switches, taking in the kitchen on the right, the bathroom on the left, the living room with its floor-to-ceiling windows sparkling with downtown lights. Nothing. She darted into each of the two bedrooms down the hallway to the left of the living room. "Daniel!"

The bed was unmade, dirty white socks on the floor next to his side. On the dining table, a *New York Times* was haphazardly folded, a dirty coffee cup next to it. In the bathroom, a towel lay crumpled on the floor. In the kitchen, dregs in the coffee maker. Patches of green floated on top of brown liquid in the carafe.

She calmed her staccato breath and raced through the possibilities for the ten thousandth time. He could be busy helping, digging people from the rubble, sleeping in the tents for rescue workers. He could be injured, lying prone in a hospital bed, unable to communicate. Or trapped, alive, somewhere where rescuers would find him soon.

Or dead, a nagging voice said. *He could be dead.*

She stood in the middle of the living room, staring south. The lights of the sleeping city blinked back at her. She imagined people slumbering in all the tiny apartments spread out in front of her. How many weren't in their beds tonight, would never be in their beds ever again?

Daniel was out there, somewhere.

A good wife would go straight downtown and start searching. But Erin was emotionally numb and exhausted to the brink. She had worked so hard to get here; she couldn't give in now. But the simplicity of defeat lured her in.

At the door, a light knock.

She opened it to Jess with Orlando behind her, carrying their bags. Erin burst into tears.

Chapter Seven

September 15, 2001

Sweat drenched the comforter and light streamed in through the east-facing window. Erin hadn't closed the blackout shades before she fell into a dreamless sleep the night before so that she would wake at first light. Judging from the sun's position in the sky, well above the buildings on the east side of the park, she must have slept through sunrise and beyond.

Daniel. He was the last thought when she fell asleep and the first when she woke up. Instinctively she kicked her feet to his side of the bed, feeling for his warm, hairy legs. There was nothing there, nobody there. She walked out of her room and into the living room to check the couch, but he wasn't there either.

Before she went to the bathroom, she checked her phone. No calls from Daniel. It was almost 8:00 a.m., and she'd already wasted valuable daylight. She went back into her room to change into clean clothes.

Jess wouldn't let her go anywhere last night after they got home. She said there was nothing they could do for anyone at zero dark thirty. She said there wouldn't be anywhere to go, that it would be unsafe on the streets and too dark to search. She convinced Erin to get a few hours of sleep in a real bed so that she could start fresh in the morning.

Every fiber of Erin's being wanted to run downtown. For over three days her goal had been to get back to New York, get home, find Daniel. But at the same time, she knew that Jess was right. So she had taken one of her sleeping pills and turned out the lights, crashing in her bed without even changing her clothes.

Now, she ripped off her travel clothes, threw on jeans and the first T-shirt she saw, ran a paste-caked toothbrush over her teeth and a hairbrush through the tangled mess on her head, and headed to the kitchen for coffee.

Jess wasn't awake yet, which was just as well. Erin would go down to the site on her own. While she waited for the coffee to brew, she skimmed the basic facts from the papers stacked up at the door. Both towers hit, both towers fell. Nineteen terrorists. Commercial airliners. Thought to be 4,700 people missing. A terrorist group called Al Qaeda, led by a man named Bin Laden, claimed responsibility. Our president vowed punishment.

None of it told her where Daniel was, what happened to him, how to find him.

It was possible he'd made it out. She had to believe this was possible.

The coffee in her mug was black, because the milk in the refrigerator had turned. The expiration date was September 10, 2001. A day before Daniel went missing. Two days after she left him.

Erin drank two cups, black. But no pills. She was stone-cold sober, jacked up on caffeine, on razor's edge, the opposite of complacent. She grabbed two flashlights, a bottle of water, her cell phone, wallet, subway card, and keys and threw it all into a crossbody bag. She stopped, forgetting something. What did one take when one was looking for a missing person? And then she remembered, with a sickening lurch of her coffee-filled stomach—a photo of Daniel. She pulled a few albums from the cabinet beneath the china and flipped through them. She removed three, the most recent ones she could find, slipped them into an envelope and put them in her bag. She tried not to think about what it meant when you had to search for recent photos of your loved one. Smiling faces staring out obligingly from paper flyers and milk cartons.

Before she walked out, she grabbed a notepad to leave Jess a note. The ballpoint pen hovered over the yellow sticky pad for a moment as she contemplated what to say. *Went to Daniel's office*? *Went to dig my husband out of the rubble*? Finally, she settled on: *Went to search for Daniel.*

She was going to Ground Zero, which was what the whole world was calling the place where her husband worked. The moniker didn't give her much hope. She had no idea what she'd do when she got there, but she would figure it out. Her plan was to get as close as she could, look for him in the faces of the rescue workers, visit hospitals and the makeshift aid stations she had heard were set up around the area, show his picture at all of the fire stations. Ask if anyone had seen him, as a patient in a hospital or a volunteer participating in the rescue effort. She imagined him, sleeves rolled up, digging through rubble to find survivors. If he were alive and well, that's where he'd be.

He had taken a job on Wall Street, but at heart Daniel wanted to be a firefighter. His father and grandfather were both New York City firefighters for Engine 63 (Top of Da Bronx). His father, Pat, who died of a heart attack at age forty-eight while Daniel was a junior in college, worked his way up to battalion chief. But Daniel did well in school. He got good grades and was recruited by all the top schools. So instead of following in the footsteps of the O'Connor men straight away, he went to college.

They'd been together a few weeks when they had to declare majors. The previous night they stayed up until four in the morning, cramming for a physics test, eating pizza, and talking about what they were going to be when they grew up. That's when Daniel told Erin he was majoring in mechanical engineering and materials science but what he really wanted was to be a firefighter one day. At the time she laughed as though he were joking, but in hindsight she thought he was serious. Part of Daniel's vision for their life together involved him working as a volunteer firefighter in the small New England town where they ended up with their farm and their picket fence, wherever that might be.

Out the door, down the hallway, and onto the elevator, empty at eight in the morning on a Saturday, the fourth day after the end of the world as she knew it. Down twenty-one floors, into the lobby of the building. The space was old-school, dark and wood paneled. Management wouldn't renovate because they didn't want to touch the pristine cherrywood—apparently the panels were very expensive. But it'd been a source of contention for the residents on the co-op committee, some of whom wanted a more modern look. Erin was on the side favoring modernization. At this moment, on this day, it seemed like trivial nonsense.

Orlando was gone and a new doorman was on duty, someone she didn't recognize. He nodded at Erin and she nodded back but didn't stop to introduce herself as she normally would.

She pushed through the revolving door and walked briskly to the subway station to catch the 2 train. As she hopped on the subway, she felt for a moment as if it were just another day and she were on her way to work. The feeling passed almost before she recognized it, replaced with the dull pain of reality.

The train stopped at every station. It used to be an express but now seemed to be a local. The commuters seemed different. More attuned. Instead of lifeless, bored faces, people registered shock. It's an unwritten rule of New York City subway riding that you never look someone in the eye, not even to smile, but today people were searching and vulnerable, baldly eye to eye. As if trying to find and measure the humanity inside, to reassure themselves people were still basically good. One thing the same, though, was that everyone still wore black, as if the city, perpetually in mourning, had been prepared for this.

After the smell, the first thing Erin noticed on stepping out of the subway at Canal Street was the flyers. The white subway tile walls, normally lined with nothing but grime, were plastered with letter-sized sheets of paper. On them were faces, names, phone numbers to call, and one word that followed her with each step, like the gaze from an old portrait, as she went up the subway stairs—Missing! MISSING. *Missing*. It was written in black and red, Times New Roman and Arial bold, and by many different hands. It hovered large over smiling, happy faces of men and women. The flyers followed Erin to the street level, papering the windows and brick walls of first-floor shops and delis. On the corner was a makeshift shrine with wilted flowers, candles, letters, teddy bears. More flyers, with messages scribbled on them in crayon or marker. *I love you. Always in our hearts. Rest in peace.* Erin pried her eyes away and continued south toward the World Trade Center.

Paper, shoes, and unidentifiable objects covered in gray ash littered the streets. The absence of normal sights and sounds—traffic, honking—made everything seem eerie, like she'd stepped into a lost world. People wandered the streets looking like extras in a postapocalyptic movie. A thick, hazy poltergeist hung over everything. Erin breathed in burnt concrete and jet fuel, fire and ash and charbroiled steel. Using her jacket, she covered her mouth and nose and kept moving.

A block east and across the street was a tent with a Red Cross symbol. She crossed the street but stopped short, people crisscrossing around her. If she looked south, over her right shoulder, she should have a clear view of the towers.

She swallowed hard and turned.

Head up, eyes focused.

She clamped a hand over her mouth to stifle the cry.

Until this moment, even with the smell and the flyers, the flowers and teddy bears, she had lingering doubts that it was real. In the way that Siamese twins or Antarctica or the pyramids of Egypt might be make-believe, she believed the whole thing might have been an elaborate hoax. But there the towers were not, felled like the two tallest trees in the forest, a seething black cloud in their place.

A policeman walked by and saw the look on her face. "Can I help, ma'am?"

She clutched his hand in both of hers and pleaded. "I need to get down there, to find my husband."

"Nobody's allowed past the barricades, ma'am." He pointed

south, where bystanders were wedged along the south side of the intersection of Canal and Varick. "If you want to report a missing person, you can do it at the State Armory, 26th and Lexington."

The policeman continued on his way, navigating unwieldy crowds. She followed him, hoping to get closer to the site. He walked west toward West Street, where three police SUVs passed by heading north. A cluster of firefighters in full gear trudged behind them in the middle of the road. They were grimy and grizzled, layered in dust. The crowds burst into applause, and the firefighters put hands up in acknowledgment.

Trucks approached from the other direction with a low rumble. A line of FedEx trucks, at least twenty, all identical, in procession. They moved south, where Erin wanted to go. She picked through the crowd on the sidewalk, making slow progress. At Canal Street, police barricades were manned by NYPD officers in full flak gear, agents in navy jackets emblazoned with *FBI*, US Army soldiers in green camo. The gatekeepers.

Erin marched up to one of them, who looked barely a man, and summoned a brave voice. "Excuse me, sir. My husband is missing." But instead of brave it came out shaky, ending on a high note like a question mark. She cleared her throat and tried again, lower this time. "He works down there. I need to get by."

He looked at her skeptically. "ID, ma'am?"

She dug in her bag and pulled out her Texas driver's license, cringing as she handed it to him. He'd think she was a lying tourist. "He worked in the World Trade Center. He needs my help."

The soldier glanced at her license and handed it back. "Sorry, ma'am. Only emergency personnel allowed past this point."

"He could be injured or hurt."

"They're doing everything they can to find survivors, ma'am."

She wished he would stop calling her *ma'am*. "I'd like to help look for survivors. Can I do that?"

"No, ma'am. Not unless you're police, fire, reserve, or national guard. No civilians allowed past this point."

"What about on the other side? The east side or the south side?" She pointed in those directions. She strained for a hopeful look, but the guard wouldn't look her in the eye.

"Whole area blocked off, ma'am." He was tiring of her questions. She had to make it personal.

"His name is Daniel O'Connor." She shoved one of the photos she brought under his nose. "He worked on the 101st floor. Do you know how many people got out from the 101st floor?"

The guard focused somewhere above her head, eyes fixed on a faraway target in a look of stoic self-preservation. "Sorry. Can't let you through without an escort."

She stood her ground, keeping her eyes on his. "Please."

Finally, his veneer broke. "Listen, ma'am, I understand. I've got a cousin who worked there too. There's people doing everything they can to find survivors. But I can't let you go down there by yourself. It's not safe."

"Then what do I do?"

The soldier shrugged. "Check all of the hospitals. Report him as a missing person at the armory building, 26th and Lexington. Put up missing person flyers. And then pray."

Erin wandered uptown along West Street, making her way to the armory. She'd planned to visit all of the hospitals along the way, until she realized she didn't know where any of the hospitals in New York were.

To her left, a slow-rolling motorcade emerged from behind the barricades. It looked like an entourage for a visiting dignitary. Three motorcycle cops led the way, blasting their sirens now and then to warn people out of the way. They were followed by an unmarked police car with red lights flashing, a fire truck with two somber firefighters in back, then another police car and two police motorcycles.

It was quiet, dignified. A procession for a dead person.

She broke into a sprint, dodging around people to get to the front. What if it was Daniel? She had to know, either way. As she dodged through the barricades, a policeman on a motorcycle yelled at her to get back.

She got as close as she could to the fire truck, her own lunatic voice ringing in her ears. "Who is that? Is that Daniel O'Connor?" Behind the wheel was a middle-aged woman with frizzy hair and big eyes. The ambulance swerved and arms grabbed Erin from behind, pulling her back behind the barricades. As the procession passed she stared after it, wondering what strange world she'd entered, where her husband was missing but nobody would help her and prayer was one of her best options.

Along 26th Street, the line to report missing persons was hours deep, snaking from the entrance on Lexington Avenue all the way to Park. Erin stood close to the end. In the thirty minutes she'd been there, she'd moved maybe fifteen feet. Flyers had followed her here, on every surface imaginable. Taped to the red brick walls of the armory, the blue police sawhorses, the light pole on the corner, the yellow and red newspaper dispensers. Even the mailbox was reptilian with them, its paper scales layered one over another, anchored at their ends by tape.

As she stared at the faces, thinking she should have made one for Daniel (How did all of these people know what to do? Had they lost loved ones before? Was there some missing person protocol she didn't know about?), her gaze settled on a face she knew. She broke out of line and ran to the light pole, ripping his face from the sea of other Missings.

He was sitting at his mother's kitchen table, a plastic fork in his hand and a slice of chocolate cake in front of him. A recent photo, one Erin didn't recognize, but it was her Daniel. His crooked smile. His floppy brown hair, with just the right amount of wave. Her husband. The man she'd planned to spend the rest of her life with. Typed across the top was his name, with *101st floor* and *Schaeffer McKesson* beneath it. They included his height, weight, and eye color. Erin shook with disappointment. The flyer made it real, somehow, that Daniel was gone. Reduced to one sad image among thousands on a pulpy, hope-filled shrine.

The line moved by inches. Erin clutched the flyer to her chest, shifting from one foot to the other. As she waited, the sun crossed from late morning to early afternoon, shining briefly on the corner of 26th and Lexington before dipping back behind another tall building. News crews came by occasionally, panning the crowd with their huge cameras. Faces sought them out, holding up photos of their missing and crying that they'd never give up hope. Erin turned away, not ready to play the hysterical widow.

She was getting angrier by the minute. The grieving were expected to stand in line for hours, patiently, like shoppers eager for a Black Friday deal. Nobody told them how long the line would take, or why they had to wait in it. Those around Erin compared stories. A woman in front of her was missing a brother on the ninety-first floor of the south tower; an older man behind her was searching for his wife, who was wheelchair bound and worked as a legal assistant on the fifty-seventh floor; a teenage boy searched for his father, who worked for the Port Authority on the sixty-sixth floor, north. When asked, Erin gave basic information, holding the flyer out but avoiding eye contact so she wouldn't see the look of pity when she said *101st floor*.

When Erin finally made it into the building, she was given a stapled packet of paper and told to fill it out. She asked the woman handing them out if there was a list of survivors, but the answer was not yet. Once she filled out her information, she'd be contacted immediately if they found anything or anyone. Dread rising, she grabbed a pen from a table and began to fill out the paperwork.

It was eight pages long. On the first page were all the basics: name, age, date of birth, hair color, eye color, employer, place last seen or heard from. She filled it out numbly, as if she were in the dentist's office. The second page asked questions about dental records (partial plate, braces, no teeth?) and objects in the body (pacemaker, bullets, steel plate, artificial limbs?). Daniel didn't have anything artificial in his body. She didn't think.

A haggard-looking woman next to Erin stared at her own form. The gruff, dirt-covered man next to her pointed at a line and said something softly. The woman began to weep, burying her head into his shoulder. To Erin's right, another woman was on the phone—"Is the birthmark on Jenna's calf more flesh colored or pink?" The question was clinical, as if they would find Jenna once she filled out this form correctly. Another man on the phone told someone, loudly, that he needed his son's dental records and could they email them right away?

Erin bent her head back to the form. On page four there were checklists for race, skin color, build, and physical identifiers like scars, birthmarks, tattoos, wigs, and toupees. Erin's pencil hovered at birthmarks. She was about to check "café au lait" and circle the human outline's stomach, but she realized that was *her* birthmark. She didn't know if Daniel had a birthmark. What kind of wife was she? She wrote *Unknown* on that line and kept going, as dry-eyed as if she were filling out an insurance application. At the line for facial hair style (Fu Manchu, whiskers under lower lip, mutton chops, pencil-thin upper lip, n/applicable), she wondered whether the lack of novelty in Daniel's physical appearance would diminish the effectiveness of the search. She never considered that tattoos or toupees might provide an advantage.

When it was complete, she handed the form to a haggard police officer. He was tall and thin with a dark mustache and bushy eyebrows. She wondered how his wife would describe him on a missing person form and whether his facial hair would expedite his rescue.

He took the form and said thank you.

Erin blinked. "What do I do now? Can I go look for him?"

The officer shifted his eyes back to Erin, and she noticed the dark shadows beneath them. "I'm sorry, but nobody's allowed down there."

She felt betrayed. What was she doing here, if not to verify she had a loved one missing so that she could look for him? Her voice was sharper than intended. "Then what am I supposed to do now?"

He shrugged his shoulders and smiled a sort of smile—lips stretched over his teeth and flattened into a line. "Pray. Don't give up hope."

Aside from praying, Erin didn't know what to do next. She stood at the intersection, watching cars stream by and New York go about its business. A swig of water kept her traitorous hunger at bay. The plume of gray ash hovered in the distance, and there was the smell, but otherwise the city seemed the same up here. It felt vulgar and wrong and unfair.

She looked down at the flyer in her hand, then called Aidan. He answered on the first ring.

"Erin! Where are you?"

"I'm staring at a flyer with Daniel's picture on it. Where did this come from?" Her voice was shrill and accusatory.

"Cathleen put it together. We needed something to hand out."

"Why didn't I know about this? I found it taped to a light pole. I've never even seen this picture before." A bus sped by too fast, whipping Erin's hair. She tried not to cry.

"I'm sorry, Erin. That must have been jarring." He used a soothing voice.

What's jarring, she thought, *is listening to Aidan—divorced, depressed Aidan—treating me like a mental patient.* She breathed in deep. "Does Daniel have a birthmark?"

"A birthmark?"

"I filled out forms and it asked for his birthmark. I don't even know if my own husband has a birthmark." Her voice hitched and she began to cry. "What kind of wife am I?"

Aidan kept a quiet, calm voice. "Erin, why don't you get a cab and come up here. Mom, Cathleen, and I are at the Pierre. Schaeffer's got tables set up for the families to work the phones and exchange info. We'll figure this out together."

In the cab on the way uptown, Erin dialed Daniel's number for the ten thousandth time since Tuesday. If only he would answer, all of this would go away. Life could go back to some sort of normal. But after five rings, she got his recorded voice. She hit redial repeatedly. If he was alive, buried in the rubble, a ringing phone might be heard.

At the hotel, a uniformed porter stood watchful under the awning that shaded the black-and-white tiled entrance. He opened the door for Erin without any questions. Inside was opulence—gold-embossed ceilings, crystal chandeliers, marble floors, lavish floral displays. Erin had been there once with Daniel, attending a charity event in a life that felt far, far away. She remembered climbing the curved staircase in an evening gown, Daniel in a tux next to her. The memory made her shudder. She didn't appreciate then how charmed her life was. She'd never take things for granted again.

Upstairs was the grand ballroom. Along the hallway, tables were set up with various signs: *Investigative Tips, Hospitals, Police, General Information.* There was a place to fill out missing person reports, and she felt so stupid. Of course she should've called Daniel's family first and asked them what to do, what they had already done. She was spinning her wheels. Being stuck overseas had made her ten steps behind, time she might never make up.

The ballroom was stunning—high arched ceilings, rococo chandeliers, a grand piano at the far end. At odds with the background were the people sitting at the banquet tables—haggard and disheveled, most in T-shirts, shorts, and flip-flops, looking like they hadn't slept or bathed for days. The tables were draped with white tablecloths and labeled with numbers—*99, 100, 101, 102, 103*. Floor numbers. Erin headed left toward the tables for the 101st floor.

As she got close, Helen O'Connor rushed toward her. Erin had never felt so happy to see her mother-in-law. "Erin, honey, we're very glad you're home safely." Helen was short and stout with salt-and-pepper hair and pale, freckly skin. Her green eyes, shot through with tiny vessels, were swollen and red. But they were just like Daniel's. As Helen folded Erin into her arms, the tears flowed.

"Where is he, Helen? Where is he?"

Helen rubbed Erin's back. "We're looking for him, dear, we're looking."

They'd never had a good relationship. Helen thought Erin was uppity and overly ambitious, not warm and sweet enough for her Danny. And Erin always thought Helen was too provincial, her talents not extending much beyond corned beef and cabbage. But now there was a mutual understanding. They were on the same side.

The room buzzed with subliminal stress and the low hum of conversation. Two small children darted past, laughing. A hollow ache struck Erin with each peal. Their mother shushed them, pulling them back to the table. Erin wanted to say, *Be happy, at least you have children.* She thought back to four short days ago when she was mad at Daniel for pushing the children issue. She'd been so wrong. Now she'd give anything to tell him she'd changed her mind, she was ready. Life's too capricious to wait until tomorrow.

At the table sat familiar faces. Aidan, looking even more weathered and creased. Cathleen, the oldest, her reddish-gray hair cinched back in a rough ponytail. Robert, Daniel's little brother, looking small and red-eyed. The table was littered with papers, water bottles, and half-empty coffee cups. An American Red Cross leaflet was open to the middle:

> *After the disaster, the following common, normal reactions may be experienced: disorientation, difficulty concentrating, trouble sleeping, headaches, skin disorders, sadness/apathy, guilt/self-blame, moodiness/irritability/ emotional outbursts, increased use of caffeine, alcohol, or drugs.*

Poking out underneath it, a word in red caught Erin's eye: *MISSING.* She snatched it up; it was the Daniel flyer she'd seen at the armory.

"When was this photo taken?" Erin demanded.

A baby at a nearby table screamed. Cathleen ran her hand gently over Daniel's face on another copy. "I'm sorry we did this without your input. But we had to put something together. This was the most recent photo we had, from Ma's party last Sunday."

Aidan put his hand over Erin's, rough and calloused and

warm. He'd taken on a protective role to his siblings after Daniel's father died. Erin always thought Aidan disapproved of her—the way he looked at her from under his heavy brow, knitted with deep thoughts. He never said anything, but it was his overall demeanor—brooding, never smiling.

But now, he was surprisingly kind. Which made Erin feel worse. If he'd been a jerk, she could have yelled at him, but instead she felt nothing but guilt. She should've been in that photo, on Daniel's left, fork in midair and a look of surprise on her face, wondering why the O'Connors never had wine at their parties. If she'd been there, Daniel might be with them now.

She stood up and walked away.

"Where are you going?" Cathleen asked.

Erin stopped, not sure where she was going. "I want to talk to someone from the company."

"All right," Cathleen said. "Come with me." She led Erin to a long table set up on the side where company representatives sat and answered questions.

Erin pushed to the front and addressed a woman with her head down, writing something on a printed spreadsheet. "What's being done to look for survivors?"

The woman looked up and blinked excessively while she spoke. "Mr. Riggs just made the announcement. The operation at Ground Zero has been transitioned from a rescue operation to a recovery effort."

Erin wasn't in the mood to interpret. "What does that mean?"

The woman's mouth made that familiar flat-line smile. "Meaning . . . that nobody else who's missing is expected to have survived the tragedy."

"So you're just giving up?"

"The company is doing everything it can."

"How many are missing from Schaeffer?"

The woman paused to take a breath. "Right now, we cannot account for 256 of the company's employees out of a total of 616. Everyone who was in our World Trade Center offices at the time of the attack."

Erin's head shook involuntarily. "Nobody who was there got out?"

"None that we know of."

The room began to spin, stars dancing in the dark edges. Cathleen guided Erin back to the table. She squeezed her head and rocked back and forth in the chair. When she was stuck in Europe, the full impact hadn't hit her because she had a goal: getting home. Now there was no immediate goal to occupy her attention.

Helen wrapped up a phone call—"OK, dear, call me if you hear anything else"—and stood next to Erin, rubbing her back. "Erin, dear. We have to be strong for Daniel."

Erin looked up. "Do you think he's dead?"

Helen sat down heavily. She flattened her lips over her teeth and shook her head. Cathleen put her hand over her mother's and leaned toward Erin. "There's not much hope. It's been four full days, one hundred hours with no news. And they say they've dug out the survivors. They've found only a few people alive." Her voice broke at *alive*. Helen handed her daughter a tissue.

"Can't we do something? Anything?"

Helen shook her head. "We've looked everywhere we can look. Every street, hospital, triage station, and rescue tent downtown."

Cathleen picked up the *Missing* flyer. "And this is taped up in every subway station, window, and bulletin board we could find."

"I know." Erin looked away. Quiet people poured coffee, shuffled papers, typed into laptops, pushed faces into hands. "I just feel so useless. What if I had been here sooner? What if I hadn't been stuck overseas? Maybe I could have gotten to him, or at least spoken to him."

Aidan shook his head at her. "There's nothing you could have done, Erin."

Helen looked around the table. "We're all exhausted. We haven't slept properly in days." She turned to Erin. "Why don't you go home, get some rest. Tomorrow's another day."

"Can't we go look for him ourselves?"

Aidan's voice was gruff. "We've tried every connection we have. It's no use. We can't get onto the pile."

"Then what am I supposed to do? Just go home, have dinner, sleep? How can I act normal, not knowing where he is?"

Cathleen wrung her weathered hands. "Erin, we're all hoping that he's still alive. But we have to start accepting reality."

Erin stood up. "They haven't found a body yet, have they? As long as there's no body, there's hope." She glanced around the table, but nobody would meet her eyes, as if they were embarrassed by their own resignation. She grabbed her bag and walked out the door.

Chapter Eight

September 16, 2001

It was Sunday—day six of Daniel being a *Missing*. As she'd done each morning since, Erin called his phone immediately when she woke up. But this morning, something was different. She couldn't leave a message. After his greeting, instead of a beep, a woman's voice politely dashed her hopes: *This mailbox is full and cannot accept any messages at this time. Goodbye.*

An optimistic voice said a full mailbox meant people were leaving him messages, which was good. She wasn't the only one hoping he was still alive. But then a nasty little voice said, *They're your messages, and he hasn't listened to them. I told you he's dead.*

One of her means of communication had been cut off, and it seemed irrevocable. She could still email him, sending messages into the void. But now she couldn't tell him in her own voice how much she missed him and loved him. Until now, there was a flicker of hope that he was listening.

She pulled herself out of bed and walked into the bathroom, feeling the dagger of silence in Daniel's absence. Usually he was the one to wake her up—he'd bound in after jogging, just as the sun was rising, and kiss her awake before he got in the shower. He was the morning person, and she was the miser. He usually worked the funk out of her by the time he left for work. If he were really gone, how would she pull out of her dark places?

After showering, she made coffee. The smell of it nauseated her, but she poured a cup anyway. Coffee was quotidian comfort. A cup of coffee in the morning meant the world still existed, for today. She left it black though. She'd have cream and sugar again when Daniel came home. Erin closed her eyes, thinking of Daniel and sugar, their love affair open and unabashed. He grew up eating junk food and never outgrew the habit. When he grocery shopped, he'd come back with Pop-Tarts, Count Chocula, and grape Crush in addition to what was on the list. His coffee was more cream and sugar than coffee. His sugar-spurred joie de vivre was childlike, untainted by fear of weight gain or diabetes.

Thinking of Daniel and his sugar crush, she felt a burst of progressive energy. She hadn't chased down all leads, looked everywhere, done everything she could do. She carried her black coffee, a notepad, and a pen to the table and sat down. She would make a list. A list of things to do to find her husband. A list was exactly what she needed. Lists were objective, organized, progressive, optimistic. Lists were filled with possible things.

At the top, centered, she wrote "Finding Daniel" and underlined it twice. Below that, she wrote "Hospitals" and listed each one she could think of, in bullet-point format. When she was finished, there were only five listed.

Erin stared downtown, where a gray plume jutted into the sky instead of the towers. Even the air in her apartment was tinged with the stench. As she stared, she imagined being in the cloud of smoke, inhaling as it wrapped its tentacles into her nose, throat, eyes, and ears, her body slowly being absorbed into it, molecule by molecule.

She shook her head to focus and called Cathleen. She asked her to email a copy of the Daniel flyer, and for the names of hospitals to check.

"I will, Erin, but just so you know, we already checked all of the hospitals in the area. Twice."

"I have to do it again, Cathleen. I have to make sure." An image from *The English Patient* haunted her. Count Almásy, unrecognizable, his face and hands burned into rivulets of scar tissue. Maybe unable to remember his own name. A nurse tending to him faithfully. Erin and Daniel had seen the movie a few years before, and Erin cried through most of it. She never imagined she'd find herself at a place where burnt anonymity was best-case scenario.

After speaking to Cathleen, Erin brainstormed more items to put on her to-do list. There were four things, in addition to visiting hospitals: file a missing persons report (which she had already done, so she checked it off), walk the site and ask people if they'd seen him (done, but she'd do it again), make her own flyers and post them everywhere, and call everyone who knew him. The last was probably a waste of time because anyone who knew anything would have called her.

Erin sat for a moment, trying to focus, but her eyes kept crossing and uncrossing. Surely there was something she was missing, something else she could do. Another task to add to the list.

She ripped the paper from the notepad and tore it into tiny little pieces. Lists were awful, terrible reminders of the futility of life. Lists were pointless, a waste of paper and ink.

When her parents knocked on the door two hours later, Erin was sitting on the floor with her head between her knees, trying not to throw up. Instead of feeling hopeful at their arrival, Erin felt a sinking sensation. Fitz and Eleanor in New York City, looking like fish out of water, here to help.

Erin had called her mother by her first name since she was eleven, when *Mommy* became too juvenile. She still wanted to call Eleanor *Mom*, but as she got older she realized the term made her mother uncomfortable. One day Erin called her *Eleanor* in front of her friends, and there was no flinch. It just seemed to flow. Though she still called Fitz *Daddy*, unless she was mad at him.

Her father dropped his bag in the hallway and gave her a great big bear hug. "Daddy!" she said, the tears flowing. Erin was like a little girl again, her father holding her after a bad dream. If only she could be comforted so easily this time.

Eleanor fluttered in after Fitz, chirping, "Oh, Erin, honey. Darling, are you OK?" Thin arms wrapped around Erin's neck, an air kiss grazed her cheek. "My dear, look what you've been through. We came as soon as we could." She looked svelte and sophisticated—a smooth, gray wrap sweater, flawless black dress pants, black suede boots, polished nails. Her blond bob was perfect. Erin searched for the gray that should have been there, but there was no trace. Eleanor wrapped her arms tightly around her shivering, cashmere-clad torso.

Nerves. Fitz told Erin once, in a candid moment when she was in high school, that her mother suffered from nerves. At the time, she hadn't fully understood. She just knew that her mother was odd, not like other mothers. Sometimes she made dinner, and other times she hid in her room all day. But now, nerves showed through in her mother's forced smile, uncontrollable shakes, and how she shifted her gaze to Fitz for support.

Fitz brought their bags in and dropped them in the guest room. Then both of her parents stood in the living room, taking in the surroundings, looking lost as nuns at Mardi Gras.

"Thank you for coming," Erin said.

"Of course we came. We're here to help you get through this. And we will get through it—we always have and we always will."

Erin looked at her father eagerly. "We'll find Daniel? You'll help me, won't you?"

Fitz and Eleanor exchanged a look. It was the same look they shared when Erin wanted to drive their new BMW convertible downtown to the R.E.M. concert, when she asked to do a semester abroad in Australia, and when she told them she was marrying a boy from the Bronx. Fitz guided her to the table. The three of them sat down, and Fitz covered Erin's hand with his. "Erin, they're doing everything they can to find him. And you'll bounce back. You always do."

Erin shoved away from the table, hard, and stood up. "Bounce back? What do you mean I'll bounce back?"

"From this terrible tragedy. We all will. This whole country will bounce back. Those Muslim bastards. We'll bomb the hell out of those raghead sons of bitches, and we'll hunt down every last one of them and slit their throats, and we'll build those towers again in the same place, bigger and better than before!"

Erin looked at her father as if he were speaking Chinese. "I don't understand anything you're saying."

"Fitz, dear, she probably hasn't watched any television." Eleanor grabbed Erin's hand and pulled her back down into the seat, then patted her leg under the table. "Everything's gonna be just fine."

Bounce back? Everything's gonna be just fine? Erin stood up again, backing away from the table. She knew her parents were shallow and stereotypical, but until now she hadn't experienced it viscerally. Their discomfort at dealing with difficulty was etched on their faces. The faces of well-to-do people accustomed to good times, unable to cope with unexpected tragedy.

"You didn't have to come. I'm sure you're missing a golf game or a spa appointment or something." The anger surprised even her. The thought that they weren't upset enough pushed into Erin's head. According to Fitz, his daughter settled a few stations below her. Daniel O'Connor from Woodlawn Heights, North Bronx, was not the ideal choice for the Jameses' only child. Or not Hubert Fitzpatrick James III's choice—Eleanor Blanton James always agreed with her husband. Sure, Daniel was smart, made it to Princeton, and managed to woo their daughter, but he was Irish working-middle-class from the Bronx, and he was nice. Too nice. Not smart or ambitious enough for Fitz James's prized possession. His pride and joy, heir apparent, and the son he never had.

Fitz and Eleanor exchanged that look again. The one that said they were afraid that Erin might go off the rails, that they wouldn't be able to control her.

Erin grabbed her purse. "I'm going to look for Daniel."

Eleanor assumed a maternal face. "Erin, do you think there's anything you can do down there?"

"I don't want to hear it, Eleanor. Daniel's missing. And I'm going to look for him."

Fitz stood up with difficulty, hefting his paunch and groaning. She'd never thought of her father as old before, but he looked it now. His thick hair was solid gray, and there were deep creases on his weathered face. He moved more slowly than before. "Where are we going?"

Erin and Fitz stood at the northern perimeter of Ground Zero, at Greenwich and Park. The ancient sun hung low in the western sky. This was the side Daniel's office was on. From the rooftop terrace of their apartment on 79th Street, he would point to the windows of his office, using binoculars to find the exact window nearest his desk. Erin never understood his fascination with locating exactly where he worked, but now at least she knew the direction it had faced.

She looked up again, to make sure. Nothing but sun-obliterating, nasal-searing smoke.

Of all of the things Erin had accomplished in her life—Harvard Law School, the New York bar exam, long hours at the office—nothing prepared her for this. According to the *Times* that morning, people on Wall Street were moving forward with business as usual, but there were no answers for Erin, no blueprints for solving her problem.

Huge dump trucks lumbered by, streaming from the belly of the disaster. The once-white trucks were now dirty and dented, *M-A-C-K* in silver letters along the front. Hauling loads of concrete rubble and twisted steel beams, metal shards, nameless dust embedded with wires, all of it covered in gray. Even the drivers were caked with it, grim looks on haggard faces. Crucifixes hung from rearview mirrors.

They'd spent most of the afternoon looking for Daniel in hospitals. The closest ones first—St. Vincent's, Presbyterian,

Bellevue, NYU, Mount Sinai, St. Luke's. Then up to Lenox Hill, Columbia, and four hospitals in the Bronx. Each time the result was the same. They went in armed with the Daniel flyers, asked to speak to hospital administration. Showed photos to everyone they passed. Pinned the flyers to bulletin boards. Spoke to the head nurse in charge on each floor. Asked to see all of the unidentified patients. They were met with sad looks and negative head shakes. Nobody who looked like Daniel, no anonymous patients. No Count Almásy.

Eleanor stayed home to answer calls and be the point person if there was any news. There was none.

Though it seemed hopeless, Erin dragged her father down to the site, compelled as if by magnet. They'd tried every guard on the perimeter. Fitz told them all he'd served in 'Nam, 101st Airborne, but it didn't help. There was no breaching the perimeter. When Erin asked a guard who was in charge, he bore his eyes into hers and said, "God, if we're lucky. Or Bush, if we're not. But neither one is available right now."

They turned around and walked aimlessly for a few blocks, not speaking. They stopped when they came to a corner with a clear view of the thick gray smoke rising from the pit in the distance. Finally, Erin spoke. "He didn't even try to call me. We were in a fight. It was so stupid. It kills me, thinking that he was in a burning building and I was on the beach, drinking margaritas."

"Oh, baby." Fitz squeezed her hand. "Don't blame yourself. It's not your fault."

Erin shook her head and choked on tears. "It feels like it's all my fault."

Fitz's phone rang and he took the call, turning his back to her and walking a few paces away. Erin walked to the middle of the street, devoid of cars and most people. She stared at the untainted blue sky crowning the cloud of devastation a few short blocks away.

A siren whined from the direction of the West Side Highway. A fat pigeon waddled by, pecking at invisible crumbs. A dystopian sight, pigeons instead of cars on Broadway. The world turned upside down.

A gust of burning stench blew past, bringing all the bad thoughts. Was that the smell of Daniel's death? Was Daniel there, now, all around her? Could he see her, hear her? She kneeled and coated her index finger with a fine layer of gray silt. She brought it to her nose and inhaled, closing her eyes. Rubbed it along the bridge of her nose and up onto her forehead, like it was Ash Wednesday.

She tried to cry, but the tears wouldn't come.

It wasn't him. She had to believe he was still out there, still breathing, until she was faced with evidence otherwise.

When Fitz came back, he took off his glasses, wiped them with his shirttail, and put them back on. Finally, he turned to Erin and put his hands on her shoulders. His eyes, shot through with tiny blood vessels and underscored by purple bags, were grim. "Erin, honey, I know you don't want to hear this. But it's been five days since anyone heard from Daniel. His family and his friends have been looking for him nonstop." He tilted his chin down and shook his head. "You need to face the possibility that he might not have made it."

"Who was that?" She almost wanted him to tell her they'd found Daniel's body. That he was dead, so that at least she would know.

"It was Helen. They're writing his obituary. They want you to look at it before they publish it. They've scheduled the memorial service for next Friday, the twenty-first."

"How can they give up like that? We can't have a memorial service—there's no body. There's no proof that he's dead."

"And there's no proof that he's alive either. It's been five full days." It went unspoken that people couldn't survive that long, injured and buried under rubble. "Erin, a lot of people are worried about you."

"Worried about me? They should be worried about Daniel."

"They're worried about both. That you're not accepting reality."

With the toe of her sneaker, Erin traced lines in the dust on the sidewalk. "I think they've given up too easily."

Fitz nodded. "Be that as it may, they are writing his obit. Do you want to be involved or not?"

Erin kicked up a cloud of dust. She didn't want to think about obituaries or memorial services or death, and the thought of planning a funeral made her weak. She put her forehead on her father's shoulder and shook her head no.

A few days later, Erin held an empty plastic bag with an orange zip lock, *Police Evidence Bag* written across it in blue, and opened the medicine cabinet. Inside was Speed Stick and aftershave, a white styptic pencil, prescription allergy meds. Her fingers lingered on his razor, sleek and silver. She pulled it from the base and inspected it. Dark stubble was wedged between the blades. She pushed in the direction of the blade, popping chunks of hair into the bag. His red toothbrush went in, along with hair she pulled from his small blue brush.

In the bedroom, she picked up his pillow, which hadn't been washed. A few days before, Erin caught her mother stripping the sheets off the bed and screamed at her to stop, bolting over to Daniel's pillow and clutching it to her chest as if it were a baby. "No! You will not wash this pillowcase." Now she closed her eyes and buried her face in it. There was his smell, buttered corn and warm cotton, so faint she might have imagined it. She closed her eyes and visualized that she was hugging him, burying her nose in his neck. As she pulled back to reality, she noticed a few short dark hairs on the pillow that must have been his. These went into the bag too.

The City of New York had set up a victims' assistance center at Pier 94 along the Hudson River and asked that family members bring DNA samples to help identify victims. Daniel's mother and siblings would take the bag later today, and would have their cheeks swabbed and their hair pulled for identification. Since Erin didn't share his DNA, she wouldn't be expected to go. Instead, she'd do her part by filling this bag with the remnants of his body.

She zipped the orange strip and set the bag on her desk, hoping it'd be enough. She didn't care that much, actually, since this was part of a plan for finding him dead, not alive. She shuffled to the kitchen where, as usual in her new reality, her parents were sitting at the table drinking coffee and reading the *Times*. As she poured coffee into a mug, she wondered how many times Daniel used this mug. If this was the last mug he used on the last morning he was here. She cursed herself for not setting aside his cup, the one that had been on the table when she came home. But she hadn't, and her mother had washed it on her first day there. The DNA people probably didn't want moldy coffee anyway.

As she took her first sip, her father pushed away from the table, walked over to her, and set the newspaper on the counter beside her. It was carefully folded in half and then in quarters, obituary side up. At the top was the date—*Tuesday, September 18, 2001*. Below that, Daniel's name.

She read every word, then set the newspaper back on the counter. And then went into the bathroom, locked the door, and cried until there were no tears left but only stars, twinkling around the edges of her vision. A beautiful aura, like the northern lights. Silver, shimmering, but with more and more darkness around the edges. She gave in to it, finding the darkness alluring. Another half hour of slow progress and the sparkles encompassed everything in their path. And then the pain set in. Throbbing, jaw-wrenching agony on the same schedule as her heartbeat, as if someone were squeezing brain matter from her skull like toothpaste. Before, she thought migraine sufferers were constitutionally weak, but now here she was, lying on the cold bathroom floor, head wedged between toilet and cabinet, immobilized by a headache.

She stayed there for what could have been minutes or hours, trying not to move her head. Her mother knocked on the door occasionally and Erin answered that she was fine, because if she didn't Fitz might break down the door. Outside the door, Eleanor and Fitz spoke to each other in frantic whispers, probably debating whether their daughter was suicidal. Erin did wish at this moment that she would just die, that the building would close in around her and she wouldn't have to wake up tomorrow and go through another day of this torture.

The migraines continued each morning after, and each time she went to the same spot of cold white tile in her bathroom and lay there, still as a rock until it passed. Once it did, she'd go down to the site again and all of the hospitals, passing out flyers and asking if anyone had seen him. Sometimes Fitz came with her, sometimes he didn't.

On the fourth morning, as she focused on keeping her head and body still, she seriously contemplated letting this be the end. But a knock on the door and a reminder that they needed to leave soon meant today was not a day for suicide. Today, Erin would officially be declared a widow. Play the role and say the words and accept the fate.

Over the din of Fox News, the door opened and closed. Twenty minutes later, it opened and closed again. There was a knock on the door. "Erin, please, honey. I've got some medicine for you. The doctor says it will help."

"I don't want help."

"You need it today. To get through the memorial service. We have to leave soon."

She groaned. Her mother was right. She couldn't play the widow without drugs to penetrate her bloodstream, make her functional, take away the migraine, and coat her words and thoughts with a sheen of chemical affability. Carefully, slowly, she lifted her head from the floor, slid toward the door, and unlocked it.

Eleanor knelt down beside her with a vial of pills and a glass of water. Erin propped herself up on her left elbow and opened her mouth. Her mother put two small pills on Erin's tongue and pressed the glass to her lips as if she were a third grader.

After she swallowed, Erin fell back down to the floor.

Eleanor tried to help her up, but it was no use; Erin was dead weight. "Fitz, come help us, please?"

Fox News paused and Erin's father walked into the bathroom. Together her parents hoisted Erin off the floor and propped her against the under-sink cabinet. She tucked her knees into her chest and rested her head there, waving her parents away.

Within thirty minutes, the pill had sunk in and she could stand. After brushing her teeth and hair, she emerged from the bathroom. It was time to prepare for her husband's funeral.

Eleanor must have gone shopping at some point in the last week, because a somber black dress and a box with a black-veiled hat were waiting on her perfectly made bed. She was begrudgingly grateful for her mother's shopping abilities—the dress fit perfectly, and the hat would give Erin the cover she needed.

Once dressed, she looked into the full-length mirror on the inside of her closet door. She was shocked by what she saw. Pale, sickly face. Purple shadows under her eyes. Frizzy, straw-like hair. Instinctively, she reached for her makeup drawer and pulled it out. She grabbed the powder case and rubbed the pad into the beige powder cake vigorously, spreading a thick layer over her face and onto her eyelids. She reassessed. Normally she would move on to blush, eye shadow, mascara. When her gaze fell on a gold tube of red lipstick, she shuddered.

Before, when she wore lipstick as her signature, she'd been seeking color and impact, something to set her apart from the crowd. Now she wanted the opposite—to hide, tuck her body back in bed and never get out again. She shoved the lipstick to the back of the drawer, hiding it behind old blush compacts and makeup brushes.

Helen had planned everything. The location, the order of events, the people who would eulogize him, right down to the polished wooden coffin that Daniel wasn't lying in. In fact, Erin hadn't done much at all surrounding Daniel's funeral, occupied as she had been with trying to find him alive. To be fair, they had asked her if she wanted to help. But still, it bothered her that Helen assumed her role in charge of Daniel's funeral by right of reversion, as if the thirteen months of marriage didn't matter. There weren't any children, after all, nothing left of the marriage's existence but a piece of paper filed away somewhere in Texas and an apartment of shared possessions. Erin hadn't even changed the name on her driver's license yet.

Fitz escorted her into the sanctuary. He paused, hesitant, at the holy water in basins before the nave. Erin considered genuflecting and crossing herself as she'd seen Daniel do but couldn't remember if she was supposed to or not, as a non-Catholic at a funeral. But if it was her husband's funeral, would it be rude not to? And then she found herself wondering why Daniel's funeral was in a Catholic church when they weren't Catholic. Maybe he still was. She didn't actually know how someone becomes un-Catholic. She was starting to feel like an uninvited guest. After an awkward moment, she tugged on her father's arm and kept walking, without genuflection, shrouded head held high.

The church was standing room only. A pianist in black played somber dirges. They were supposed to sit in the front pew on the right side of the church facing the altar. As they approached, Erin caught glimpses of people she knew. Jess was there, sitting with her boss, Craig, who Erin knew from weekends in the Hamptons. There were Erin's friends, Daniel's friends, Daniel's coworkers, acquaintances, and lawyers from Erin's firm. Even her secretary, Judy, was there.

Erin looked straight ahead as she passed, avoiding faces bent with temporary sorrow. Their presence and civility a reminder of the unspoken acceptance of the possibility of death around every corner, that the floor could buckle beneath you at any moment. These people's tears might have been real, but their grief wouldn't last. And that was socially acceptable. Copacetic. Expedient. The covenant shared among the living—that life must go on.

What if Erin couldn't go on?

Centered at the altar at the end of the long nave was a shiny, dark coffin. It was open, draped with numbered jerseys and rosaries. A blown-up photo of Daniel as a high school senior sat on an easel next to it. Lilies were everywhere, their sickeningly sweet smell belying the fact that they were dead too. Just before Erin sat, she caught a glimpse inside the coffin.

She knew what was in it. Old photos, notes he had written, stuffed animals from his childhood, a wad of hair his mother saved from the DNA bag, postmortem letters from family members telling him how much he meant to them, how valuable his short life was to theirs.

More telling, she knew what was not in it.

They'd asked Erin to write a letter too, but when she sat down with a pen and paper she found herself devoid of feeling, mind blank, nothing but a cold stare making its way onto the paper. This wasn't how she would remember Daniel. This ceremony, this empty coffin, this Catholic service was so that his family and friends could move on, not Erin. That would take a lot more than a Catholic mass.

As Erin listened to a priest she had never met talk about her husband as a child, Erin imagined how embarrassed everyone would be if he turned up, injured but alive, in a hospital somewhere. They who were so eager to say goodbye to him, fair-weather friends and family. Erin vowed that she would never give up on Daniel.

Chapter Nine

October 10, 2001

Nineteen days later, Erin stood on Greenwich Street north of the Ground Zero barricades, in front of the café where she got coffee every postapocalyptic morning. Its plate-glass windows were plastered with flyers beginning to curl and yellow at the edges, tearing at the seams where paper met tape. But Daniel's was pristine, white, new. Erin replaced them all, frequently.

After the funeral, denial and hope ran away together, and grief descended in their place.

She had become obsessed with reenacting their last days together. There may have been a first time for everything, but there was a last time too. The last time Daniel hugged her (outside, on the street, as she was getting into the cab to leave), the last time they ate at their favorite restaurant (Pastis, at lunch on a Sunday in August), the last time they made love (Sunday, September 2, in the morning after his run). The last time she held his hand, smiled at him, brushed her fingers across his stubble (she couldn't remember). The last time Daniel called her his wife.

Now she'd be called his *widow*. The word ripped through her head, wrapping its cruel, ugly angles around every neuron. She couldn't be a widow. Widows were old, salt-and-pepper-haired women with shrouds covering their faces. They wore long, flowing black gowns and pointy-toed shoes and scared little children who trick-or-treated at their doors. Erin was too young, too optimistic, too ambitious to be a widow. Death didn't happen to her and Daniel, it happened to unfortunate people.

When Erin married Daniel, she did it for the long term. She loved him enough to know she would have regretted losing him. So she said yes for her future self—the woman who was going to have his children and watch him become a father, who was going to grow old and travel with her loyal, steadfast husband. She never considered one of the possible outcomes was ending up a *widow* before the age of thirty.

She handed flyers out to the exhausted-looking workers on their way out, coated in dust, and to the freshly showered officers and firemen heading in the other direction. To sympathetic passersby, to anyone who looked her in the eye, she said, "Please let me know if you've seen him."

Almost always, they shook their heads, avoided her eyes, and hurried away. Occasionally they stopped and squeezed her hand and told her they were sorry for her loss.

A plane traversed the sky overhead and Erin stopped and stared, even after it passed.

Almost every day since coming back to New York, she'd been down to the site of the former World Trade Center, a seething pile of rubble, smoke, burning toxins, and recovery workers. She watched the Mack trucks drive along the West Side Highway bearing their unthinkable burdens. She had become intimately familiar with the route, the officers and guardsmen manning the barricades, the volunteers handing out food and water, the burned smell of death.

Erin had visited every hospital from Staten Island to the Bronx, Manhattan and Brooklyn and Queens, even Long Island and New Jersey. Some multiple times. She'd asked to see unidentified patients and had been met with pitiful headshakes. She'd made her own flyer for Daniel, with all the same information but using her favorite photo of him and her phone number on the bottom, and she'd plastered copies on blank walls and bulletin boards all over the city. She carried them as she walked, her messenger bag slung crossbody-style to keep her hands free. Recovery workers and hospital staff knew her by name.

After a few weeks of hospital rounds, she gave up, frustrated with the looks of pity and the closed doors. Now she spent hours each day walking the perimeter of Ground Zero, hoping for a miracle. It was the closest she could get to Daniel.

Now that Daniel was gone, he was everywhere—in the messenger boy on his bike, in the white-aproned worker sweeping the street in front of the deli, in the man with the business suit walking briskly to the subway, newspaper and briefcase in hand. He was the father sweetly holding his child's hand, the child Daniel never had and the father he would never be. He was the shift in the wind's direction, the structure in the wandering clouds, and the voice that whispered just behind her ear, the one that disappeared as soon as she turned to it.

As Erin continued to bump along at rock bottom, almost everyone else had disappeared. Fitz and Eleanor had gone back to Dallas a week ago. The phone calls and visits from friends had died down. Even Jess had been distant. She called every once in a while to check in, but the calls were few and far between now. She blamed it on work and being busy helping with her company's recovery efforts, but Erin suspected it had more to do with not knowing what to say, the awkwardness of being around someone who believed her life to be over. Nobody wanted to be around depressed people. Erin also suspected the main reason had to do with a rumor she'd heard—Jess was dating one of Daniel's best friends and coworkers, Nick Messina, and she was all wrapped up in him. Nick also worked at Schaeffer. In fact, Daniel had recruited him there, but apparently he wasn't in the office yet on the morning of September 11. Jess probably knew that Erin wasn't ready to deal with that yet, but still it angered Erin that she had to hear it from one of Jess's friends rather than Jess herself.

Erin's law firm sent someone to talk to her. The woman, who Erin had never met before, offered grief counseling, discussed benefits, and told her to take as much time off as she needed. A sort of temporary disability leave. Though they hadn't put a limit on it, it wouldn't last forever. But money and clients were the last things on Erin's new priority list. Eventually they would probably fire her, and building management would lock her out of the apartment, and the utility companies would turn off her electricity and water and gas. In the meantime, Erin would keep searching.

Aidan was the only person who hadn't abandoned her. He called her every day to check in, brought her breakfast, and even helped her pass out flyers around the site on weekends. She suspected he didn't hold out hope anymore, that he was just doing it to keep her company. He had gone back to work after the memorial service, but he stopped by her apartment every morning with coffee and every night with takeout. The night before, though, he came without food and told her, gently, that it was time to start the process of healing. That it was now October, and the time for hoping for a miracle was over.

"You need to get out of the house, and not just to look for Daniel. Come on, let's go to the Greek place on the corner. Baby steps."

Erin had been on the computer, scrutinizing a just-released map of Ground Zero. She was wearing sweatpants that hadn't been washed in three weeks, because the pile of dirty laundry next to the closet was so high she couldn't open the closet door. Her hair was in a messy ponytail and she wore glasses, not having bothered with contacts for days.

She pushed her glasses up and looked at Aidan as if he'd said, *Let's fly to Jupiter*. For a moment, her heart jumped as though she were looking at Daniel. Other things about him were not at all the same—where Daniel was muscular and proportioned, Aidan was cut from a slab, thick and rectangular. Daniel's skin was smooth and clear, while Aidan's was rough and prickly with hair. Daniel always smiled; Aidan rarely did. But their faces and voices were eerily similar, in a way Erin couldn't pinpoint.

"I can't imagine going to dinner ever again," she said.

Aidan shrugged. "I understand. I loved him too. I don't want to move on either, but we don't have a choice. At some point, you might want to start living again. And when that day comes, I'll be here to help you."

Erin stood in the middle of Chambers Street, watching the sun set over the Hudson. Smoke and haze flung fiery oranges and reds across the sky—rich, deep colors Erin couldn't enjoy because they wouldn't exist without particulates from the depths of hell.

Two women bustled by, speaking in loud New York accents and looking behind them, where a dark plume still smoldered and the towers were still gone. "Did you hear there were jumpers? I heard from a friend of mine who was in the Garment District that she could see them, dots dropping from the top of the tower. She didn't know what the things falling were then, but now everyone knows. Can you imagine falling that far down, knowing you're about to die?"

They came to an abrupt stop, their conversation over. The women glanced at Erin and then at the Daniel flyers, facing out, tucked into Erin's crossed arms. Their eyes dropped and they scurried away.

Could Daniel have jumped? The crash spanned floors ninety-three to ninety-eight, just a few floors below his office. The fires would have been raging, the heat and smoke intense. She closed her eyes and imagined the view from his office, then imagined falling from it. One hundred and one floors down. Her lungs squeezed tight and she forced shallow, hyperventilating breaths. The papers fell to the ground and caught a breeze, skittering along the sidewalk into the gutter and down the metal stairs of a café basement.

She backed up until she was against a brick wall. Thoughts rushed her head, of people falling, their stories and hopes and dreams falling with them. How many were there? What were they thinking as they fell? Why did they do it? How bad must the conditions have been to cause people to do that?

And then certainty hit her like a baseball bat. Daniel was really and truly gone, possibly in the worst way imaginable. She would never see him again. His face was becoming harder to conjure; his strong, deep voice would never calm her again. She closed her eyes tight and tried to picture his face, his dimples. His hand on her cheek, his lips on hers. Her traitorous brain brought only wispy memories. She pleaded with the universe and whoever ran it: *Please please please. I need a miracle.*

In response, a loud voice boomed out, "Superman, don't save me!"

A busker on the corner stood on an upturned wooden crate, a black felt hat sprinkled with coins and dollar bills at his feet.

Let me fall

I said, you came a long distance, but I don't need your help

Let me break it down to you, in simple physics

I said to the Man of Steel

If mass hits a terminal velocity of 122 miles per hour and you're faster than a speeding bullet, then you catching me while I'm falling would do more harm than good

So, Superman, don't save me, let me fall

Let the ground be my cushion

Because I'd rather my body be broken than my fall

My spirit is already broken, and you're not my lucky token

So, Superman, don't save me, let me fall

Let the wind massage my skin

Let gravity do its job

Erin bolted away and toward the barricades, escaping from a poltergeist. A police sentry caught her in an embrace, stopping her solid. His chest heaved as he wrapped his arms around her. Her knees buckled, and she fell to the New York sidewalk, coated with the smudges of thousands of pieces of chewing gum, the officer gently releasing her. Curled up on her side, Erin closed her eyes. She was like a homeless person, this street the closest place to home now. Lying on the ground that caught him, held him, embraced what was left of him.

She flattened her right hand on the ground and pressed her left cheek to cold concrete, closed her eyes, and breathed Daniel in.

She lay there a long while, long enough to lose awareness of her surroundings. It was, strangely, like death must be. People passed by. She sensed them starting to form a cluster. Did she hear them talking or just imagine it? Whispers, murmurs. *A 9/11 widow. Still trying to find her husband.* The officer who caught her shooed onlookers away.

The air shifted and cold clouds pushed out the sun. It was the first time she'd experienced peace since the day the world changed, and maybe ever. She didn't want to leave, but the officer eventually roused her, told her it'd be getting dark soon and she should be getting home.

The next morning, she woke up disoriented and fully clothed, lying on top of her bed. In the kitchen, a half-empty vodka bottle sat on the counter. She screwed the top back on and made coffee. While it was brewing, she opened the front door to get the paper, but it wasn't there. She stood for a moment, trying to remember the last time it came. Whether she got a renewal notice.

The door across the hallway opened. Erin's neighbor Fiona, red hair fresh from bed, looked wide-eyed when she saw her. She was a young mother, married to Angus. Both from Scotland. Erin had heard them coming and going with the baby since the disaster, but she hadn't seen them. "How are you?" Fiona asked, looking genuinely concerned.

Erin ran her fingers through her hair, eyes crinkling with tears. "It hasn't been easy. You know about Daniel?"

Fiona bit her bottom lip and squinted. "Yeah, love, I heard. Can I do anything for you? I didn't want to intrude before . . ."

"Do you have a paper?"

"A paper? Sure." Fiona seemed eager, probably relieved at the small favor she could help with, and that Erin didn't want to talk. She disappeared into her entryway and returned a few seconds later with the *New York Post*.

"The *Post*?" Erin hadn't pegged them as *Post* people.

"We don't take the *Times*, sorry."

Erin glanced at the cover—a photo of one of the hijackers. The face of evil. Erin felt like she was going to throw up. She nodded quickly to Fiona and closed the door. Inside, she poured black coffee and opened the paper, hiding the face of her husband's murderer.

She sipped hot coffee without enjoying it. In the apartment all was quiet except the ticking of the baby grandfather clock on the mantle—Erin's gift to Daniel on their first anniversary—and the occasional honk from the streets below. The ubiquitous noise, so familiar to New Yorkers, had recently started up again after a period of détente.

The front of the Metro section caught Erin's eye. It featured a photo of a familiar-looking woman wearing a long-sleeved black knit top, jeans, a bag strapped across her chest. Curled up in a fetal position, eyes closed and cheek pressed to sidewalk. Blue barricades loomed behind her along with an uncertain-looking, barrel-chested police officer standing guard. Against her wrapped arms, propped up as if staged, was a flyer, the words *Missing* and *101 North Tower—WTC 1* in red caps across the top. The headline beneath the photo read, "The Weeping Widow of 9/11: Loyal Wife Refuses to Give Up Hope."

It took Erin a few seconds to connect the dots. She glanced down at the clothes she was wearing. Black long-sleeved top, jeans. She was the woman in the photo.

She closed the paper without reading the article and finished her coffee with a shaky hand. After the last bitter sip, she called Aidan.

Chapter Ten

December 16, 2001

Erin couldn't breathe.

She sat perched on the edge of the bed, hands in lap, as Helen O'Connor rifled through Daniel's closet, pulling clothes off hangers and underwear out of drawers, separating everything into three piles, labeled *Keep*, *Donate*, and *Trash*. Before Helen, Cathleen, and Aidan showed up, Erin had put aside the few items she wanted to keep—the frayed Mets baseball cap that Daniel wore every weekend and not just to Mets games, a set of gold Texas-shaped cufflinks Erin gave him on their wedding day, and his favorite T-shirt, which said *Ewing Oil: Keep on Pumpin'* above a pump jack and which Erin had bought for him when they were dating. She kept his driver's license, a Princeton sweatshirt, and his favorite pair of boxers, sprinkled with tiny green shamrocks and *Luck o' the Irish* printed across the butt.

Other than these items, some wedding photos, and her pixelated memories, after today there would be nothing left of Daniel in her life.

From the kitchen a clanging noise reverberated, as though someone dropped a skillet. Cathleen was packing everything away into boxes. Erin had decided to sell the condo and move, though when and where hadn't been settled. What she did know was that she couldn't live here anymore. Everything reminded her of him, beginning with the walls themselves.

Erin and Daniel had bought the condo less than a year ago, after Daniel got a promotion. They found it a few days before Christmas last year, four months after their August wedding. They searched in every neighborhood in Manhattan for months before they found it. In Midtown, a "two-bedroom" was really a one-bedroom with a mattress and an alarm clock inside a walk-in closet. In Greenwich Village, the two bedrooms were each the size of walk-in closets, one only slightly bigger than the other, both oddly angled. The East Village was too sketchy, Gramercy too dull, Upper East too stuffy and expensive. The Upper West Side was just right. It was on the red subway line, which Erin and Daniel could take together, Erin getting off at Times Square and Daniel riding all the way downtown. They were able to find a two-bedroom with a view. There were babies and dogs on the sidewalks, quiet evenings, late-night bars and Sunday brunch hot spots, and few tourists.

It'd been January when they moved in—cold and gray, banks of sooty snow lining the crusty streets. Erin had decided they needed to start their married life anew, with furniture they bought together. They moved in with only a couch from Erin's law school apartment, a rug she bought on a summer adventure to Turkey, and a full-sized mattress they threw on the floor by the bedroom window and covered with blankets. They didn't own a television. Those first few weeks, before they pulled their wedding gifts out of storage and spent weekends at furniture stores, they got by with the bare necessities, sleeping on a mattress on the floor. At night after work, there was nothing for the newlyweds to do but eat dinner on the couch and make love on the floor. They were in the process of hiring a contractor to renovate the kitchen and paint the walls; in the meantime, they doodled on the walls and wrote notes to each other in magic marker as they came and went. Daniel drew amateurish portraits of Erin in every room, one with flowers in her hair, another with a halo over her head, and one a caricature where she looked like an alien (*a beautiful alien*, he had corrected her when she pointed it out). Somehow in those silly drawings, buried now underneath several coats of paint, Daniel had managed to capture the essence of her.

Looking back, Erin realized that having Daniel and few possessions was the happiest time of her life.

Helen went about her business with brusque efficiency. "Honey, what about these? Couldn't you wear them?" Helen held up a stack of crisp white T-shirts.

Erin took a few steps toward her and skimmed her shaking fingers along the top shirt, shivering in a draft of closet air. She shook her head. "No. Donate them."

Helen tut-tutted, putting the T-shirts in her *Keep* pile, then moved on to his jeans, hung neatly on thick plastic hangers. "And all of these? They're like new."

Erin might have been offended by Helen's insinuation that Daniel's jeans would fit her. She had a twenty-six-inch waist, and Daniel's jeans were size 32. Instead, she closed her eyes and spread her lips into a smile. "Helen, why don't you take them?"

Helen raised her stubby eyebrows and put the stack of jeans next to the T-shirts. "They're perfectly good jeans. I'm sure I can find someone who can use them." Helen had a hard time letting go of possessions. Her cluttered, tchotchke-filled house was one of the reasons Erin rarely accompanied Daniel on the occasional Sunday when he went to Woodlawn Heights to take his mom to mass and have lunch with the family. That and all the chaos—Aidan and his two girls, Cathleen with her husband and three children, and Robert would all be there. They were a boisterous family, and it was a small house.

When Erin called Aidan two months before, ready to move on to stage two of her grief (goodbye denial, hello anger, depression, and bargaining all swirled together), Aidan had taken her just a few steps away to the restaurant on the corner, as promised. They were big steps for both of them. Aidan was broken too—by his little brother's death, but also by divorce. A few months before September 11, Aidan's wife left him for a hulky firefighter neighbor, taking the kids and moving across the street from their house in Washington Heights. He told Erin about watching his life continue on outside his window, without him. That he was so close made it easier on his two girls, five and three, but harder on Aidan, watching the newly happy family come and go. On Wednesday nights and every other Friday, the girls walked across the street to Aidan's place, carting their little suitcases filled with essentials—stuffed animals they couldn't live without, toothbrushes, favorite pajamas, picture books. Even when his sunshine-filled girls were with him, and before the divorce and Daniel's death, Aidan tended toward dark and depressed. Erin guessed it was part of the reason he wasn't married anymore.

The two of them hadn't had much of a relationship before—they had nothing in common, and there seemed no good reason to be friends. Aidan was always awkward and formal, barely looking Erin in the eye. Now Daniel's death had given them something in common. At dinner that first night in October, they discussed Daniel incessantly, hungrily. Aidan had access to the parts of Daniel Erin never knew. Aidan had his DNA and his history. It was as close as she could get to Daniel now.

Helen was bent over in the closet, digging through Daniel's shoes. Erin left her to it and went to help Cathleen in the kitchen. "How's it going in here?" she asked.

Cathleen looked up, pushing a lock of faded hair from her pale face. "It's good. I've got most of the cabinets packed up." She stood and pulled out the drawer by the refrigerator. "I left you some silverware and a few cups and bowls. How long do you think you'll stay?"

"One more night? Maybe two. The phone will be turned off tomorrow and the water and electricity on Saturday, so I have to be out by then."

"Where are you going?"

"I'll find a hotel, and then I'll look for a small studio on the Lower East Side. Or maybe Brooklyn—Cobble Hill or Park Slope." Most of the furniture would be sold with the condo, whether the buyer wanted it or not. Erin would start over, again. The china and silver and other things she'd received as wedding gifts would go to an estate-sale company to be sold at auction. She'd keep her clothes and toiletries, her computer, and her files.

"Erin, don't stay in a hotel. Come stay with me."

"Thanks, but I'm not the best house guest right now." The truth was, Erin didn't think she could handle living with a family right now. Happy kids, functional people. Grief is better nurtured alone.

Aidan came out of the second bedroom, holding a file box labeled *Important—Keep*. Since he was an accountant, he had taken the job of wrangling files. He set the box down with a *thud* next to the kitchen table and said, redundantly, "These are your important files. Vital records, marriage certificate, insurance, mortgage documents, stuff like that. You need to hold on to this stuff."

"OK."

He disappeared into the bedroom and emerged again, holding another box. "And this stuff is all Daniel's. It's his work files, college transcripts, stuff like that." He pointed to a smaller file inside of it. "Oh, and this one has all the files related to Wheelchair Warriors."

"You mean Weekend Warriors?" That was the name of Daniel's flag football team that played Sunday afternoons in Central Park. But Erin didn't understand why Daniel would have a file for a flag football team.

"No, Wheelchair Warriors. You know, the charity Daniel was starting?"

No, Erin didn't know Daniel was starting a charity. "What are you talking about?"

He sat down and ran his fingers through his hair, looking at her from under his brow. "Geez, you guys lived together, and you didn't know he was starting a charity?"

Erin swallowed a lump in her throat.

"Come on, Aidan," Cathleen said, hopping down from the counter where she'd been emptying a cabinet of plastic containers. "I didn't know it either. Just tell us."

"All right. So you know we ran the marathon last year, right?"

Erin nodded, relieved. She did know that much. "Yes, of course."

"And Daniel's goal was to qualify for Boston."

Erin remembered. She'd been working that weekend preparing for a trial and couldn't cheer Daniel on like she'd wanted to. He hadn't qualified, and she told him she was sorry, but he hadn't seemed that upset. She hadn't heard anything more about it.

"Well, there's a reason he didn't. We were up in the Bronx, close to the finish, and we were both on track to qualify. But then Daniel saw his friend Greg Grady on the sidelines cheering him on. Cathleen, you know Greg, right? Went to high school with us, a year older than Daniel?"

Cathleen nodded as she packed.

"Anyway, he was standing next to his son, Nate, who has cerebral palsy and has never been able to walk. The kid was cheering, arms flailing, huge smile on his face. Before I knew what was happening, Daniel ran over and grabbed the wheelchair. He pushed Nate the rest of the way to the finish line. Must have been six miles at least. Big kid too." Aidan raised his eyebrows. "Kinda heavy."

"I had no idea," Erin said, sitting at the table across from Aidan. "Daniel told me that he didn't qualify and you did, but nothing else. Why did he do it?"

"I don't know. Even pushing Nate, Daniel almost qualified. But he didn't care. Daniel said after the race that it was the best feeling ever. And Nate was so excited. He cried with joy when he reached the finish line." Aidan wiped his eyes and took a deep breath. "After that, Daniel was on a mission. He wanted other runners to feel that, and other kids like Nate to be able to participate in races. And not just races for kids like them, but real, competitive races. He had gone and talked to a nonprofit lawyer. He was working on getting a tax-exempt entity. He called it Wheelchair Warriors. If you don't mind, I'll take the file and see how far he got with it."

"Yeah, of course," Erin said, staring at her hands. Daniel had done something amazing, something that moved him enough to want to start a charity, and she knew nothing about it. Had he been afraid to tell her? Afraid she would criticize him for throwing away his shot at Boston? Or did she show such a lack of interest in sports that he thought she wouldn't care? Her husband had been an amazing person, a kindhearted soul who cared about other people. How could she have been married to him and not really known him at all?

That night, after all the boxes were packed, files were sorted, and Daniel's closet was cleaned out (Helen took most of it to her house, where she said she'd find people who needed it, but everyone knew Helen would keep it all and someone would have to deal with it again at some point), Aidan was the last to go. He stayed behind to help Erin sort out some legal and financial documents relating to Daniel's death. It was almost the shortest day of the year and already pitch-dark outside, the sun having gone down over three hours ago.

As Aidan stood at the door, buttoning his black wool jacket and pulling on his skullcap, he turned to Erin. "Are you sure you're ready to leave this place?" He looked out the windows at the view toward Midtown. "It's a great place."

She did have mixed feelings about it. It had taken them so long to find the perfect place. They'd gotten into a bidding war and won. What if Daniel came back, somehow, miraculously? They still hadn't found a body. That was nonsense, of course. She knew he was gone. But even so, would Daniel have wanted her to stay here?

But no, there were too many memories. "Yes, I'm sure."

He nodded and jammed his hands into his pockets. "Well, then we need a closing ceremony. What are you doing for dinner?"

"I think Cathleen left a box of mac and cheese in the cabinet."

"Come on," he said. "I'm taking you to dinner."

Erin smiled. She was exhausted and hungry. "That sounds nice. Greek place again?"

Aidan shrugged. "Thought we might try something new this time."

As they were walking out the door, Erin's phone rang. The landline. She checked the caller ID. It was an international number, +44. Probably Alec. He'd been calling to check on her, still oddly feeling like he needed to, and she'd been ignoring him. Talking to him brought back too many memories from that day.

Phone still ringing, Erin closed the door and locked it.

A waiter poured red wine into Erin's glass, the deep ruby liquid crashing in and cresting like a wave. Candles flickered and glowed. All around them people smiled and laughed, engaging in civilized conversation. Erin ordered a Caesar salad, followed by the best spaghetti carbonara she'd ever tasted. The pasta was fresh, made that day. Someone poured more wine. All the time she'd been going through hell, other people had been doing this. She couldn't help but feel a spark of hope. She was still alive. The thought was exhilarating and heart-wrenching, hopeful and guilt inducing. Daniel was lost in a void, having suffered a horrible death, and Erin was sitting at dinner, enjoying a glass of wine, moving on with life.

Aidan was telling stories about his brother. "So Daniel was maybe eleven, and his friend Greg was at the house. God, those two. They were fine on their own, but together they came up with the most cockamamie schemes." Aidan leaned back in his chair. "They were obsessed with gasoline, for some reason. Probably because it could make things burn."

Erin smiled and nodded, trying to ignore that it had been jet fuel that caused the fires in the towers. She'd heard this story a few times—not from Daniel, but from Aidan in the last few months. She'd had no idea when he was alive that Daniel had been so mischievous growing up. "So they wanted to spell their names in fire on the driveway. They took a couple of red Solo cups, you know those plastic cups?" Erin nodded. "And dripped out their names. But Greg's name was shorter than Daniel's, so as Daniel was finishing his, Greg had already lit them both. I happened to walk outside at that moment and watched as the flames hit the cup Daniel was holding. Daniel freaked and threw it in my direction. It almost got me, and it would have if I hadn't jumped out of the way." Aidan shook his head, a nostalgic look in his eyes, and then he started laughing. "If you look at his school picture that year, you'll see half his eyebrows are singed off."

Erin laughed until tears streamed down her cheeks. "Wait, there's a photo of him? I've got to see that."

"Yeah, I'm sure it's at Mom's house somewhere. Next time I go, I'll dig it out for you."

Flames licked the wax candle into drippings on the red-and-white checked tablecloth. They'd ordered one bottle of wine at least—had Aidan ordered two? As the main course turned into tiramisu and riesling, the candle's flame became larger and more intense, flickering wildly. In the wavering glow, Aidan looked almost like Daniel.

"Come on," he said, standing up and grabbing her hand. "It's getting late." They spilled onto Mulberry Street, wrapping their coats against a cold December. A street sweeper rumbled by, while after-hours workers swept sidewalks and closed up shop. Along the cobbled street, a cab ambled past, its marquis numbers lit.

"Taxi!" Aidan yelled, then he whistled with his fingers, strong and clear. Daniel called cabs exactly the same way. Erin slid onto the cool black vinyl of the taxi seat, feeling warm and dizzy from the wine.

"Two stops. First one is 101 West 79th Street," Aidan called out to the driver, without hesitation. His voice sounded like Daniel's but lower, more gruff. Erin wondered when Aidan had memorized her address. He never came over when Daniel was alive, but of course they hadn't really entertained much. They had been gone all the time, working, out with friends, or in the Hamptons for the weekend.

The cabbie turned the heater on high. The warmth and the wine combined to make Erin sleepy, so sleepy. As the city whizzed by, she rested her head on Aidan's shoulder, imagining for the briefest moment that he was her husband and they were on their way home after a night out.

Back at the apartment, Erin handed Aidan a twenty-dollar bill, and he shoved it back at her. She slid out of the cab, tripping on the curb. She stumbled and caught herself with one hand on the sidewalk. Orlando swung open the door. "Mrs. O'Connor! Are you OK?"

"Fine, Orlando. I'm fine." Erin giggled, keenly aware of the pointlessness of her life. Coming and going and working and going out and searching for Daniel and then giving it up and then drinking so much that none of it mattered anymore anyway. "I'm going to be fine. Just fine and dandy!" She stumbled again, into Orlando this time. An older woman carrying grocery bags, swathed in black wool and bent against the cold, walked past, frowning at Erin.

Orlando quick-glanced to Aidan, who got out and leaned toward the cab's window. He said something, handed over a few bills, and the cabbie sped away. Aidan turned back to Orlando and nodded, answering an unasked question. "I've got her." Then he grasped Erin by the elbow and guided her to the elevators.

Upstairs, Erin threw off her coat, kicked off her shoes, and turned on the CD player for the first time in over three months. Soundgarden was still on deck. The parquet floors were cold under her feet as she swayed to the music. She tried to focus on the twinkling city lights, feeling the absence of the giants that used to shine in the distance. She hadn't thought much about the lyrics of this song before, but now the singer's words, about nothing breaking him no matter how hard he fell, strummed at her bones.

Her eyes were closed and her head beat to the music as if she were at the concert in Boston where they'd gone to see Chris Cornell two years ago, her last year of law school. She imagined Daniel there, next to her, dancing with her, kissing her.

And then his arms were around her and he was really there, moving with her, and she didn't know where he came from but she didn't want to ask, like a dream you never want to wake from. He smelled like Daniel, and when he whispered in her ear, "You're so beautiful," he sounded like Daniel. She felt his stubble on the back of her neck as he kissed her, raising the hairs on her arms and legs. She kept her eyes closed the whole time, blowing up the outside world, imagining her eyes were open and the towers' lights were downtown again. When she turned and put her arms around him and kissed him, it really was Daniel, just thicker and rougher. And when they fell onto the couch and she let him take off her clothes, straining to feel his flesh against hers, it was Daniel's body that pressed up against her. Daniel's breath on her neck and his whispers in her ear and his hands on her ass as he pressed himself into her, over and over and over again until they both exploded into lightness and darkness and regret.

Chapter Eleven

February 22, 2002

Erin pushed spaghetti with meat sauce around on her plate, bumping it into a piece of garlic bread. On the plate next to her was a blue-cheese-drizzled iceberg wedge, which her mother had made her order. She sat on a brown and maroon pleather chair at a white-tablecloth-covered table in a beige and mauve room. Around her, wealthy people sat and forked steak and fake smiled. It could have been any Friday night from her childhood, with one exception: the way people around them acted. On a normal country club Friday night, there would have been many handshakes and back slaps, a few impromptu conversations with Fitz standing and Eleanor sitting looking pretty, ending with a *Call me! We'll have lunch*. But since Erin had come back, people had been dodging her and by extension, her parents. They would walk the long way around to avoid eye contact, pretending to be engrossed in a phone call or a menu. It wasn't that they were bad people. They just didn't know what to say.

"How's the spaghetti?"

Erin nodded at Fitz. "It's fine." And it was, for her *After* life.

Erin's life had been split into two parts, *Before* and *After*, severed neatly between that moment on the beach, when everything had been sunshine and sea salt, and the next, when she realized it was all a facade, her happiness nothing but a shaky Potemkin village sent tumbling with one swift kick.

But even for the lowered expectations of her new *After*, it had been a huge mistake.

Sleeping with Aidan.

First, because she was not attracted to Aidan.

At all.

Despite his passing resemblance to Daniel.

Second, because he wouldn't leave her alone after.

The next morning, once she came to and had her coffee and recreated what had happened, however hazy and with some gaping holes in the timeline, she had been absolutely horrified.

Aidan? She slept with *Aidan*? Boring, gruff, depressed, sad *Aidan*?

Before she married Daniel, Erin had slept with only two other men. Two. Not that many, compared to most of her friends. She'd been very picky in her Before life. Never in a thousand years would she have slept with someone like Aidan.

Yes, there were certain biological similarities between him and Daniel. But that was where it ended. Daniel had intelligence, liveliness, a spark that set him apart. He had something indescribable, the X factor. Aidan didn't. But even more than that, it was such a betrayal. What was she thinking? It'd been just three months. If there'd been a body, it would've barely been cold.

It could only be explained by the wine. She drank too much. Pure and simple.

Maybe she could have put it behind her if Aidan had gone his own way. Recognized it was a huge, terrible, awful, disgusting, heretical mistake and quit trying to talk to her, just like she planned on doing. But no. He stepped up his efforts. The next morning he called her, excited about their new relationship. He told her he expected her to have mixed emotions, but he was in it for the long haul. He told her she'd come around eventually, and he would see her through it all. That he knew he was in love with her but if she needed more time, he'd wait as long as it took. He was a patient man. He wasn't going anywhere.

He said she would grow to love him.

He was such a saint.

Aidan was convinced they had a relationship ordained by the Bible. He'd researched it, or remembered it from his Catholic upbringing. He even had a name for it: *levirate marriage*. "It's when a man marries his deceased brother's widow. It's from the Old Testament," he said, excitedly. "Look it up. Deuteronomy 25:5–6."

"I don't have a Bible."

"What? I'll bring you mine. I have it highlighted."

Erin reminded him that in the Old Testament, women were possessions to be taken care of. Like cattle. "I don't need to be taken care of."

"Now that's where you're wrong. Maybe not physically, but emotionally you do. You wanted to be with Daniel, and I'm not that different from him. We have almost the same DNA. You'll grow to love me," he said again.

Erin had told him she needed to go, and hung up. Then she called a moving company.

The next day, her packed boxes and what was left of the furniture were put into a storage room in Harlem. Everything but one suitcase, which she loaded into the red Mercedes she'd had since college. She even canceled her cell phone with its 917 area code so that Aidan couldn't call her anymore, and to cut any lingering ties to New York. She drove to the only place she could think of as home now—Dallas. She arrived the day before Christmas Eve.

On Christmas Day, she stayed in bed. Her parents checked on her now and then, and she smelled food, so she knew they were going about the business of celebrating, but the thought of attending services at First Baptist Church, staring at her parents over honeyed ham, mashed potatoes, chocolate pie, and Sister Schubert's rolls and pretending everything was fine, that Daniel was in a better place, that she believed in any of it, was unbearable.

She stayed in bed the day after, and the day after that, and many more days after that.

A handful of her old friends had called her since she arrived in Dallas, most of the conversations lasting less than five minutes. They were check-the-box conversations. Only one—Blair, her best friend from high school—came to visit. Even with Blair it was awkward, because their relationship hadn't evolved beyond high school, and what happened to Erin couldn't be discussed with a high school lexicon. Blair was married to Bryce, her high school sweetheart, and her most pressing concern was whether to distress the kitchen cabinets during her kitchen remodel. Erin agreed she should. When Blair left, Erin went back to bed.

It was mostly quiet while they ate, except for the sounds of soft jazz pushed through the fingers of a piano player in the lobby. The hum of civilized conversation, the clinking of silverware on plates, and the occasional clattering of a dropped serving tray created ambient noise. Fitz and Eleanor made conversation occasionally—Eleanor mentioned someone's daughter getting married; Fitz wondered aloud if Eddie Samuels was still at the top of the leaderboard for the golf tournament going on that weekend.

When they could think of nothing else to say, Fitz turned his attention to his daughter, putting his hand over hers. "Erin, I know this is a difficult time for you, but your mother and I are here for you. We're going to help you through it, just like we helped you through things in the past." The words were hollow, almost rehearsed. Acted out by someone playing a part.

"What things, Fitz? What things have *we* been through before that are like this?"

Fitz looked at Eleanor, brow furrowed. She chimed in, helpfully. "Well, middle school was tough. How mean you girls were to each other."

"You think losing my husband in a terrorist attack is like middle school?" They were trying to be supportive, but Erin couldn't help herself. Her chest was a smoking, seething cauldron. "He's my husband! And he's gone!"

Fitz stabbed at his steak. "We're just trying to say that . . ."

Erin dropped her fork. "None of us are up for this. You guys can't help me. Because you're here and I'm here and we're all on the same side and he's on the other side. There's nothing between us and him. Nothing to bridge the divide except death itself."

The rest of the dinner was eaten in silence.

Before she left the city, after everything was packed up and the movers had gone and there was nothing left to do, Erin had visited once more the place where she now accepted Daniel died. The north side of the northern perimeter of Ground Zero. To say goodbye the only way she knew how, in the only place she knew him to be.

Cars were allowed again, even below Canal Street. Yellow cabs honked; pedestrians were back on sidewalks where they belonged. Cafés opened their doors again. The world, even in lower Manhattan, was returning to normal. She couldn't get as close as she wanted to, but there was a sort of viewing area at the south end of Greenwich Street, just past Park Place. She walked slowly south toward the metal fence, breathing in heavy air, and waited patiently behind a group of women holding maps, speaking in hushed tones, and snapping photos. Mercifully, they left after a few minutes. Erin took tentative steps, a believer approaching the altar.

The fires were still burning, but the pile had dwindled. The distinctive facade of one of the buildings, four or five stories up, still stood, but the debris around it had been cleared. Wide swaths of dark gray ground had been stripped and leveled. A yellow truck with "New Holland" on the side clawed at wire and twisted metal, loading it onto a dump truck.

For a long moment, she just watched. She closed her eyes and tried to feel Daniel. Brought back his warm smile, his dimples. A slight breeze became the feel of his arms around her. It was brief; soon she was brought back to the beep of horns and the far-off whine of a siren. She gazed toward the cold gray sky, clouds mixed with wisps of smoke, and wanted to cry. She wanted to fight for Daniel. She wanted to stay. But she had no cry or fight or stay left in her.

After a few minutes, she reached into her bag and pulled out the plain white piece of paper inside, "Daniel O'Connor" written in blue ink across the front. After folding it carefully, she taped it onto the plywood amidst missing person flyers, miniature American flags, wilted and dried flowers, notes with *I love you, Daddy* scrawled in crayon.

Written on the paper was a simple message:

D,

I'm sorry I wasn't here for you. You were so much more than what I thought I wanted. I love you now more than ever. I'll never stop loving you.

I'll look for you always, everywhere I go, in every face I see.

Love, E

The next morning, Erin woke up in thousand-thread-count sheets and padded across the handwoven rug to her bathroom, where the cabinets were topped with marble. Before, she had enjoyed this kind of luxury, but now she found it hollow as a bird's bones. She slid out of silk pajamas and put on two-hundred-dollar Seven jeans from ten pounds and half a country ago. The jeans, her favorites, used to fit like a glove. Now they slipped down and hung loose at her hip bones. She yanked them off and threw on black sweatpants instead, pairing them with Daniel's Princeton sweatshirt.

There was a knock at the door, and her mother walked in as Erin came out of the bathroom, slipping into well-worn flip-flops. Eleanor assumed a bright expression. "Good morning. Are you going to wear that all day?"

"Honestly, I haven't thought that far in advance."

Her mother clasped her fingers together. "Well, I thought maybe we could do some shopping today. Get your hair cut, pedicure, maybe a massage if we have time?"

Vanity outlived beauty with the women in Erin's family. They clung to it until the bitter, collagen-deprived end. Her grandmother, Evelyn McKenzie Blackwood, lived to eighty-one and was a princess until her last breath. She wore full makeup until the very end, even when she could no longer apply it herself. At Erin's high school graduation party her grandmother emerged from the powder room with a burst of Coty Airspun Face Powder in a perfect circle around her lips, red lipstick applied over the top.

But Erin couldn't lie, the massage sounded nice. Getting out of this house also sounded good. "OK, sure. I'll go."

Her mother looked thrilled. "Great! Don't you want to take a shower? Maybe fix your hair, put on some lipstick? Daniel wouldn't mind if you look pretty while you're mourning him."

Erin was like an angry windup doll that had been twisted to the brink, then released. She whipped around to face Eleanor. "Look pretty while I'm mourning him?" she growled. "He's dead, Mother. Dead! Don't you get it? And you're worried about my fucking lipstick? Well, this is what I think about lipstick!"

She grabbed a gold tube from the top of her chest of drawers, twisting it up for maximum exposure. She smeared it on her lips, cheeks, forehead, and neck. Then she slashed at the closest thing to her—the oval mirror that swiveled above the white-painted vanity table that had been in her bedroom since she was six—leaving behind a violent smear of red and the letters *D E A D*. While Eleanor stood watching, mouth gaped and eyes wide, Erin ran to the bathroom and colored the wall-to-wall mirror in Rich Red until she hit rim. One tube down. She hurled the empty tube across the room, yanked open her makeup drawer, and grabbed every lipstick inside, including each of the eight tubes that were stashed inside various handbags and drawers in Manhattan and consolidated during her move home, as well as some old tubes from as far back as middle school.

She opened one and shoved the others in her pocket, screaming, "Dead!" at the top of her lungs. She ran from her room, streaming lipstick along the walls as she went. "Murdered!" Gashes of red wax covered family photos in traditional frames adorning the hallway walls. Erin as a baby, then a toddler, one frame with all thirteen of her school pictures under one mat. "Vaporized!" As a cheerleader in her red-and-white St. Mary's uniform, arms akimbo and pom-poms planted on her waist. "Crushed!" Erin at camp, the only time she ever had bangs. "Mutilated!" The family, in white T-shirts and jeans, barefoot under the spreading live oak, her dad holding Henry, the family dog. "Obliterated!" Red lipstick obscured her parents' wedding photo—"Dearly departed!"—streaked the no-glare glass covering her high school senior photo, her hair long and silky, her lips painted the perfect shade of red.

Eleanor stood as if in shock, forearms over skull protectively.

Erin faced her in a battle stance. Veins bulged and pressure exploded in her head. She shook the lipstick at her mother. "Kaput! No more! Totally gone! Not even so much as a fucking toenail left of him. And you care what color my lips are?"

Erin tossed the second empty tube over her shoulder and started on the living room. Eleanor darted past her into the kitchen and punched numbers into the wall telephone.

By the time Erin's anger was spent, Rich Red was slashed across designer-painted drywall in the living room and shimmered from the white custom slipcovered sofas from Quatrine, coordinating Scalamandre Chinoise Exotique drapery, throw pillows covered in linen, and simple white lampshades. Wax lay thick on burgundy leather Manhattan chairs and crystal decanters filled with single-malt scotch, was ground into the authentic zebra skin from her father's African safari hunt, and cut wide swaths across the refrigerator and the painstakingly distressed cabinets in the recently remodeled chef's kitchen.

All of it glowing red with his transubstantiated blood.

Only when the last dollop of red wax from the last tube in her fist was gone did it end. Empty gold tubes littered the hardwood floors like spent shotgun shells. Erin sat on the cold marble entryway, knees to forehead.

Within a few minutes, she heard the wail of an approaching siren. A bang on the door. Eleanor, whimpering and holding a tissue to her nose, tiptoed around Erin to open it.

"Officers, thank God you're here. My daughter, I think there's something wrong with her. She just smeared lipstick all over my house."

"Lipstick, ma'am?"

"Yes. You should see it. It's awful." Her voice shuddered. "It's going to take weeks to clean it up."

"Can we come in?"

"Please." Two sets of heavy boots thudded across the entryway.

Erin sat up and backed herself to the wall, rage still simmering her limbs. There were two of them. The one in front was of medium height and build, young, dark skinned with a kind face. The badge sewn to the right shoulder of his navy blue short-sleeve shirt looked fake, like it was handed out in a Girl Scout ceremony. It had a blue asterisk, a red flower, and a star. It didn't say *police* anywhere—instead it read *Department of Public Safety.* The monogrammed letters on the right side of his shirt spelled *A. Vasquez.* The other officer was small, thin, beady-eyed, his red hair in a buzz cut. His shirt said *T. Kendrick.*

T. Kendrick looked amused.

Erin put palms to forehead and exhaled audibly.

Vasquez said to Kendrick, "Stay here, watch her." Kendrick stood with legs apart, hands clasped behind him, in the middle of the entryway. He didn't look at Erin.

You don't know what it feels like not to know, she wanted to say to him. The rage had dissipated, leaving behind a soulless heap. *How can I live with myself? One day we were both fine, maybe fighting but fine, and the next he was gone, without a trace, without a word.*

He didn't even call me. Some of them called. He didn't think of me at all.

Eleanor showed Vasquez the living room, the kitchen, hallway, bedrooms. A few minutes later they returned, Vasquez with his head bent over a pen and a pad of paper. "Ma'am, I'm sorry for your damage. But, um. What do you want us to do?"

Eleanor blew her nose. "She's a danger to us and herself. She needs to go somewhere. Where they can help her. Is there somewhere you can take her?"

"We can't take her to jail, ma'am." Vasquez glanced at Erin, skeptically. "Unless she's committed a crime?"

"Just look!" Eleanor's arm swept across the lipstick-laden living room. She hesitated, tissue to nose, and broke into tears. "It's just too much. I can't take it."

My husband was murdered, but Eleanor can't take it?

Erin pushed herself off the ground and walked toward Vasquez, arms outstretched in *cuff-me* position. "Please just take me. I can't stay here any longer."

Her mother quivered by the living room, avoiding her gaze.

Officer Vasquez hesitated a moment, eyebrows raised. He glanced at Kendrick, and they both shrugged their shoulders and shook their heads. Vasquez pushed Erin's hands down. "I'm not cuffing you." He grabbed her right elbow and escorted her out the mahogany double doors.

At least four neighbors were outside, speaking in low whispers. A dog barked. Keeping her head down and arms behind her as if cuffed, Erin slid into the back seat of the cruiser.

Kendrick pulled something out of his pocket and handed it to Eleanor. "If you want her back, she'll be at the Highland Park Department of Public Safety, 4700 Drexel Drive. Here's my card. You can dial the main number."

Eleanor nodded and shut the front door.

At first, the ride to the police station was quiet and peaceful. Erin breathed in and out steadily, feeling strangely free. And then Officer Kendrick piped up, turning to his partner. "Lipstick rampage? What kind of crime is that, Chief?"

Officer Vasquez shrugged. "Defacing private property?"

"I don't think that's a crime if you live there."

"Intimidation? That woman was clearly intimidated."

"Yeah. Don't think intimidation is a crime either. We're gonna get laughed out of the shop." He turned to Erin. "What happened there, Lipstick Girl? Why'd you make your mommy so upset like that? Boyfriend didn't ask you to the dance?"

Erin glowered at him, then gazed out the window as they passed through the neighborhood where she spent her childhood. Huge, columned mansions with verdant manicured lawns. Seasonally planted pink and red flowers, Valentine's Day hearts still on doors, the hope of spring around the corner.

The rage began another wave. What did these people know of love? True love was a paradox—an emotion made possible only after everything to love was gone. These rich people who didn't understand pain or suffering or death had no right to pretend they knew anything about love. Half of these people were cheating on each other, based on Erin's knowledge of her friends' parents and parents' friends. She and Daniel might have ended up like this too. All married couples get there eventually, or worse. Even if Daniel had lived, there would have been cheating, and if not then fights over money, familiarity that breeds indifference, a 50 percent chance of divorce. There's no happily ever after, not really.

Believing this didn't make her feel better. A traitorous tear escaped from her eye and slid down her cheek, stopping at the waxen lipstick barricade in its path.

Vasquez glanced at her in the rearview mirror. "Not going to talk to us then?"

"The police don't really help anyone."

He harrumphed. "You're way too nice of a girl to be spouting off such liberal nonsense."

"I'm not a girl. And you're not even real police. Working the Highland Park beat, like that's real exciting. What do you do, rescue kitties from trees? Give people tickets for parking on the wrong side of the street?"

Kendrick chimed in. "Yep, that's right. Just doing our job, protecting this community from the dangerous crimes perpetrated by lipstick vandals."

They both laughed, pleased with themselves. Prepping their stories for the boys down at the station. Erin didn't speak to them again.

The police station looked more like a brand-new La Quinta with its Spanish architecture, red-tiled roof, and water fountain in front. The officers led Erin past the front desk, where the bleached-blond receptionist stared at her with disdain, through a set of locked doors and into a small room with a table and two chairs. It looked like a room where they would question witnesses on *Law & Order*, except it was well lit with freshly painted walls and framed modern art prints on the walls.

Vasquez offered her a chair. "Can I get you anything to drink? Coffee, water?" When she didn't respond, he said, "Maybe some makeup remover?" Then he slapped his belly and laughed on his way out of the room.

From the doorway, Kendrick said, "Someone will be in

shortly to take a statement. You should be thinking about who you want to call with your one phone call. Like maybe your makeup artist?"

They walked away, chortling like middle schoolers. "Hey, Chief, we got a Code Twenty-Five in there. Assault with intent to wear makeup." Loud hoots. "No, no, no, it's a Code Thirty-One, criminal mischief with a beauty product." More guffawing and then a door slammed and the noise was gone.

Sergeant Brower must have pulled the short straw. He walked in some time later to take Erin's statement, reading a file and twisting the hairs around the bald spot in his curly light-brown hair. He wasn't laughing at her. Instead, his face, softened and creased by time, was haggard and bored. The coffee-stained white button-down and khakis said he was an office worker, not a field guy. Maybe he already did his time, or maybe he couldn't cut it. When he looked at Erin, finally, his head whipped back in a startle reflex.

"Whoa there, darlin', what'd you do to yourself?" He lowered himself into the chair opposite Erin. His accent was deep East Texas Piney Woods.

"You mean they didn't tell you?"

"Oh yeah, there's some stuff here." He glanced at the file. "Took a tube of lipstick to the entire house, scared your poor mama to death. What it don't say is why."

"Does it say on there what kind of crime I committed?"

"What's a sweet little lady like you doing vandalizing her house and scaring her mama?"

Erin stared him down with as much disgust as she could muster and spit the words back at him. "Sweet little lady? How do you know anything about what I am?" This was a new Erin, one who destroyed her mother's house and then became sullen and peevish with the police. It felt good. Like ripping off a scab.

"I need to call the psych ward then? That what we're dealing with?"

"I don't have anything to say to you Keystone Cops. I want my lawyer."

"You refusing to answer any more questions without counsel present?"

"Damn right I am."

He leaned back in his chair and put his hands behind his head. "Honey, now, you could be in a lot of trouble here. Even if she don't press charges, which she might, your mama gonna kick you out of the house, at the least. Where you gonna go?"

Erin straightened her spine and calmed her voice. "Sergeant Brower. I am a twenty-eight-year-old woman, and I am perfectly capable of taking care of myself. This is a domestic dispute between my mother and me, and it has nothing to do with you, Barney and Gomer in there, or anyone else." Her voice rose as she spoke. "And I clearly and concisely stated my desire for counsel to be present before any further questioning. By asking me additional questions beyond that point, you are violating my Miranda rights. Even though they have not been read to me, as an attorney I am quite familiar with them. Now, unless there is a crime you are planning to charge me with, aside from excessive use of makeup, I strongly encourage you to release me." Erin imagined fire sizzling from her eyes.

Sergeant Brower smiled at her. "Well now, darlin', thank you for that little speech, but I'll be making the decisions around here."

Erin couldn't take it anymore. She stood up and leaned over

the small man across the small table in the small room and yelled, "You don't get it. Here you are, questioning me about lipstick, when there are real, live terrorists flying planes into buildings and making people jump from a hundred floors up for no reason. For their stupid two-thousand-year-old beliefs! And you're fucking wasting your time on me?" She grabbed the hair on either side of her head and yanked. "He's gone, vaporized into tiny pieces. Not a shred of him left. Who fucking cares what I look like, what my parents' house looks like? Where I'll live from now on?"

Erin released her hair and sunk back into her chair, leaning face-forward onto the table in front of her. She didn't speak again, not to Vasquez or Kendrick when they came in sheepishly to apologize, not to the yellow-haired receptionist who'd looked at her with contempt at first but later came in with cookies and a cup of coffee, not even to Fitz James when he showed up sometime later, sporting a grim look and spewing apologies, to collect his daughter.

Chapter Twelve

February 24, 2002

Light filtered through the curtains and Erin closed her eyes tighter, breathing in HVAC-controlled Texas air. She didn't want to see the outlines of her former bedroom still smudged with lipstick. After he showed up at the station to bail Erin out of jail, Fitz called the housekeeper, Liza. She and three of her sisters rushed over, cleaning up as much as they could. But lipstick was hard to remove. There were still remnants throughout, traces of her spent anger.

Erin's mother wasn't equipped to handle her daughter and her grief. Tragedy wasn't her thing. Eleanor was a Styrofoam doll coated in glitter floating on the surface of a country club swimming pool. Now Erin understood, if she hadn't before, why she was an only child. Fitz probably wanted boys—stock, hardy young men that he could teach to hunt and fish—but Eleanor was overwhelmed with one well-behaved girl. Boys would have put her over the edge.

Obviously, Erin couldn't stay long after what had happened. But she had no idea where she would go. New York was full of painful memories; Texas was big and superficial. Like Goldilocks, she'd have to find her "just right" in a world not meant for her.

In the bathroom, she tossed back two Valiums before the migraine could take. Threw on the first jeans and T-shirt she could find in the stack of clean clothes Liza had piled on her chest of drawers the day before, after mostly ridding the bedroom of red wax, and went to tell her parents she was leaving.

The kitchen smelled of coffee grinds and burnt toast. Erin wasn't surprised that her father was sitting at the kitchen table alone, mug in hand, reading the paper. He didn't look up when she came in, feigning deep interest in the sports section. Erin poured a cup and sat down at the other end of the table. Only then did she notice the black wooden box on the table between them.

"What's that, Daddy?"

Fitz put down the paper and pulled the box toward him. "This came for you yesterday by FedEx. I was going to give it to you when I got home, but it didn't seem like the right time, given the circumstances."

"What is it?"

He stood, picked up the black box, and brought it to her. "The O'Connor family sent it. They thought you should have it. It's ashes from the World Trade Center site. They sent it to the families of the victims for whom they, um," Fitz cleared his throat, "couldn't find anything else."

Fitz rapped softly on the top of the box.

Tick, tock, tick, tock went the grandfather clock.

When she could take it no longer, Erin opened the top panel. Inside was a lump wrapped in a blue velvet sack, silk drawstring tied in a bow. She pulled it out and probed the outline of something curved and solid inside. Untied the bow and let the sack drop away, revealing a funeral urn made of polished cherrywood engraved with *9-11-2001.* It was no more than five inches tall, the top sealed tight with two screws.

Feeling the smooth wood under her fingertips sent a shudder down Erin's spine.

Other than a few photos and some clothing, this box was all she had left of her husband.

But this wasn't him. Daniel couldn't be reduced to a box of dirt. It would be a constant reminder of that day.

She pushed it away. "I don't want this. Please send it back to the O'Connors."

Erin stood up from the table and went to pack her things.

Traffic was heavier than usual on the last Sunday in February, people out enjoying the sunny day. Past the spaghetti bowl of the city's freeways the cars thinned out, and Erin could breathe again for the first time in months.

Northwest on 287 toward Wichita Falls. The monotony of the highway, the constant whoosh of pavement passing under her tires. Fields with small houses and old windmills. Cows in dry pastures chewed grass and swished their tails at flies. With each mile that passed, Erin felt free, disappearing into North Texas oblivion.

The countryside became flatter and flatter. Used-up rows of farmland stretched into a distant horizon cut razor-sharp against the sky. An unobstructed view, with only the occasional homestead or oil well to interrupt it. When Erin was a child, her parents would take her to visit her grandparents at their West Texas ranch. After riding a horse or crawling through a maze of hay bales or playing with the mangy flea-ridden cowdog named Beau, Erin would lie flat on the ground and gaze at the top half of the world. Expanding her field of vision to a bowl of blue marbled sky, she could forget she was tethered by gravity to the scrubby, dirt-filled ground and pretend to be a denizen of the clouds.

Now she felt the half-moon sky envelop her as if she were inside a snow globe. The terrain couldn't have been flatter had it been poured from a concrete truck and scraped level with a trowel. A few lonely trees stood stark against the seam of earth and sky. In the distance, a speeding freight train blew its horn.

Erin drove for hours without stopping, pulled as if by magnet toward northern New Mexico. In a place called Santa Rosa the sun went down, and Erin stopped to get gas. Farther down the road a red rectangular sign announced the place within as "Restaurant." It was called Route 66, and it seemed right that she should eat there. She sat in a worn red leather booth next to a window shielded with yellowing lace curtains. A couple ate at a nearby table, the man with stooped shoulders, the woman with a leathery face and dyed-red hair. They ate in silence as old couples do, looking more at Erin than at each other. Sparse words occasionally about the food or the weather. The man tipped his cap and winked at Erin as they left.

Next to Route 66 Restaurant were a Travelodge and a La Quinta. She checked in to the Travelodge and parked her car outside the door to room number 11. Powered by sleeping pills, Erin slept without moving for eight hours. She woke before dawn, drank coffee from a Styrofoam cup served in the breakfast room next to the check-in desk, threw her bag in the car, and hit the road again, with no more than a vague pull toward the north and west.

Northern New Mexico was flat hard mesas and red rocks, sun-scorched earth and cactuses. Miles upon miles of nothing at all, as if humans never existed. From the side of a mesa a juniper tree grew, trunk bent and gnarled, clumpy green canopy striving toward the sun. Erin was struck by its will to survive in a harsh climate. It reminded her of a Georgia O'Keeffe painting she saw at the Whitney in her Before life—a skull with antlers, sharp angled and angry. Below it, flowers in full bloom. Death cutting to the heart of life.

She realized that without life, there would be no death. Without Erin to mourn Daniel, death would lose its edge.

Through New Mexico to Colorado, the state line delineated rocky, dry, and desolate from green, lush, and rolling. In Durango, snow fell and a river rushed. Onward through Utah; Moab to I-70 and then I-15 North, where the traffic was all dirt-covered semis and Jeeps and Subarus. Erin cringed behind the wheel, the red Mercedes sticking out like a runway model at Walmart.

At the next gas station she took the windshield squeegee and squeezed brown soapy water from the narrow sponge all over the car, from the top down. She refilled the sponge repeatedly and covered the car in wet. After the gas was pumped, she drove into the dusty field of grass next to the station, turning hard doughnuts and kicking up dust. She threw it into park, got out of the car, and evaluated. Still not enough. She dug into the sandy dirt with bare hands and smeared it over the shiny glossy red until the car was thick with grime. When her nails were bloody and raw and no more red shone through, Erin slid back into the driver's seat and merged onto the interstate.

Through Provo and Salt Lake City and Ogden and into Idaho, where she stopped for gas at a Flying J truck stop and ate meatloaf and instant potatoes and lifeless green beans. She'd driven more than half the day, from sunup to well past sunset. She spent another night at the Days Inn next door.

In the morning, she knew where she'd been headed all along. The West Coast, as far from New York as she could go without driving into the ocean.

Between the sidewalks along a boulevard near the center of Portland, Oregon, was a narrow strip of green space where children screamed and ran as they played at a park. It was late afternoon by the time Erin arrived, but the gray sky rendered the hour indeterminate.

Her friend Laila gave her a bear hug, then held on to her shoulders and looked her square in the eye. "I'm so sorry about your husband. I can't imagine what you're going through."

"Thank you." Erin would have cried, but Laila's energy was too commanding for tears. There weren't many people who made Erin look like a shrinking violet, but somehow Laila, with her big bones, cropped spiky hair, and booming voice, always stole the show.

Laila was a party girl, that friend in college who always drank too much, said exactly what she thought, and got into fights at bars. She was fiercely intelligent but addicted to life in large doses. She voraciously consumed everything from books, sex, and reality TV to alcohol, drugs, and careers. Her tendency was to follow the men she was dating wherever they took her. She'd lived as a financial analyst in New York, a volunteer firefighter in Memphis, a dental assistant in Minnesota, and joined the Peace Corps in Rwanda, where she taught hundreds of African orphans how to speak English and dance the Texas two-step until she was caught having sex with a twenty-year-old native who was there for job training.

After she was kicked out of the Peace Corps, Laila landed back in her hometown of Lubbock, where she met a drummer in a band. She followed him to Santa Monica, working for a temp agency during the day and hanging out with the drummer at night, until she found him in flagrante delicto with another groupie in her bed.

After that, for the first time, Laila moved for a job. Her boss at the last temp job liked her so much that she hired her as a full-time web designer, and so Laila moved to Portland, where the weather was dark and mysterious and there were plenty of soulful musicians to choose from.

Somehow through it all, Laila and Erin kept in touch. Laila had called Erin the morning after the incident with the drummer. Erin had been surprised that Laila expected fidelity from a guy in a traveling band, but tried to be sympathetic. Erin encouraged her move to Oregon, telling her she needed a fresh start. At the time, Erin's life had been on track, and she thought there could be nothing more depressing than to be aimless and wandering like Laila.

Barely six months later, here Erin was at Laila's doorstep, the latest mournful girl escaping her tragedies.

"Let me help with your bags!" Laila said, bouncing quickly from the topic of grief. Subject raised and addressed, maybe now they could avoid it. Erin popped the trunk and Laila helped her with her one suitcase and a bag with a blanket and pillow, all she needed or wanted to bring, the rest of her things still abandoned indefinitely in the storage room in Harlem.

Laila slung the bag over her shoulder. "You got lucky because my roommate just moved out. So the room's available as long as you need it."

"That's great. Thanks so much." Erin followed Laila to the door of a five-story rectangle of red bricks, walls flat and straight as a box. The bottom floor was a Chinese restaurant. Molecules of rancid vegetable oil and fried soy sauce wafted out, permeating everything in their path.

Laila's apartment was on the fifth floor, and there were no elevators. As Erin panted up the steps behind her new roommate, Laila looked over her shoulder and said, "The rent's seventeen hundred a month. Your share is eight fifty."

"OK."

"It's kind of small, but it's cozy."

"I'm sure it'll be fine."

"You're easy."

At the top, Laila walked to the end of the hallway and stuck her key in the lock of a scratched wood door with "#54" in gold stick-ons. The place was small—a narrow kitchen on the left, beyond that a living room overlooking the boulevard park. Laila's bedroom was down a short hall to the right, and the other bedroom was on the opposite side of the living room. The furniture was college-era: a purple velvet couch with bald patches and a quilt thrown over the back. Two tweed armchairs, a beat-up coffee table, assorted mismatched throw pillows. A tube television on a small table was propped in the corner with a VCR under it, cords everywhere. Some VHS tapes sat in a plastic milk crate next to the television.

A musky litter box smell suffused the air. "How many cats do you have?" Erin asked.

"How'd you know? There is a pretty boy in here. He must be hiding. Butternut!" Erin was allergic to cats, but like furry little sadists, they always took to her. She experienced a jolt of panic, the feeling of being too far down the wrong path, wondering what she'd gotten herself into. It jarred her with its normalcy—an emotion predicated on the expectation of happiness.

It passed quickly. Erin followed Laila and the cat smell into the bedroom on the left. She unpacked a few things into the beat-up brown bureau with drawers that bumped along, wood grating on wood. The apartment, the expectations, the weather, the smell of the air were as far as she could get from Dallas, from New York, from any life she'd led before.

She walked back into the living room and sat on the purple couch.

Laila called out from the kitchen, "You want some coffee?"

"No, thanks."

"You hungry?"

"Not really."

Laila rummaged around in the kitchen for a few minutes and came out holding a steaming cup of something. She sat across from Erin. "Listen, you don't have to talk. I know it's been rough for you. You may want to just be alone."

Erin stared at the coffee table and took a deep breath. She no longer had a compulsion to fill silences.

"Actually, I have no idea what you want or how you'll be. I've been nervous as shit wondering what I'm going to say to you."

Erin looked out the window overlooking the park. "Is it always this cloudy?" She didn't know what she wanted or how she would be either, but she knew she didn't want to talk about it.

"Yeah, mostly." Laila stood up and walked to the window, clutching her cup. "Some days it's sunny. On one of those two days of the year, you can see Mount Hood out there." She pointed across the park and to the right, south, then turned back to Erin. "You should have chosen someplace sunnier, like Southern California. Anywhere, really."

Erin shrugged. "I like the clouds. They suit my mood."

Laila nodded. "This should work out just fine then." She turned on the CD player—Pearl Jam. The music hit the natural frequency of Erin's sorrow. She closed her eyes and leaned her head against the worn quilt, allowing herself to be carried up and away, her consciousness becoming a floating thing. She felt herself crest inside a bubble on a wave, rattle around metal beams of a New York City skyscraper, ebb and flow with the clouds.

That night, she took two more pills and lay in her new room on a cheap springy mattress covered with a pilled maroon bedspread, letting the meds work through her veins. As she drifted off, a small, warm body curled against her, purring.

Chapter Thirteen

March 22, 2002

Portland was the right fit. The daylight held no interest, and with the near-constant clouds and rain there wasn't much of it. Erin became nocturnal, spending short, cloudy days in bed and long, black nights awake with only Butternut for company. The cat believed Erin's room was his. He curled up with her while she slept and purred next to her while she watched TV. She tried to push him away, but he just stared at her with lazy eyes, purring and thwacking his tail against the bedspread. Eventually they declared a truce, which involved Erin giving up completely and taking Benadryl to reduce the sneezing and itchy eyes. It also worked as a sleep aid.

A few weeks after she arrived, Erin emerged from her bedroom in the late morning. Laila was buttering toast and watching the news. Erin poured water from the tap and swallowed two pills, then focused on the ticker at the bottom of the television screen: *First-class stamp to cost 37 cents; Peru official: car bombing tied to Bush visit; Scientists test first human cyborg.* The rest of the world had officially moved on, and so had Erin. Her life was nothing like it'd been before. She'd left New York behind, left

Daniel behind. She felt like a coward, running away from her problems. But if she hadn't run, she'd have suffocated from the stillness.

"What are you going to do today?" Laila asked.

Erin sat on a barstool and propped her elbows on the counter. She hadn't thought about what she'd do today, or the next day, or the next. She was still on disability leave, but that was set to expire soon. Maybe it already had. She had no interest in finding a job as an attorney again. A professional career was another thing she was running from. "Oh, I thought I'd run a marathon. Maybe start a new business."

"Well, all right!"

Erin rubbed her swollen eyes. "I'm joking."

"I know, but that means you have a sense of humor!"

"More a sense of doom. Can I have some coffee to go with it?"

Laila pulled a cup from the cabinet above the coffee maker. "Black?"

"Black."

As Laila was pouring coffee, Erin looked at the *Portland Tribune* lying on the counter. It was dated Friday, March 22, 2002.

Laila handed Erin the coffee and assessed her face, worriedly. "Listen, I'm not working this weekend, so I thought you might want to walk around with me. There's a lot to do within walking distance." She pointed to the left beyond the living room. "There are lots of little cafés if you go that way." She gestured in front of her, opposite the front entrance. "And in the other direction, across the park, there are some galleries and museums. A few more blocks is the river and a nice walking path. We could also do some shopping, maybe take a yoga class."

Erin took a gulp of black coffee.

Laila cleared her throat. "And then, of course, there are coffee shops everywhere. This is Portland, after all."

Erin wasn't really listening. She was wondering if she had enough pills to get through the day, and whether she'd have to call Jess's shrink, who she'd seen once in late September and never again, to get a new prescription. She shrugged her shoulders. "OK."

"Want some toast?" Laila held up a loaf of bread and a butter knife.

"No, thanks. Maybe later." Erin stood up and went back into her room, closing the door.

Around midnight that night, Laila came home with someone. Erin was in the bathroom when they came through the door. They were quiet at first and then became louder, his deep voice booming and southern. Erin's bedroom door was open and the bathroom light off—she never turned it on—so it probably looked like she wasn't there. Except that she was always there. The laughter retreated to Laila's room and the slammed door shut most of it out, but not all. Raucous laughter and some bumping around, the typical fare. Lots of moaning. A little later Laila screamed—"Right now!" Erin went back to her room, closed the door, and waited for the noise to subside—which turned out to be eleven minutes. After a long period of silence, she went to the living room and turned on the TV.

Butternut sat next to her while she watched home-decorating shows, QVC, true ghost stories. The middle-of-the-night shows were punctuated by loud men yelling at her to call them if she'd been injured in an accident and *For Adults Only* ads showcasing busty women with big hair and 1-900 numbers. At about two thirty she tiptoed into the kitchen and rummaged around for a snack. She found Captain Crunch and passable milk, eating it out of a chipped white bowl in front of another decorating show. Put her bowl in the sink, then sat on the bathroom counter and clipped her toenails. Stood in the shower for thirty minutes letting warm water rush down her back. Put on a robe, tried to sleep and failed. Went back to the couch and flicked the television on.

Laila's guy came out a little before six in the morning. Late thirties or early forties, bald spot, slight gut. Salesy type, the kind who used to be good-looking and still acted like it. He was standing at the door, putting his wallet in his pants and sliding his wedding ring back on, when he noticed Erin.

With startled eyes, he quick-glanced the room to see who else was there. Fake smile. He said something, so Erin took off the headphones. "Excuse me?"

"I said hey, darling, what are you doing?"

Erin shook her head and put the headphones back on. The man looked bewildered, and a little angry. He hesitated a few more beats. Then he slipped on his scuffed brown loafers and ducked out the front door.

After the departure of Mr. *Right Now!*, a restless Erin threw on jeans, boots, and a jacket and left the apartment just a few minutes behind him. The streets were quiet, slick with drizzle. The air was cold, but not like New York in December. This was a heavy, dank cold, the kind that seeps into marrow. She searched the street for movement, but Laila's man had already scurried off.

The pre-dawn morning was strangely illuminated, the moon high in the western sky, fuzzed around the edges by wispy clouds but still fat and round. Stretching higher than the five-story building she came out of was a huge, ungainly tree, bereft of leaves, limbs at awkward angles. Moonlight backlit its arthritic canopy, hard and rigid at the joints and thinning out into asymmetrical sticks that would hold the leaves when they came back in spring.

Across the street at the park, swings hung forlorn and slides curved down for nothing. In her imagination, Erin stood in the light of morning, holding hands with Daniel while they both drank coffee. She heard their daughter yell, *Watch, Mommy!* and watched her zip down the slide. Daniel laughed, picked the little girl up, swung her in the air.

A metal swing creaked and flapped in the empty breeze.

The darkness of night was starkly honest, the true state of the world, the condition to which everything would return one day. Feeling the night on her face, Erin tried to imagine, as she had when she was a child, that there was nothing instead of something in the world. Her mind flipped inside out for a sweet moment of nothingness, and then the moment was gone. She opened her eyes, feeling like an uninvited guest in a world that shouldn't exist.

A food-service truck rumbled down the road. It rained off and on, thick fat drops pelting the olive-green Barbour jacket she'd taken from Fitz's closet at the last minute, thinking that wherever she was going, she might need a rain jacket that wasn't hot pink. She stood between a metal-loop bike rack and a fire hydrant, considering which way to go. In front of her, across from the park, a few low buildings displayed framed art. She tried to remember Laila's directions from yesterday. Museums and galleries across the park, grocery store to the left? Bars and restaurants behind her, which held no interest. The river in front of her, past the museums, a few blocks maybe. She would see where that took her. Maybe she'd sit and watch boats go by as the sun rose.

After four blocks the sidewalk was bordered by squat office buildings, all two or three stories. Few buildings in this neighborhood were higher than four stories. There were apartment buildings, warehouses, restaurants. She passed an open parking lot taking up an entire square block. After eight blocks she came to an intersection with a four-lane thoroughfare. It was now twilight, the promise of sun peeking from the horizon. The roads should have been busier, but other than the occasional car, they were desolate. Maybe it was the weekend.

Beyond the intersection lay green space and wide sidewalks. A street sign pointed to a bridge, which meant she was close to the waterfront. She crossed the road and walked across dewy grass to the edge of a wide, slow-moving river. She turned right and followed the waterline along a sidewalk. To her left was a metal fence that delineated a steep drop to the river. Sprinklers came on in the midst of foggy drizzle, catching Erin off guard. As she walked, she squeezed water from her hair and sheared teardrop-shaped droplets from her jacket.

After several blocks she came to a sunken semicircle-shaped plaza. A performance venue. Beyond it was a round, flat area with a fountain in the middle, but there was no water spraying in the early morning chill. This was a place where families took their kids to play on sunny days.

Erin walked until she reached a line of park benches facing the water, where she sat. A few early joggers passed by, a handful of cyclists and rollerbladers. Out on the river a long boat glided quietly, a team of rowers propelling it in synchrony. Good people up before the sun, working their bodies, living healthy. Erin vaguely remembered what that was like.

The sun crept into day. The peak in the distance looked like someone's science project, an exploding volcano made with baking soda, the tip formed as if with clay pressed between small fingers. Noises got louder as the sun rose—people laughing, talking, setting things up. Still Erin didn't look back until a band struck up a Dave Matthews cover song. The road behind her was blocked off from cross traffic by orange cones. White canopy tents with metal poles were set up along the pavement. People dressed in running gear with numbers pinned to their shirts milled about, eating doughnuts and drinking coffee.

Erin thought of Daniel and his charity. The one he never got to finish. Pushing children in wheelchairs in races like this. He would have been the first one there, helping everyone set up, passing out doughnuts to kids, laughing and chatting. Putting smiles on people's faces. Except there would have been a whole contingent of kids in wheelchairs, smiling from ear to ear, waiting to race.

Erin crossed the plaza for happy families and sat on a park bench adjacent to the street to watch smiling people run for charity. Across the street was a stout stone building with cylindrical pillars holding up the entrance. A sign above the pillars announced the building as Three World Trade Center.

On a double take, the name didn't change.

She crossed the road, dodging fit thirty-somethings and

babies in strollers, a boy in roller skates, kids riding bikes. Up close, it was unmistakable: this cluster of buildings was called the World Trade Center complex.

What were the odds? That she would find this after just a few weeks in Portland. That she would stop here, to watch the race festivities. That she would notice the sign on a building. That she would have been thinking of Daniel and his charity because of a race in Portland and that the race would begin in front of a complex of buildings called the World Trade Center?

She'd never really believed in God, especially not after September 11, but now she believed the universe was trying to tell her something.

She ran all the way back to Laila's apartment, making a few wrong turns and missteps along the way. It'd been dark earlier, and she hadn't paid much attention to all the turns she'd made. When she finally made it back, panting from the exercise, she found Laila on the couch in her pajamas, a half-eaten powdered doughnut balanced on her tummy. Laila was apple-shaped, with skinny hips and legs and a generous belly. She looked a little green from the night before. *A green apple*, thought Erin.

Erin threw open the curtains to the small deck outside. "Wake up! It's a beautiful day."

Laila covered her eyes with her forearm, making *ugh* and *isk* noises like a vampire adjusting to daylight. Erin was the one whose husband had died, but Laila looked like the one in mourning. "What are you doing up so early?" Laila asked.

"I have an idea. I'm going to try to fulfill Daniel's dream. Make his charity come to life."

Laila sat up and the doughnut fell to the floor. "What charity?"

"Daniel wanted to set up a charity to help kids in wheelchairs be a part of real races. And now, I'm going to do it."

"You think you're up for that?"

"Of course." Erin still couldn't admit to weakness, not out loud. "I'm an attorney. I can do it. Daniel's brother told me that they got hung up with the legal work and didn't know how to go forward. I can help with that."

"Honey, you know it's not going to bring him back, right?"

Erin shrugged off Laila's concern. "That's not what I'm doing. I just want to do something good for a change." She might have been scraping bottom, but she was still capable. And now she had something to live for.

Buoyed by a wave of humanitarianism, Erin called Daniel's little brother, Robert, right away using Laila's landline. She'd never gotten a new cell phone, choosing to stay below the radar. She wouldn't have answered it anyway, given that she didn't want to talk to anyone. Her parents still didn't know where she was, and she was avoiding Aidan too. She'd given her forwarding address to Schaeffer so she could continue to collect benefits, but with strict instructions not to give out her whereabouts to anyone, not even family.

As the phone rang, Erin started hyperventilating. Did Robert know what happened between her and Aidan? Erin had left the city two days later. She didn't know what the fallout had been, or even if there was any. She hadn't spoken to Aidan since she canceled both her phones and drove away from New York.

Robert picked up after four rings. In a shaky voice, she said, "Hi, Robert. It's Erin."

"Erin! How are you? *Where* are you?"

"I'm in Portland, Oregon. And I'm OK. But listen, I wanted to find out more about the thing Daniel was doing. The charity."

"Yeah, Wheelchair Warriors."

"What's going on with that?"

"Nothing. After Daniel died, we tried but couldn't get the application together. I started grad school and I don't have time, and Cathleen started working again, and Aidan, well, you know Aidan." There was a pause, during which Erin wondered how much Robert knew. She chose to say nothing. "And Mom, she won't say it, but she doesn't have the energy these days. It's all been too much for her." Erin didn't know any of this, because she hadn't stopped to think of anyone's grief but her own.

"Where's the box with the files?"

"I think Aidan has it. Why?"

"Daniel needs a legacy. I want to make this happen."

From across the country, Robert breathed an audible sigh of relief. "It would be so great to get your help. It's been weighing on me. I feel like I'm letting him down, but I just can't function. It's like none of us are whole without him." He choked up but pushed through. "Turns out, Daniel was our heart and soul."

"He was mine too."

Robert agreed to get the box from Aidan and also agreed not to tell anyone she called. He emailed her several documents later that week. She didn't waste any time. There were Word documents, a pdf of a tax form filled out in Daniel's hand with scribbles and question marks all over it. Photos too, with a note about including these in the marketing materials. Some must have been taken by the O'Connors because Erin had never seen them before—Daniel with his family, playing sports, and one of Daniel pushing a boy in a wheelchair, a number pinned to the boy's chest, during a race in New York City. They were at the finish line, Daniel's right hand up with his index finger pointing toward the camera. The boy in the chair, tousled blond hair, chapped face and rosy cheeks, was smiling ear to ear. This must have been the race and the boy Aidan told her about, Greg's son. Erin enlarged the photo and made it the background image on her laptop.

Erin had never done tax law before, but she could figure it out. She was an attorney, after all, and how hard could it be to fill out a few forms? Even if the form was long and complicated, and after she spent a few hours on it there were more question marks in the margins than answers.

She went to work, putting together a mission statement, a budget, and a description of the charity's activities. She researched tax laws, poring over the instructions and the IRS's website. Robert sent her a box full of information that arrived one afternoon with the mail. She unloaded the box onto the dining room table. There were more photos, marketing flyers for other charities, and business cards of attorneys, accountants, marketing and public relations people. Several pages of notes torn from a legal-sized yellow pad in Daniel's sprawling and confident hand detailed Daniel's vision for his charity. The notes, jotted down over a period of several days, included things like *from 5Ks to marathons, kids in wheelchairs, recruit runners by word of mouth, donate proceeds to charities for disabled kids.* He'd probably written this at their apartment, maybe while Erin was asleep. One of the pages was splattered with coffee. She closed her eyes and rubbed her fingers over the indentations in the paper, as if she were reading braille.

She dried her eyes and kept going, more motivated than ever. Erin worked on the application nonstop, through tears and fatigue and emotional mood swings that ranged from numbness to intense anguish to punch-drunk laughter.

And then late one night, two weeks after she'd started, she got to a point where she couldn't continue. She was faking it. She couldn't envision this project, couldn't see anybody wanting to participate. She had no hope or optimism for the future or those who would be present there.

Cursor blinking at her, she blinked back.

Laila walked in. "What are you doing?"

Erin turned around slowly, as though the air were sluggish and murky. "I'm fulfilling Daniel's dream. But I don't know how to do it. It'll never work."

Laila looked over Erin's shoulder. "Wheelchair Warriors. I like it."

"But I can't do it. I don't know any kids in wheelchairs or people who run. None of my friends will participate. I don't even know if I have friends anymore. They're all too busy making money. Going to clubs. Or at least they were before September eleventh. Now I don't know what they're doing. Are they all still trying to get past the ropes at Lotus? Eating at Pastis and Bouley Bakery? Are they still shopping in SoHo and going to Montauk for the summer? Are those places even still there?"

Laila knelt down beside her. "I'm sure those places are still there. And you do have friends. New York is rebounding, and so will you."

"I can't, Laila. I don't have the tools. I'm lost without him. I had no idea how much I loved him, how much I needed him in my life."

Laila stood up. "You need to start going out with me. You need to get out of the house and meet new people."

Erin turned back to the blinking cursor. "I don't want to meet anybody new. Ever."

"OK. Suit yourself." In the kitchen, Laila poured water into a blue plastic cup. Erin had learned that most people weren't good with other people's grief. Laila took a deep gulp of water and tossed the cup in the sink. "I'm going to bed."

Seven hours later, gray morning light filtered through the living room blinds. Erin lifted her head from the desk, wiping drool with the sleeve of Daniel's Princeton sweatshirt. She brewed strong coffee and poured a cup. Then she sat back and double-checked the Wheelchair Warriors application spread out in front of her. She'd answered all the questions, filling in blanks and checking boxes. She read over it all again, signed the form, threw on jeans, and walked three blocks to Kinko's, where she made a copy and bought a manila envelope. At the post office a few blocks away, a long rectangular three-story building that looked like it was built in the sixties, she waited in line for fifteen minutes, clutching the envelope to her chest. When it was her turn, she approached a bored-looking clerk, feeling as if she were about to hand over her child. If this failed, Erin would be a failure. Daniel would have died for nothing.

Erin began to hand her the envelope, then hesitated.

The clerk looked confused. "Can I help you?"

Erin ran her hand over the address, *Internal Revenue Service.* Checked and double-checked the return address.

"You want to mail that?"

"Yes."

The clerk's purple nails clacked on the counter. "Then you're gonna have to hand it over."

After relinquishing control of her future to the federal government, Erin slept the rest of the day, tossing and turning over the questions and the visions roiling in her head. Was that it? Would the charity happen now? She envisioned people signing up, children in wheelchairs rolling themselves out to the starting line, where they'd be matched with runners. Erin would stand on the sidelines, cheering for them, and the world would be OK again because Daniel's wishes would be fulfilled. She almost believed that if she did all of these things, got it all organized and stamped with approval and watched volunteers making it happen, Daniel would come back and would be standing there at the finish line, cheering with her.

Chapter Fourteen

May 31, 2002

Two months after she mailed in the application for tax exemption, a letter arrived in the mail addressed to *Wheelchair Warriors, c/o Erin O'Connor*. Erin's heart beat wildly as she ripped it open. The first line stated *Dear Ms. O'Connor*. She still read the *Ms.* with a pang, even though she'd reconciled the fact that she was now one letter short of being married. It sounded almost the same, some professional married women even preferred it, but to Erin it stood for a lonely widow.

> *We received your application for exemption under section 501(c)(3) of the Internal Revenue Code of 1986, as amended. Unfortunately, we find the application lacking in key respects. Specifically, the following items are missing or insufficient:*

Thirteen items were listed. *Thirteen*. Not just one, and not just oversights. If she were practicing law at a firm, this would constitute blatant malpractice. She'd missed an entire page of financial information, leaving it blank. She picked the wrong basis for exemption, checking the box that declared the entity was a private foundation while representing that it would be a publicly supported charity, apparently two mutually exclusive categories. She didn't sign it everywhere she was supposed to, and she didn't include the required application fee. The list went on.

She was a failure at the one thing she should have been good at, the only thing she was trained to do—practicing law. Daniel would have been able to figure it out. Smart, determined Daniel who did everything right, excelling even at the job he didn't want to do. But restless, self-centered Erin couldn't pull it off.

The truth was more devastating than a simple failure of legal acumen: she couldn't find enough hope in her own heart to believe anything good in the world would ever prevail again. What did it matter? What was the point of any of it?

She stuffed everything back into the envelope representing her failure and hurled it across the room, where it slid like a Frisbee underneath Laila's worn velvet couch.

Hearing the commotion, Laila came out of her bedroom office. "What's going on?"

"I'm an incompetent *widow*, that's what." Erin threw herself onto the couch and curled into a fetal position.

Laila sat next to her and rubbed her back. "If it makes you feel better, I'm feeling pretty shitty today too." She tossed a letter on Erin's lap.

The return address was *Texas State Penitentiary at Huntsville* with a name and number written below it: *Barnhart 07031-078*. "What's this?"

"An invitation to visit my dear father. In prison."

Erin sat up. "Oh, geez. I'm so sorry." Erin felt ashamed she'd been claiming all the sadness in the world for herself. She'd been so wrapped up in her own issues she hadn't bothered to ask Laila about her life. All she knew about Laila's parents was that they divorced when she was five. "Are you going?"

Laila whooped in laughter. "Aren't you the comedian? Me, spending hundreds of dollars to fly to Texas and visit my manslaughtering dad just because it's his birthday and he misses his baby girl." There was a catch in Laila's voice as she grabbed the letter and ripped it up. "Nah. Maybe next year, Daddy-O."

Erin rubbed her eyes. "Manslaughter?"

"Bar fight. Long story."

"How long is he in for?"

"Another five years. Less for good behavior." Laila stood up. "Let's not talk about that. We both need a night out. We're going to have some fun, Portland style. Take a nap and get yourself together. Be ready to go at eight o'clock."

Laila took Erin to a restaurant called Mint with a long, curved bar and exposed brick walls. It was loud and dark and vibrant, packed with twenty-somethings and yuppies. Erin wore a simple black dress with long sleeves and a hemline that fell just above the knee. It'd been her favorite little black dress in her Before life, the plunging neckline showing off what she'd been proud of. Now it draped in places it didn't used to.

"This place is amazing, better than anywhere in New York and cheaper by half," Laila said.

Erin doubted it was better than anywhere in New York, but she wasn't in the mood to debate the relative merits of hipster restaurants.

The hostess showed them to a small, dimly lit table in the back.

"What should we order?" Laila asked after they sat, eyeing the cocktail menu.

"Just no margaritas, please," Erin said.

"No worries there. People here don't even know what a margarita is." When the waiter came, Laila ordered them both dirty martinis. "Drink up," she said, holding her drink aloft. "I'm going to make you forget your troubles the only way I know how."

Erin eyed her martini glass warily, remembering the last time she drank too much. It hadn't made anything better. But then a Chris Cornell song came on, "Seasons," one of Daniel's favorites. Trying to move forward was impossible when everything reminded her of Daniel. Maybe numbing herself was the best way to forget. Erin raised her martini glass to Laila's, clinked, and took a deep gulp of her prescription—raw vodka and bitter vermouth tainted with briny olive juice. Within minutes it warmed up her chest and spread to her arms, legs, and brain cells.

Two more martinis were followed by a round of champagne at the club they went to next. After champagne they switched to shots—several of them, fast and furious. Erin forgot who she was, where she was, and why she felt so sad. She forgot that she was a broken widow in the middle of her grief who had slept with her husband's brother, and she let the house music carry her away. The songs flowed together endlessly. Laila bumped and grinded with a blond guy, then an Asian guy, and then a guy who looked like Tiger Woods. She was moony and heavy-lidded, and Erin must have looked the same. There were at least three men in and out of her vision, illuminated by neon lights flashing in time with the beat, bumping up against her, fighting for her attention. She kept her eyes closed and let it happen, the warm bodies around her reminding her that she was still alive.

She ignored the tiny flicker of judgmental Before-Erin inside her, telling her that intelligent, ambitious women didn't lose control and gyrate on dance floors like wild animals.

When her legs started to give out and her mouth went dry, Laila grabbed her hand and led her out of the club. Hands grasped at both of them, and a panorama of eyes watched them go. As they poured out onto a dark Portland sidewalk, Laila let out a loud holler. "Girl, you are manbait! I'm taking you out with me every night. The dregs alone are better than I usually get."

"It's not me, it's you." Erin wasn't even wearing makeup. She couldn't imagine that any of those men wanted her, with her sunken cheekbones and black cloud of misery.

"Oh, honey. Not even close."

"Well, why didn't you pick one up then?"

"There's plenty of time for that later. You're not ready for men yet." Erin didn't tell her about Aidan, nor did she tell her that she knew about Mr. Right Now.

The next day Erin woke up next to Butternut with the worst hangover of her life. Combined with the nasty weather, it gave her an excuse to stay in bed all day, which seemed like the answer to all of her problems. She'd sworn off daytime anyway. The harsh spotlight of the sun belonged to producers and overachievers, not drug-addled widows throwing in the towel on life. But night hours formed a widow's shroud. They passed without comment or judgment, without the useless activity that occupied the day. There were no banal platitudes or affected smiles, only drinks and pills and shadowy corners. The self-inflicted physical pain of a hangover was far better than grief-induced emotional pain, and there was the benefit of the blissful numbing that preceded it.

Erin had found her cure.

A few weeks later, a guy at the club whose name Erin couldn't remember nodded at the martini in Erin's hand. "Why are you drinking that?"

"What are you, the cocktail police?"

He shrugged. He was blond, but rough-cut rather than pasty. High cheekbones and blue-green eyes, perfect teeth, a Brad Pitt nose. A perfectly symmetrical face. Hours at the gym were displayed under his white T-shirt. *He would have made a good Nazi*, she thought. And then she thought of Daniel with his crooked smile, slightly chipped tooth, and soft belly. Kind, crinkly eyes. Sometimes awkward social skills.

"No, but if you want to party, that's not the way to do it."

"Who said I wanted to party?"

The guy took stock of the dance floor. Beautiful people surrounded them. Women in short skirts and stilettos and men wearing black and charcoal gray pulsated to the deep house beat. Waitresses in plunging halter tops wended their way through, bearing drinks on round trays.

He smirked at Erin. "This isn't exactly where you go if you're the stay-at-home type."

The familiar vodka haze settled into Erin's veins and smoothed the hard, anguished crevasses of her brain. "Right. Maybe I just want to get drunk and be left alone."

"That's no fun. Try this instead."

He pulled out a clear bag full of small round pills in different pastel shades: green, blue, pink, yellow.

Erin's heart raced with excitement. "They look like Easter eggs."

He laughed. "Only this ain't the Easter Bunny, it's the Energizer Bunny, and he's bringing you nothing but happiness." He pulled out a blue one and pressed it into Erin's palm.

She looked at the pill skeptically. "What is it?"

"The love drug, baby. Because it makes you love everyone."

Erin nodded at the bag. "You go first."

The guy shrugged and popped a yellow one just as Laila and Ben walked up, bearing second drinks for everyone. Laila handed Erin a drink and squealed at the plastic bag. "Ooooh! Scooby snacks! Gimme one."

"All right," he said, grinning. "Now there's a girl who knows how to party." He took out two pills, yellow and pink, and handed them to Laila and Ben, who downed them with their martinis. Laila leaned over and stuck her tongue in Ben's mouth. They made out on the edge of the dance floor, sloshing their drinks.

Ben was Laila's man du jour. They were deep into each other's souls, according to her. The guy with the pills was Ben's friend from Los Angeles, a documentary filmmaker, in Portland filming something about the rise of Buddhism among young Americans. Maybe his name was Stewart, or Spencer.

"What do you say, princess?" Ben's friend grabbed Erin's wrist and stared at her hungrily. She turned the pretty blue pill over in her palm. The other side was stamped with one word: *Sky*.

Erin thought of Daniel, going to his office in the sky. In her dreams he had wings and sometimes he took flight, soaring over the devastation and landing smoothly on elysian fields, succeeding even in choosing his own death. The image of him falling cut through her alcohol-numbed brain, faster and faster and faster. And then the part her dreaming mind never let her see but her waking mind was fixated on. The part where she always woke up. She didn't want to imagine it, but she couldn't stop. The more she told herself to stop, the more her brain pulled up the footage, like a truculent child disobeying a parent's feeble orders.

Erin closed her palm around the pill, digging fingernails into flesh. She raised her fist to her mouth and licked the Sky pill out with her tongue. She swallowed quickly, chasing it with vodka.

Love. Overwhelming, intense, crushing love. She felt it for Daniel, for Stewart-Spencer, for Laila and Ben, for everyone at the club. She even felt it for the people who flew the planes into the towers. Pure and complete understanding that everything that had or would happen in the world was done out of love. How could it not be?

She tried to make the guy understand, and it seemed to work, because he was nodding his head. "When love is this good, it just takes everything else out, you know? It's all I feel. It's all there can be, all there ever will be." Neon lights from the disco ball danced around Erin, illuminating the man's face, his white teeth, his keen eyes.

"Yeah." He blew smoke rings above his head. "That's deep."

"I mean, you can see it. Right there and there." Erin pointed to the sky, which in the club was the balcony, the rafters, the silver ducts crisscrossing the ceiling. "Love and fear, that's the choice. All there is. All there ever will be."

"Yeah, you said that already." He pulled her into him, right hand crushing her into his chest, cigarette in his left.

She threw her arms around his neck. He stubbed out his cigarette on the table, pulled her to the dance floor pulsing with throngs of people with hands in the air, moving to the beat. The love in this pretty little pill was her savior, a pharmaceutical Jesus Christ.

Chapter Fifteen

August 14, 2002

A few months passed in a haze. Ben's friend went back to California, leaving behind a handful of pills and the name of a dealer in town. After he left, Erin got a job at Threadz, a vintage women's clothing store a few blocks from Laila's apartment. It didn't pay much, but it was an easy job. Twenty-something women came in searching for clubbing outfits, inexpensive and edgy, and Erin picked things out for them. She had seen the sign on the window while walking by one afternoon and applied without too much thought, feeling that a job as a clerk would be a good way to pass the summer hours. When the shop's owner, Candace, hired her, Erin was surprised. She had convinced herself the world had no use for her anymore, a lonely widow. Of course, Candace didn't know Erin was a widow when she hired her. She later told Erin that she looked like a younger version of herself—thin, ghostly pale, and always wearing black. Erin liked the job because nobody cared if she was quiet and moody. It added to the shop's allure. She could even work while drunk and high. It was worlds away from her high-stress lawyer job in New York. The girl she had been felt like a fictional character she had loved once, wanting to live in her shoes and experience her life, but had since forgotten about.

Erin walked into the apartment at half past eight after closing up the shop. Laila's door was closed and the Gipsy Kings were playing. They used to be one of Erin's favorite bands, but not anymore. She tried asking Laila not to play their music, but Laila said she'd been working to it for years and it was part of her creative process now. Erin could push the issue—*Please don't play the Gipsy Kings because their music was playing on the beach where I was drinking cocktails while my husband was dying.* But instead she let it drop, settling for Laila agreeing to keep her door closed.

In the kitchen, she threw a frozen dinner in the microwave and flipped through yesterday's mail. Advertising circulars, catalogs, flyers from local restaurants, bills in Laila's name. Apart from the box of documents Robert had sent a lifetime ago and the rejection letter from the IRS, still lying among the dust bunnies under the velveteen couch, Erin didn't usually get mail.

The microwave dinged as a different-looking envelope in the stack of junk mail caught her eye. It was addressed to *Erin James O'Connor*. Printed in dark blue on the upper left corner was *September 11th Victim Compensation Fund* and the image of a rippling American flag. Erin tore open the envelope.

Dear Ms. O'Connor,

On September 22, 2001, Congress established a fund for victims of the September 11 terrorist attacks as part of the Air Transportation Safety and System Stabilization Act (49 USC 40101). You are listed as the surviving spouse of Daniel F. O'Connor, 28, DOB April 12, 1973. We are contacting you to let you know that we have evaluated the claim filed on your behalf and have determined a settlement amount based on several factors, including Mr. O'Connor's age and salary on the date of death, and his earning potential over the course of his natural life expectancy.

There was a number at the bottom, a big number, and she couldn't read beyond that. Daniel had been pulverized by terrorists and she was getting paid for it, as if he were nothing more than a rare Ming vase. It felt wrong somehow to accept the money. Was this blood money? She was getting this offer because somebody—the government or the building's owner or the airlines or all of them—needed to assuage their guilt, cut short their liability, tie up the whole unfortunate incident with a number and a bow.

Erin ripped up the letter and threw the pieces in the trash. She took a shaky sip of water. Then she rushed into the bathroom and threw up, because she knew she was going to take the money. It was too much money not to take.

Daniel's death was all Erin's fault.

Without Erin in his life, Daniel wouldn't have been at the World Trade Center that day, because he wouldn't have been working as a financial analyst. Instead, he would have taken a job with a smaller firm somewhere else, or maybe a position doing what he really wanted to do, developing better ways to fight fires, and he would have watched the towers fall with the rest of the world, been horrified with everyone else, maybe even volunteered for the rescue and recovery effort. But he would have lived.

Daniel often came home from his job stressed out, wondering what the meaning of it all was. He enjoyed the challenge of deciphering market movements and he liked the people he worked with, but he wasn't passionate about the job. He complained that he was just making rich people richer, exploiting inefficiencies in the system. Not doing any good in the world. He didn't believe that finance was his destiny. But they had their dream of moving to the country and raising kids, and Daniel wanted to do it right. He said he didn't want them to have to worry about money, because the primary reason couples divorced was money. Erin didn't try to persuade him otherwise.

And so he didn't quit, even though he wanted to. He stayed in a finance job where he made a lot of money, and where he had the potential to make even more. They had a great life together that first year—summer weekends in the Hamptons, the Belmont Stakes and the US Open, ski trips to Vermont in the winter—and still managed to save a little money toward buying a place in the country one day. In hindsight, they already had everything they could have wanted. But still, they had wanted more. And because of that, everything was gone.

Erin got drunk that night, as usual, and slept in a cocoon of pills and booze. The next day, she woke up stone-cold sober with a screaming headache. But before she took a pill, she walked into the kitchen, pulled the trash can from underneath the sink, and dug through it, pinching out every torn piece of paper. She wanted desperately not to take the money, but she wasn't strong enough to stand on principle. With this settlement, she wouldn't have to worry about working for a while, maybe ever again. And despite everything she had been through, everything she thought she had learned, and the fact that she was a completely different person from Before-Erin, deep in her twisted soul she knew she still needed money. *I guess people really don't change*, she thought, as she shoved the trash can back into its place.

She fit the ripped pieces together like a puzzle, then carefully taped them back into an 8 1/2 x 11 piece of paper. And then she called the number at the bottom.

After she hung up, she brewed coffee and drank it with milk and vodka.

Within two weeks, the sum of two and a quarter million dollars, tax-free, was deposited into her account.

Because Daniel was working hard to provide for their future, he was dead and she was rich. She ended up with exactly what he was working for, everything she'd thought she wanted in her Before life. Money, freedom, independence. Nobody telling her what to do. She had it all. Except him.

She may as well have pushed him off the building herself.

When Laila found out, she let out a low whistle. "Damn, girl. I know it doesn't make up for your loss and all that, but that is a *Pretty. Little. Penny*."

"I know."

"Drinks on you tonight?"

Erin leaned over the railing of a balcony at the club where she first met Ben's friend, whose name was definitely Spencer, a few months before. It was called Halcyon, or maybe Judgment Day? Something like that.

"I didn't know you were coming back," she yelled over the house music. His face was fuzzy around the edges. She focused harder, but it was a blur, the lines of his face pulsing with neon lights from the dance floor. Erin put her hands on his cheeks, feeling his face the way a blind person would.

He swished his martini around. "I had some work to do." They had just popped more X, or rather Erin had. Spencer said he took his in the bathroom.

"Still interviewing Buddhists?"

He grinned at her. "Got that all wrapped up, on to the editing phase. Now I'm working on an exposé of the porn industry."

"If you're looking for material, you've got the wrong girl."

"Don't worry. It's not field research." He laughed at his own joke.

She furrowed her brow at him, trying to concentrate. "Then why are you here?"

He threw his hands up in mock surrender. "OK, OK. I missed you. Laila told me all about the fun you two are having, and I couldn't stay away."

Erin's lids relaxed down her eyes, chemical joy radiating with her pulse. People grinded on the dance floor below. "She told you about the money, didn't she?"

The music picked up, a crescendo of house. He had to yell over it. "What money?"

"I know, right?"

Spencer pointed to his ear and nodded his head, mouthing

at her, *I can't hear you.* Erin took his hand and led him to the dance floor, getting lost among all the beautiful people.

That night at the club, she felt the first flicker of life since Daniel died. The bartender looked into her eyes, and something in her chest fluttered. He said his name was Ryan, and he wanted to know hers.

His hair was dark, his eyes like glistening coal. Smiling and bright, a window to his spirit. And out of all the pairs of eyes in that club, his locked onto hers. She looked into them and saw goodness. Earnestness. Something ineffably hopeful and right. A commitment to life. The same core qualities Daniel had possessed.

"Her name's none of your business." Spencer hadn't acted possessive before, and he hardly had reason to, but he must've seen the look in the bartender's eyes. "Here." Spencer pushed Erin's credit card back to her and handed his own card to Ryan. Puffed up his chest. Took control of the situation.

Erin put her card away. She glanced again at Ryan, who pulled his eyes away from her to run Spencer's card. And then she turned away from him, handed out the drinks he had made, and drank from the cocktail he had shaken. What he represented was a fathomless ocean that she could not dive into again. It held hope and joy and goodness, yes. But danger lurked there too, the potential for deep loss and despair. She took Spencer's hand, threw one more glance at Ryan, then turned her back on him.

The money festered in her bank account, becoming septic. She couldn't spend it fast enough. When she spent it on other people, she felt free, relieved that it was out of her bloody hands. When she bought something for herself, even groceries, it was as though she were killing him all over again, living off the spoils of his murder. Needing the money while it poisoned her was a catch-22, one she couldn't find her way out of.

There was a little game Erin liked to play with herself. It was called Let's Count All the Ways in Which I Killed My Husband. Number one, their marriage and plans to move to the country pushed him into a job he didn't want. Number two, she didn't make him quit even though she knew he was miserable. Number three, she left for Spain when he didn't want her to. If she had stayed home for his mother's sixtieth birthday party, if she had told Jess to hold off on their girls' trip, that they could drink away her sorrows in Mallorca a week later, there was a very substantial chance Daniel would still be alive.

Almost every morning, Daniel and Erin had left the apartment together and rode the 2 express train downtown. They would leave around 8:40, because Erin liked to be at work by nine. She would get out at Times Square and he would keep going, all the way to Cortlandt Street. This was their routine unless one of them had an early meeting. But since he didn't have to wait for Erin to get ready, given that she was on the beach drinking margaritas, he left for work earlier than usual.

She'd envisioned how it would have played out in an alternate universe. Around the time they arrived at her stop, 8:50 a.m. or so, one of them would receive an email about the attack from a colleague to a group distribution list. It would say something brief and to the point, like "Plane just hit WTC." Instead of continuing on downtown, Daniel would get out of the subway with Erin. They would stand there together at the intersection of 42nd and Broadway, staring south, watching the smoking building with horror like so many others. Holding hands. Both of them alive. Thanking their lucky stars Daniel hadn't left early for work that day.

Chapter Sixteen

September 10, 2002

Erin sat in her pajamas on the threadbare couch, hair tangled and a cat on her lap, clutching an empty vodka bottle and a half-eaten cinnamon roll. Outside, rain dusted the windows and mediated the weather to mostly cloudy. The afternoon before had felt like summer. The sun shone more jubilantly than usual, and warm, muted breezes blew in from the ocean. But today could be any season, and, with the rain blocking out the sun, any time of day.

She hadn't started the day with vodka. She woke up late, poured black coffee, and flipped on the new plasma flatscreen Laila asked her to buy. Butternut curled up next to her like a comma. Oprah came on, and Dr. Phil was her guest—the man she made famous after hiring him as her expert in the beef industry lawsuit. It happened in Texas while Erin was in her second year of law school. Her father, who had several friends in the beef industry and knew some of the attorneys in the case, had called her daily to give her updates and asked her to research some of the laws for him. She had done it, ever eager to please.

The segment ended and commercials blared. Erin sat

through them, strangely comforted by the fact there were still people out there who wanted to improve themselves by buying things. A Macy's commercial set to obnoxious music was filled with kids wearing backpacks and back-to-school outfits. Was it August already? Or worse, *September*?

She hadn't thought about the one-year anniversary, or how she'd survive it. Teeth clenched, she grabbed the *Tribune* from the kitchen counter. The date on the upper right of the front page was September 10, 2002.

That's when she grabbed the vodka bottle.

Laila walked out of her bedroom wearing reading glasses and stretched her arms above her head. "Good morning!"

Erin wiped away the last few tears on her cheek. Laila glanced at the empty bottle. "Vodka for breakfast? You OK?"

"It's the anniversary tomorrow. Why didn't you warn me?"

Laila glanced at the television looking confused, as if it would help her understand. "I thought you knew. I'm sorry."

"You have to go out with me tonight. Please, I'm begging you." Laila had slowed down in the past few months, working more during the day and not going out as much at night. Things with Ben were getting serious. Half the time he spent the night, and the other half Laila stayed at his place. Soon she'd probably move out or ask Erin to move out.

Laila grabbed the remote from the table and turned off the TV. Erin sensed she was about to get a lecture, from party-girl Laila of all people. Laila tossed the empty vodka bottle into the trash then sat next to Erin, patting her leg. "Of course we'll get through tomorrow together." Erin rested her head on Laila's shoulder. The cheap white clock in the kitchen marked the passage of seconds with stiff ticks. Someone next door flushed a toilet; water rushed the pipes. For a moment, Erin felt at peace.

"But maybe let's consider not getting drunk and high this time. How about we spend the day hiking instead? Ben has found this really great path that goes all the way to the top of Mount Hood, and the views are amazing. He could go with us. We'll pack lunches and spend the whole day."

Erin pulled her head away from Laila's shoulder. "Hiking? I can't go hiking."

Laila inspected her cuticles. "OK. Is there anything else you want to do? We could go shopping, or maybe drive to the beach?"

"Please, I just want to go out tonight. That's all. I want to stay there until we can't stay any longer, and then I want to go to another club and do the same, and after we can't go anywhere else I want to come home and sleep until it's all over." Erin wanted to recede into a dark box, like the one holding her tiny share of the dust that wasn't Daniel.

More seconds ticked away; outside a big truck rumbled by. The happy cacophony of children reverberated from the park across the street. Laila patted Erin's leg and heaved herself up. "OK. We'll go out."

Erin opened her eyes in a strange place. King-sized bed, low bureau with a television on top, white pleated curtains. The door to the bathroom was closed, and a thin slice of light glowed along the bottom. The bathroom fan rattled.

She bolted up and tried to remember, but she had no idea

who had left the imprint on the pillow next to her or who would come out of that bathroom.

She was wearing her black clubbing dress. She vaguely remembered putting it on yesterday, to go out with Laila.

A rush of realization—going out with Laila. Getting drunk and high. The one-year anniversary.

Erin crawled out of bed, pushed the curtains back, and unlocked the sliding glass door. Walked out onto the cold floor of the balcony, grasping the black metal railing.

Cars and trucks zoomed by on a four-lane road below her. It was cloudy and drizzly, the sun hidden behind a thick layer of fog. Even if she could see the sun, she wouldn't know which direction she was facing.

She was high up. From the buildings around her, she guessed about ten floors.

Her legs quavered, long stalks the color of skim milk. She hadn't worn lipstick in a year, but she was still superficial, this body all she'd ever be. Deadened synapses, air on skin, the rail at her fingertips. Pills and liquor a substrate for her own thin veneer.

She slipped bare feet onto the bottom bar and climbed to the top. Teetered as she lifted to tiptoes, grabbing the rough concrete of the building beside her. Below, a few pedestrians walked. A light breeze ruffled her hair. She wiped the strands from her eyes, lips.

The distance between Erin and the ground was the only thing separating her from Daniel.

She wondered how it would feel to just drop, let go of everything and finally know exactly what he'd experienced.

But no, she would never really know. There was no raging

fire behind her. He had been over ninety floors higher. *Ninety floors*. What must he have experienced—disbelief, horror, abject terror?—when just these ten floors caused her stomach to flip, anticipating the plummet to certain death.

Erin had always been good at math. She liked it because it was logical and universal. It applied to everyone equally, regardless of race, gender, religion. And so Erin had done the math, a million times, sick and twisted as it was:

9.8 meters per second per second
101 floors, 1,256 feet, 383 meters
Ten seconds to impact, ten seconds of flying
Speed at impact = approximately 170 miles per hour

It would have felt like getting hit by a race car at the Indy 500.

Her toes teetered on the narrow edge of the banister. From where she balanced, it would take about three seconds. Three seconds of the wind whipping her hair, her dress. Three seconds to freedom.

But she couldn't. She was a coward, not brave like Daniel. She pushed off, back to the cold concrete of the balcony, as someone shouted and a hand pulled her from behind. She fell into him, landing hard. Spencer thudded into the glass door, locked his arms over hers and said, "Not on my watch, you crazy bitch."

Spencer insisted on driving her home. He was the protective type, and she the perfect little victim. She opened the door as soon as his car came to a stop in front of her building.

"Just a minute," he said as he grabbed her arm, leaning in for a kiss. It was soft and gentle, and Daniel's face flashed in her mind, or was it a flashback of the night before, of kissing Spencer and pretending he was Daniel? "Last night was great."

He pulled away, and she was suddenly curious. "Who are you?"

He looked surprised. "I'm Spencer."

"I know, but why do you like me?"

He laughed. "Crazy turns me on, I guess." He checked his reflection in the rearview mirror, then turned back to her. "I'll call you when I'm in town next."

Erin gazed into his shallow eyes, trying to find even a flicker of hope for the future. But there was nothing there.

"Please don't."

When Erin opened the door to her apartment, barefoot, nauseated, and still reeling from the near-death experience, she was confronted by the worried, expectant faces of Fitz and Eleanor James. They stood up from the table as she walked through the door. Laila was at the table with them; she didn't stand or even look at her roommate.

"Erin!" Eleanor, looking stylish as always in a soft blue cashmere sweater, gray pants, and lipstick, stopped short and clapped a hand over her mouth at the sight of her daughter.

Erin looked at her father. "How did you find me?"

Fitz gave Erin a hug, which she returned limply, then appraised her at arm's length, top to bottom, from her feral hair to her dirty toes. He sniffed the air and narrowed his eyes. "Where have you been?"

"I was just," she pointed at the door with her shoe, "out for a walk."

Eleanor began to cry. "We've been so worried about you, Erin. Why didn't you call? Or let us know you were OK?"

Erin tried to remember why she hadn't wanted them to know where she was. A memory surfaced, tucked away under pills and drinks and pain. Lipstick smeared all over her parents' house, the police taking her away. She shrugged. "I told Schaeffer where I was. I figured they would tell you I was OK."

Fitz glared at her. "But they said you told them *and* your firm not to tell us where you were, and they wouldn't. We had to track you down using a PI." Her dad looked as if angry and upset were battling for superiority, neither clearly having the advantage. "How could you do this to us?"

"I'm sorry." An outdated personality in her head, one that was ten years old and obedient, felt bad for worrying her parents. The same girl surveyed the apartment and balked, cheeks flaring in shame at the shabby furnishings, the dishes piled in the sink, the stench of cat urine and old garbage.

That ten-year-old girl, the one who didn't just almost commit suicide, bought time. "I'll go shower, and we can go to lunch."

When she came out of her room twenty minutes later, showered and dressed, hair wet and no makeup, wearing jeans and a T-shirt and old Birkenstocks, Laila was gone. But her bedroom door was open and the room looked pristine—bed made, clothes picked up, nothing on the floor. Erin had never seen it look so clean. The rest of the apartment was just as messy as it usually was. There was so much judgment in that gesture, so much blame-shifting, that the breath caught in Erin's throat.

Fitz stood in the kitchen wearing his reading glasses and staring at a newspaper. Next to him, Eleanor tentatively rinsed silverware and dropped it into the dishwasher. Fitz picked up an envelope, *CHASE* in large blue letters at the top, and pulled out tri-folded papers. After a moment, he flashed it at Erin. "What's this?"

"What?"

"Your credit card bill is almost forty-five thousand dollars. TVs and computers? Restaurants and lounges? You're charging more in one month than most people make in a year!"

Erin waved him off. "I don't care about that."

"Well I care. And what are all these charges from Los Angeles? Have you been traveling?"

Los Angeles? She hadn't been there. But it wasn't any of his business. "What are you doing reading my credit card bill?" She yanked the papers from his hand and turned her back to him, looking at it for the first time. There was a charge from Best Buy for over ten thousand dollars, restaurant charges, bar tabs for hundreds of dollars each, Apple computers. Multiple charges in LA—restaurants, stores, gas stations. The debits went on for over four pages, small print. Everywhere Laila and Erin had been, what they had bought. Apparently what Spencer had bought too. All on her tab.

"How can you afford that?" Fitz gave her a short pause to respond, but she didn't need to justify anything to him. Was he the one who lost his spouse in a terrorist attack? He had no right to judge her. Nobody did.

He narrowed his eyes at her. "You got settlement money, didn't you? How much was it?"

"Dad, it's none of your business."

"You shuffle in here close to noon, wearing next to nothing and smelling like a distillery, your hair a rat's nest. You disappear from our lives for months, we don't know if you're dead or alive, and you don't even apologize for it."

"I apologized!"

From behind Fitz's bulk Eleanor chimed in, a toy poodle behind a bulldog. "I know you've been through a lot, Erin, but how could you do this? And how could you let yourself go like this? I mean, look at this place. Look at yourself."

"Eleanor, for Chrissake. How many times do I have to tell you I don't give a shit anymore?" Erin swept her hand across the raised bar counter separating the kitchen from the dining table, sending her credit card statement, keys, and pens flying. "None of it fucking matters!"

Eleanor pursed her lips and clasped her jittering hands. Fitz shook his fist at Erin, resorting to his default parenting tactic—yelling. "Erin, you have got to learn to control yourself! So you've had a tough time. We loved Daniel too. But it's been a year! You have to move on. It's not like you to fall apart like this. Everything we've done for you, everything we've taught you, all gone in an instant! It's impossible to take!"

"I'm so sorry to disappoint you, Daddy." Her tone was as icy as she could muster through tears, which was pretty good, given Eleanor was her example. "But this is not like middle school, and it's not like losing a puppy. I'm not going to just forget about it and move on. I think you should go."

Eleanor vibrated with anger or fright or nervousness, her lips pressed into a fine line. She swiped away remnants of tears. "I can see we're not welcome or appreciated here. Fitz, let's go."

He stood a few moments more, hostile glare trained on Erin. Something else was there. Fear, maybe. Uncertainty. "We'll go, since that's clearly what you want. But just so you know," he said, shoving the credit card envelope in her face, "I'm not going to let this continue."

Sweat trickled from Erin's right armpit, her face flushed. Her heart beat overtime. How could she have been raised by these people? Head down, she opened the door and waited for them to leave.

"We're leaving." Eleanor grabbed her lambskin jacket and Louis Vuitton handbag. Fitz walked out with their luggage, still clutching the pages of Erin's credit card bill.

Chapter Seventeen

February 23, 2003

Erin stood in the frozen aisle with the door open, cold air blasting, and threw microwave dinners into the cart. The market was artificially light and bright, chock-full of happy couples and harried mothers. Laila did most of the shopping, but Erin went occasionally, just to get out of the apartment. It'd been months since her parents' aborted visit, and not much had changed in her life. She had no family and only one friend, Laila. And even that relationship was starting to fray. Spencer used to visit occasionally, but that stopped when Erin's credit card was canceled. Fitz had taken the credit card statement with him when he left and must have had Eleanor call Chase Bank, pretending to be her daughter. Erin still had access to her bank accounts; so far Fitz hadn't managed to take those away. Maybe he would, maybe he wouldn't.

All of the striving we do to achieve a certain outcome when we're not even certain it's the right one. It reminded Erin of a parable she once heard about a Chinese farmer. His horse ran away, and his neighbors cursed his bad luck. He replied, "Maybe so, maybe not." Then the horse returned with a whole herd of wild horses. His neighbors praised his good luck, and he said, "Maybe so, maybe not." His son was bucked from one of the wild horses and broke his leg, and his neighbors told him he had rotten luck. "Maybe so, maybe not." When the military came the next day conscripting for their army, they didn't take his son because of his broken leg. When fate is determined so much by chance, why even try to plan?

She was grabbing a frozen tamale dinner when her phone rang, and she pulled it from her pocket. Her phone almost never rang. She didn't even know why she carried it. In fact, as she watched it light up in her hand, she realized she didn't even know what her own phone number was. Laila had made her buy it on one of their shopping sprees, insisting she needed it for safety. Other than Laila, she'd given the number to just a handful of people: her boss at Threadz, Robert, when she was working on the charity, and Jess, because she had emailed Erin asking how to get in touch. Not even her parents had this number, as far as Erin knew.

It was an international number starting with +44. Probably Alec. Jess had given him the number. A few months before, she'd told Erin she gave it to him after he called Jess to check on Erin. He'd called in the past, and Erin had known it was him. But she hadn't answered before, and he didn't leave messages. Out of curiosity or boredom, maybe for a brief glimmer of excitement, she decided to answer it this time. "Hello?"

"Hello, Erin? It's me. Alec." He sounded so sunny and cheery and British.

Hearing his voice, the devastation and pain of those first few days crashed down hard. Flashbacks of the beach, the pool, the three-margarita revulsion in her stomach. The uncertainty of not knowing where Daniel was or what happened to him. That was the worst part—not knowing, a lack of closure. Her breath suddenly came short and panicked in the middle of the frozen-foods aisle. Annoyed mothers pushed their carts around her, harrumphing. A kid screamed, "I want gummy bears!"

"Alec?" she said, voice thick with emotion.

"Yes, that's right. Alec Carlisle. Remember me?" He cleared his throat awkwardly, as if realizing she may not want to remember him. "From Mallorca? Well, actually I'm from England, but we met in Mallorca?"

Of course she remembered him. Every moment of that day was writ on her memory like etched glass. His blue eyes, five o'clock shadow, slightly crossed front teeth. All of it hit her in a wave of twisted nostalgia. "Yeah. Of course, I remember. How are you?"

"I'm well. Very well. I've called you a few times, you know. Wanted to check in with you. See how you're holding up."

Erin let his statement hang. She had nothing to say for herself.

"I've been in touch with Jess. She's kept me up to date. Actually, she gave me your number."

"Oh, right." Erin didn't say she already knew this. "So, why are you calling?" Erin had a strange shameful feeling, as though she were a naughty child. She always had this feeling when she thought of Alec, as though the universe might punish her for thinking his name or conjuring his face.

"Oh, forgive me. Well, Jess told me you were living in Oregon now, and, well, I just so happened to be in town. On business. So I thought I'd look you up."

Alec Carlisle was an international banker, if she recalled correctly. Erin didn't know much about international banking, but she was pretty sure it didn't go down in Portland, Oregon. When she didn't say anything, he filled the awkward pause. "I thought, maybe, I could take you to lunch or dinner. Just to check in with you. I've got some free time tomorrow, during the day and evening."

"Oh. OK, sure."

"Brilliant. When are you free?"

Erin laughed, more of a forceful exhale through her nose. *I'm always free*, she thought. Freedom was her fate. It walked hand in hand with loneliness. She had a job, but it was just a way to let her free time pass without thinking too much. "How about lunch tomorrow?"

It was a rare sunny day in Portland, close to sixty degrees. The winter sun came in at an angle, its rays bent and dappled by maple trees. It was the sort of day she would've reveled in not long ago, begging Daniel to take a walk through the park with her. They would've sprawled out on one of the big flat rocks that jut out from the bedrock of Manhattan, soaking in the waning rays of precious New York sunlight. Held hands, let the sun warm their faces, needing nothing more than to be together.

She walked along the sidewalks of the North Park Blocks, hugging her arms to her chest and shivering despite her long sleeves and fleece. Alec walked beside her, wearing jeans with a white T-shirt, brown leather jacket, and gray Converse sneakers. He was taller than she remembered, at least six foot two. Rough-cut but elegant at the same time, like his primitive nature was constantly struggling for primacy within the civilized society in which he lived. Seeing him again was strange, like a part of her other life, even though technically he was on the cusp between Before and After. His presence had unleashed a volley of emotions, most of which she hadn't identified or processed yet. Which explained the shivering.

"Are you cold? Do you want my jacket?" He was chivalrous. She remembered that about him, always willing to help when she needed him.

"No, I'm fine."

"Did you have enough to eat for lunch?"

At the sidewalk café they'd just left, Erin had ordered a side salad and a glass of pinot grigio. While she pushed around the lettuce, Alec had eyed her and her plate warily. It was true, she was gaunt. A wisp of her former self. She rarely looked in the mirror and never weighed herself, but she could tell by the way her clothes fit. Laila told her recently that she needed a steady diet of cheeseburgers. Before-Erin had been obsessed with weighing herself every morning and plastering sticky notes throughout the apartment with scribbled platitudes like *Nothing tastes as good as thin feels*. Daniel would roll his eyes at her and tell her he liked a woman with a little meat on her bones. Now martinis supplied her energy, and food was something to placate her stomach when it growled.

Erin shrugged. "I'm fine. I don't have much of an appetite these days."

They walked in companionable silence. Breezes rustled bare tree branches and toyed with Erin's hair. There was the occasional call of an owner to its dog, the distant, happy squeals of children on the playground. In spite of the conflicting emotions that shivered through her body, she felt strangely comfortable with Alec. They barely knew each other, but at the same time, they had gone through something life altering together. Two strangers who shared a once-in-a-lifetime event. Erin had depended on Alec heavily, if only for a brief period of time. It cemented a deep bond and made it feel as though they'd known each other a very long time. And took away the need for small talk.

In front of them the path split into a wide circle with a bronze elephant sculpture towering over the middle. As they got closer the detail came into focus—intricate spirals carved throughout, the heads of other elephants, a sun, what looked like serpents. Across from it was a bench.

"Want to sit?" Alec asked.

"Sure." Erin's legs and feet were tired, unaccustomed to this much exercise. In front of them was a water fountain splashing up from an art deco dog bowl. An unleashed poodle trotted up and lapped from the fountain.

After they sat, Alec spoke. "It's really good to see you again."

"You too," Erin said, looking straight ahead even as she could feel his eyes on her. After a few beats, she looked at her watch. "Do you need to get back to the office?"

Alec watched the dog run off, his owner running after him. "No, I'm good. The rest of the afternoon is pretty free."

"You're here for business?"

"That's right. It's a bank acquisition. Portland-based bank. Barclays is the underwriter." That seemed a sensible explanation. Erin felt silly for imagining he was here just to see her.

Alec turned to her and put his hand on hers. "Erin, I haven't had the chance to tell you how sorry I am. About your husband."

She nodded and blinked away tears. "Thank you." She

pressed her hands together and put them to her lips. She hoped he didn't want to talk about what happened to Daniel. Acknowledging it was enough.

To change the subject, she said, "You were engaged. You must be married by now?"

Alec dropped her hand and leaned back, gaze focused on the elephant in front of him. "September eleventh changed a lot of things."

"You didn't go through with it?"

"We put it off for a while. I had to work through some things."

"And?"

"And I'm still working through them."

"What things?"

"The reason I asked Poppy to marry me in the first place, it wasn't the best reason. But it's what people expected us to do. We dated all through university and after. I'd taken up seven good years of her life. To not marry her after that seemed cruel. I couldn't think of a good reason not to, except . . ." A songbird sang in the canopy above them. The wind rustled Alec's dark blond hair. He ran his fingers through it and turned to Erin. "Something was off. After September eleventh, life came into focus. And that something felt more important."

Erin nodded. Something pulsed beneath the surface, unanswered. "Is that why you're here?"

"I told you, I'm here on business."

"I know, but why come see me?"

"I heard you were struggling. I wanted to check on you."

Erin nodded. "I am struggling. But there's nothing anyone can do for me."

Alec looked at her and blinked a few times. "I don't have anything to say that doesn't sound clichéd."

"It's OK. There's nothing to say."

"I feel like I can be honest with you. It's just such a strange situation. What we went through. We are bonded, but at the same time, over something really horribly tragic. For you, and for the whole world."

"I understand. You can't go through an event like that with someone and not feel a deep connection."

"And also, when all of that horrible stuff was happening, I saw how much you loved your husband. I saw how devastated you were. And I wondered if I would have had that same reaction. It seemed so clear then. Perhaps I wanted to have that feeling again. Certainty, one way or another. I thought I could find it in Mallorca, but I went back there after and didn't find any answers. So then I thought, maybe it was you." He cleared his throat nervously. "You seem to be the answer to a question I didn't know I had."

As Alec looked down, Erin swiveled her engagement ring around on her finger, a one-and-a-half-carat emerald-cut diamond with two smaller triangle diamonds on either side. The sun bounced off the diamonds, and they sparkled like stars in a midnight sky. Daniel picked the ring out himself. After he proposed, he told Erin he spent weeks looking for the perfect diamond, talking to every major jeweler in the city, learning about cut and clarity and color, shopping for the best deal from the most reliable source. He spent three months' salary on it, just like he was supposed to do. They'd done everything they were supposed to, hadn't they?

The thing unspoken between Erin and Alec was too much to

bear. In another life, another world, another time, there might have been something here. But this simply couldn't happen. Erin couldn't have met someone else in the midst of her husband's death. Fate wouldn't do something so cruel to her. How could she ever be happy with this man?

She squared her shoulders and looked him in the eye. "Alec, I don't know anything about you or your fiancée. And I'm not really one to give life advice right now, so take it for what it's worth. The mad ramblings of a sad, lonely widow. But trust me: Cherish what you have. Appreciate it. They're right when they say you don't know how good it is until it's gone."

Alec looked at her, his deep blue eyes questioning. Pained. She could see she'd hit a nerve. After a long pause, he exhaled, turned away from her, and nodded. "You're right. Of course you are."

Erin's shoulders shook with quiet shudders. They sat a few more moments in silence. Alec nodded again as if confirming something to himself, looked at his watch, then stood up. "Well, it looks like I need to get to the airport then." He crooked his elbow to her. "Shall we walk?"

Erin took his arm and they walked slowly through the park to the one-way street where he'd parked his rental car, a silver Lincoln sedan. Before Alec crossed the street, he turned to look at Erin. She caught a waft of his aftershave, a crisp cedar-tobacco smell. He leaned in and gave her two slow kisses, one on each cheek.

"Please, Erin, take care of yourself. OK?" There was genuine concern in his gaze.

She nodded, crossed her arms, and looked away.

He slid into the driver's seat of the car and started the engine. Erin stood watching as he disappeared into a sea of cars heading north.

Erin ran the five blocks home, panting with exhaustion. She used to run every day, play hours of tennis, hike Colorado mountains in the summer. Now she could barely jog five blocks on flat terrain. She burst into the apartment and went straight to her room, planted herself facedown on her bed, and wept, feeling the pain of being alive for the first time in months.

Chapter Eighteen

March 15, 2003

Laila walked out of her bedroom wearing her reading glasses. "Erin."

Her tone made Erin look up from her newspaper. "What?"

She pushed her glasses to the top of her head. "What are you doing to yourself? Have you looked in the mirror lately?"

Erin put down the newspaper and swiped at a matted lock of hair covering her face. She pulled a coffee mug from the cupboard and poured a cup. "Don't start with me."

Laila pushed her palms flat on the counter, shoulders at her ears. "Fine. But your rent check bounced."

"What?"

"I know, I thought it was strange too since you're Ms. Moneybags now." Laila pulled a crumpled piece of paper from her black velour hoodie and flicked it at Erin. It bounced off her shoulder and hit the floor.

Erin picked it up and flattened out its creases. It was a check made out to Laila Barnhart, in Erin's handwriting, for eight hundred and fifty dollars, dated March 1, 2003. Stamped in red ink diagonally across its face were the words *Account Frozen*.

"There must be some mistake." But as soon as she said it, she knew it was no mistake. It took her father a while, but he'd finally blocked her from her own bank account.

Laila walked into the kitchen and poured herself a cup of coffee. She looked tired and judgmental. "No mistake. I called and pretended I was you. They've put a freeze on your account. By court order."

"You pretended you were me?"

"Whatever. You owe me money. Your credit cards are no good either."

Erin curled her fingers around her coffee cup, holding it as a shield. When she sipped, steaming hot coffee burned her tongue. "I helped you buy a car. I bought a new TV. I pay for everything when we go out."

Laila looked out the window toward the park. "And thank you. But those were gifts. They don't pay the rent."

This was rich. Laila, with her string of lovers, excessive drinking, indiscriminate drug use. The girl who got kicked out of the Peace Corps, treating Erin as the fuckup.

Ben came out of Laila's room and put his arm around his girlfriend. "What's going on here?"

Laila nodded at him. Ben took a couple of slow steps toward Erin. They'd obviously talked about this. Rehearsed it.

"Erin, you know Laila's been good to you. She took you in after the tragedy, let you stay with her." His tone was soft and manipulative, as if he were speaking to an unruly child.

"I pay rent! I'm not freeloading."

He nodded patronizingly. "Until now. You go out all night, sleep all day, and now you can't pay. And well, we've been thinking." He turned back to Laila and took her hand. "Things are getting serious between us, and we were thinking I should move in here. And that might make things a little cramped."

Erin swallowed the lump in her throat. So that's what this was. "You're kicking me out?"

"No, no, I wouldn't put it that way."

"All that I've done for you, and at the first sign of trouble you kick me out?"

Laila's eyes went wide. "I've taken care of you, Erin. How many times have I taken off your shoes, pulled random men off of you at bars, held your hair back while you threw up, made you breakfast in the morning? Do you ever make the coffee? Do the grocery shopping? Think of anyone other than yourself? Jesus, it's like you're a child. Grow up! You can't live like this forever."

"I can't believe this." Erin tried to push past Ben dramatically, but she bumped into the doorjamb. Hot coffee and porcelain cup vaulted from her shaking hands. The cup shattered into jagged pieces, the liquid scalding her bare legs. She jumped back, and a shard of porcelain sliced her heel. Hot red blood spilled onto the peeling linoleum floor, swirling with brown coffee.

Laila bolted toward her, grabbing a roll of paper towels from the counter. "Are you OK?"

"No, I'm not OK!" Erin leaned into the cabinets, standing on her one good foot. She yanked a wad of paper towels off the roll and pressed them to the cut. Tears blinded her, spilling over her cheeks and pooling with the blood on the floor. "I can't believe you're kicking me out. At my lowest point. He's only been dead a year."

Laila dropped to her knees beside Erin, her expression softening in direct proportion to the amount of blood spilling. "It's been longer than that, Erin. You need to get yourself together. It's time for us both to move on."

Laila found a roll of gauze and medical tape from a first aid kit under the sink, and she and Ben doctored Erin's foot. The sharp pain was a focal point, keeping Erin's mind off the panoply of miseries that had become her life.

Laila and Ben told her there was no rush, but Erin had her pride. As soon as the bleeding stopped and her foot was bandaged, she packed her things. She didn't want to be somewhere she wasn't welcome, and she couldn't stand to look at the happy couple one more day. Packing didn't take long. A few clothes, three pairs of shoes, her blanket and pillow, some toiletries, and her car keys. She left the new television behind, claiming it wouldn't fit in her car.

Laila stood by the door. "Do you have a place to go?"

"Yes," Erin lied, juggling her purse and jacket with her suitcase. Laila didn't ask where, probably preferring not to know whether she was lying.

"OK. I'm sorry things had to turn out this way."

Erin paused at the threshold and turned back to Laila. Cool air in the hallway collided with staleness in the apartment. "Yeah. Me too."

Laila smiled a flat smile and held out her arms. Erin hesitated for a moment and then gave in. Laila was warm and soft and smelled of buttered toast. For one weak moment, Erin thought about asking her to reconsider. She could get her shit together, be a better roommate. But that seemed impossible even to her. Without making eye contact, Erin pulled away and bumped her suitcase down the carpeted hallway.

At the door to the stairwell, she turned to look one last time.

Ben had his arm around Laila, and they looked like parents watching their wayward teen leave home. "I'm always here if you need anything," Laila called as Erin opened the door to the dank concrete steps.

Erin let the door slam behind her.

Out on the street, thick clouds blocked the sun and gave the day a sort of timelessness, no beginning and no end. Most days in Portland were like this, and they all reminded her of the day she left to go to Mallorca, in her Before life. As though Portland had opened its hazy, gray arms and welcomed Erin to the funk.

Erin opened the trunk of her car, which was parked on the street in front of Laila's building, and threw her things in. She slid into the driver's seat, slamming the car door hard. She wanted Laila and Ben to hear it and think she was angry and defiant. Not sad. Their faces weren't visible from this far down, but she knew they were both standing at the window, watching her go.

For a moment, Erin stared straight ahead at the sliver of candy-apple metal on the horizon. Dirty, never washed, yet stubbornly bright red like the hard-lacquered nails of a woman who has it all and wants more. It contrasted starkly with the gaunt, sharp-angled woman she had become. This had been her dream car. The car that belonged to Erin James, the one she drove to Harvard Law and then to New York City, keeping it at a ridiculous cost even though she and Daniel rarely used it. Daniel called her a Texas girl in a Texas car. He pointed out that if they sold it they could have bought round-trip tickets to Europe every three or four months and still pocketed money. But to Erin the car was a symbol of freedom. A level of luxury that most New Yorkers didn't have access to, and a means of escape in an emergency.

A lot of good the car had done Daniel when he was in trouble.

She turned the key in the ignition and it caught smoothly, purring to life. There was power underneath her fingertips, straining at the gears. She could release it and go wherever she wanted. Families, relationships, possessions are all sharp nails driven into the fabric of life, pinning you down. When they're ripped away, it gives you freedom but leaves you in tatters.

Erin shifted the gear stick into drive, rolling away from the curb and onto the fog-laden street in front of Laila's apartment. It was the southbound side of a boulevard lined with museums and old brick apartments and hipster restaurants. The strip of park in the median was bisected by a walkway flanked by bare-branched trees, park benches dotted along the way. Good people were acting as though it were any other day: walking their dogs, sitting cross-legged on park benches watching their kids play, drinking Starbucks coffee from paper cups.

Instead of making a decision, Erin let the impatient car choose its path. After a few blocks a red light stopped her, but the way was clear for a right turn and the car took it. Erin and the Mercedes passed churches and office buildings, trees starkly naked next to trees with bright green leaves. In front of them, a highway was the path of least resistance.

Clouds thickened and reclaimed the day from the sun. They passed low rolling hills beneath a charcoal-gray sky as rain clouds swelled and churned their way inland. Tall shrubs whizzed by, morphing into warehouses, strip malls, gas stations.

Beyond the city, orange public storage units, boat stores, and used car lots gave way to low one-story homes nestled in with trees and tucked behind fences, and eventually to yellow fields dotted with scrub and scraggly pines.

Small towns with worn gas stations and run-down churches, mobile homes and weathered markets calling themselves food stores. Rural scenes that seemed obsequiously committed to existence despite the odds.

Roads became more winding and pine trees thickened, the smell of sap tingeing the air. Low mountains made sporadic appearances from behind the clouds. For almost an hour the car drove, beckoned by the roiling clouds ahead.

And then, a sign.

On the right side of the road stood a square green highway sign on a post, the type Erin had seen many times on many other roads. Three black numbers inside a white bubble shaped like a police badge: *101 North.*

Just like Daniel's floor.

I must be hallucinating, she thought. But no, there it was again, up ahead, this time mounted to a metal truss bridge straddling the road: *101 North to Seaside and Astoria,* along with an arrow pointing to her fate.

The world sharpened and became Technicolor. Black beneath, green on both sides, blue above, red all around.

She took the exit.

Wide placid roads, grasses and scrub brush, low hills and the smell of sap. Homes and farm stands selling produce. She drove behind flatbed semis burdened with lumber. Erin embraced head-on every decision she'd made or not made, her father's betrayal, Laila's fair-weather friendship, every twisted branch of fate that had brought her here.

The tires hugged the curves of the asphalt path scratched along the Pacific coast. A ray of late afternoon sun streaked through a thinning cloud and shone off the red hood, the garish color of life—the color of fire and hostility, shiny apples and clown noses. Blood, ambition. Lipstick.

The car was an anachronism, a throwback to the brief, happy life that was destroyed along with the towers. It didn't belong in the gray purgatory of Erin's present. She gunned the engine, daring the perfect machine to veer from the painted yellow stripes.

Night fell. She crossed over a short bridge and then a much longer one, trussed with steel beams. It looked like one of the many bridges that crossed into and out of Manhattan and led to a glorious stretch of coastal highway. A thin row of boulders bordered the highway on the left and beyond that, the ocean. She cracked the window and heavy salt air infiltrated, bringing in pine and beach and seaweed.

She sped along the dark, jagged coastline and the curves came faster. Tires squealed and rubber burned. Erin gripped the wheel like a race-car driver. The gash in her foot protested as she hit the gas harder. Fat raindrops fell on the windshield, distorting her vision. She flicked on the windshield wipers as she veered left around a curve. Lights flashed behind her.

In the next instant, the windshield cleared and there was no time to react. She braced herself for impact and closed her eyes, hoping for a pain-free ending for both her and the deer. Her breath went in and out in slow motion as the car sped on. The seconds stretched into eons, time in which there was no time because Einstein was right, it was a stubbornly persistent illusion that dropped away when the veil was pulled back. Still no impact. She opened her eyes, expecting to see the deer bounding across the road and to take the next curve to the right. Instead, she stared into glassy doe-brown eyes as the car took out delicate deer legs.

A *thud-pop* on the windshield, change in air pressure. Cold wind and shattered glass rushed her nose, mouth, hair. Skidding tires, smoking rubber. Screeching of metal on metal and then the car was flying across sharp-edged boulders. Something stopped the car but Erin was flying free, floating through the air. Beneath her was the Mercedes, the boulders, the deer, and in front of her, the wide expanse of the ocean. The joy and freedom of flying.

She closed her eyes and everything went dark.

Chapter Nineteen

March 17, 2003

Are you still alive?

The voice resonated throughout her body. Her heart smiled, and she struggled to see him. It was his voice, but she couldn't open her eyes.

No, I'm not.

This isn't the end for you.

Her soul answered him, *There's nothing left for me here.* She heard the grin in his voice as clearly as his words: *But are you still alive?*

This question didn't resonate though, and she didn't answer. The presence was gone. And she realized she wouldn't be able to see him with her eyes, because her eyes were dead along with the rest of her. There was a car and a highway and a deer and an ocean. So this must have been the afterlife. Why was he asking if she was still alive? Were there jokes in heaven?

A remnant surfaced from her memory. They were at Jess's family's house in the Hamptons on Memorial Day weekend, 2001. Four months before Daniel died. Having dinner with friends outside on the patio. Talking about what they would do with their lives if money didn't matter. Jess was there, and Marc, the guy who later dumped her. Jess's boss, Craig, a Goldman guy. His girlfriend du jour, Shelley, who was about forty with bleached-blond hair and a washed-up look.

Daniel, of course, said he'd be a firefighter. Jess said a writer. Marc said he'd own an NFL team. Craig said he'd be doing exactly what he was doing—making money however he could. When it was Shelley's turn, she took a swig of her martini and said, "It's too late now, but I always wanted to be a pastry chef."

Daniel leaned forward and said to her, "Why is it too late?"

Shelley shook her graying roots. "I'm too old. Chef school is full of twenty-year-olds."

And Daniel said to her, "Are you still alive?"

They all laughed. But Daniel didn't. He was earnest with his green-eyed Boy Scout optimism. He said it again, and the laughter died down.

"Yes," she responded.

"Then it's not too late," he said.

Shelley's expression changed. She leaned forward and looked into Daniel's eyes. "You know, you're right. I may be almost forty years old, but I'm still alive, goddamn it." Then she stood up and yelled, taking up a superhero stance, "I'm going to be a fucking pastry chef!" Of course, Shelley followed Daniel around the rest of the weekend trying to lure him away from Erin, which Daniel described as trying to tear down a cinderblock wall with a toothpick.

Erin remembered a deep certainty, when she saw Shelley's expression change, that twinkle in her eye from being validated, that Daniel was too good for this world.

Come back, she thought. *Where are you?* How was she supposed to find him? She didn't know the rules of this new world. It would've helped if she believed in God. When she was alive, maybe she would've known what to do. Remembering a handful of yoga classes, she tried to clear her mind of all thoughts and focus on her third eye—the spot between her eyes. The spot where a sharpshooter might aim a rifle. But all she could see were the brown eyes of a doe, wide open and terrified. She continued to feel for Daniel but found only darkness and then, gradually, became aware of a fluorescent white glow. *If this is heaven*, she thought, *they need better lighting.*

Hearing kicked in along with the glow. The beeping of machines, voices in a hallway, an overhead speaker bleating out doctor's names. And then other senses. The feel of needles taped in her arms, her mouth dry as desert sand. Smells—chicken broth, bleach, antiseptic. Taste—sour, salty, metallic.

A change in air pressure. The voices out in the hallway became louder and then muffled again. A beeping noise, like someone tapping on a computer keyboard. These were not heavenly noises. They were pedestrian, earthbound. Her eyes flickered open. Above her, white acoustic ceiling tiles and fluorescent lights. A woman in white scrubs with a long, dark ponytail changed a bag on an IV pole, then turned toward Erin.

"Well, someone's awake! I'll page the doctor. How do you feel?"

Erin narrowed her eyes at her, confused. Was she really alive? It seemed impossible. She blinked her eyes in response. Pain set in and coursed through her body, as suddenly as if she were plunged into boiling water. Searing chest and lungs, legs raw and burned, head pounding, swollen feet and hands. She squinted, her eyes the only parts she could move, and groaned.

"You're in pain, of course. You've got injuries over most of your body. A few broken bones, deep bruises and abrasions, but nothing too serious. I've just replaced your morphine drip. Doctors say you'll be all right again soon. Your family and friends have been here; I think one is in the waiting room. I'll go get her. I know she'll be excited to see you awake."

Erin squinted her eyes and shook her head, or at least tried, but the nurse didn't notice. *Family? Friends?* She didn't have those anymore.

A few minutes later, the door opened again, but it wasn't Fitz and Eleanor. It was Jess.

"Hi, sunshine!" Jess tried hard to beam positivity, but the red, puffy eyes with dark circles gave her away. "How are you feeling?"

Erin tried for a small shake of the head but managed only to widen her eyes. Jess sat next to her on the doctor's stool. Outside the hospital window, the world was gray and cloudy. Tiny droplets clung to the glass. Her bones ached with the wet, cold feel of the day. If Erin had wanted to keep living, Oregon with its morose grayness would've been a good fit.

Jess grabbed her hand. Erin tried to squeeze back, but her fingers were like overstuffed sausages. Sandpaper coated her mouth. With some effort, her vocal cords contracted. "Water." It didn't sound like the right word, but apparently Jess understood it. She poured water from a beige plastic pitcher into a plastic cup and held it out, but Erin couldn't move her limbs. The nurse came in the room as Jess leaned in, awkwardly.

"I think she's thirsty." Jess looked relieved, her outstretched arm holding the cup toward the nurse.

"I'll get her some ice chips. Water could upset her stomach. She hasn't had anything but IV fluids for two days." The nurse bustled over to Erin, took the cup from Jess's hand, and put it back on the tray. Grabbed another cup, filled it with ice from a bucket, and with a gloved hand placed little chunks of frozen water into Erin's mouth. Though she felt like a baby bird being fed by its mother, the cold rocks melting on her tongue provided instant relief.

When she'd had enough, she leaned back into the scratchy, plasticky pillow. The nurse checked some instruments and left the room without another word.

"I wish I'd died." The words were more like croaks.

"Don't you dare say that!" Jess grabbed Erin's hand and leaned forward. "Erin, haven't you punished yourself enough?"

Erin shook her head hard, tears spilling out onto the gauze covering her face.

Jess responded through tears. "Yes, Daniel was a great guy. And he was a great husband. But Erin, please listen, because this is important. His death was not your fault."

The tears redoubled, originating from under her breastbone and streaming from her eyes, her nose, her pores. The words spilled out, raw and guttural. "I was on the beach drinking margaritas while he was dying. On a trip he didn't want me to go on. We argued about it. I left angry. Do you know how it feels, to have left things that way? Jagged knife, stuck in my heart."

Jess squeezed Erin's hand, looking stunned. She leaned forward, wide-eyed. "I'm so sorry. I think you told me that in Spain, and I forgot."

Erin nodded and cried. "And if I'd been there, he would've left for work later. With me. And he wouldn't have died."

Jess's next words were slow and strong and punctuated. "I'm so sorry, Erin. I feel like this is all my fault for making you go."

Erin shook her head but couldn't find words. They were both silent for a few minutes, the only sounds the sputtering of heating vents and an occasional doctor page. Then Jess leaned in. "But listen to me, Erin. You have to stop punishing yourself. You loved Daniel. You didn't know Daniel was going to die. It wasn't your fault Daniel died."

Erin's body shook; monitors began to beep.

Jess squeezed her hand harder. "It wasn't your fault that Daniel died. It wasn't your fault that Daniel died. It wasn't your fault, OK?"

She put her arms around Erin's neck, and together they cried. Erin cried for Daniel, for her marriage, for the children she'd never have. She cried for her lost dreams and the country home and her bakery and the volunteer firefighters who would never meet Daniel O'Connor. She cried, finally, for her country, for innocence, for everyone who was lost. Erin cried because she was finally letting go of her fantasy—the idea that it was all a bad dream or a cruel joke meant to test her, that Daniel was out there somewhere waiting to come back to her. That he would show up on her doorstep, ring the bell, tell her he'd been in a hospital all this time but didn't remember anything—his name, her name, where he lived. She cried because she didn't believe in God but she wanted to die so she could be with Daniel again.

Amid incessant beeping, Jess pulled back to arm's length. "He's gone, Erin. But you're not. You're still here. This is a sign. The doctors said there's no way you should have survived that crash. They said the entire car was crushed like a soda can except for one spot, right above your head. You should have drowned with it, but miraculously you flew through the windshield mostly unharmed. And then there was a police car following you, about to pull you over for speeding, but instead he saved you from drowning. Someone must be looking out for you. So let it go now, OK? Quit sabotaging yourself and figure out what you're still doing here, what you're supposed to do now. Because somebody, whoever it is, has plans for you."

Alec walked in the next day bearing a bouquet of wildflowers tied with twine and a worried expression. Erin was sitting up, sipping chicken broth with a spoon, a bowl of cubed gelatin in front of her. After getting over the initial shock of seeing him, her cheeks flushed with embarrassment, inexplicably, over the sad situation, the scratchy sheets, the beige plastic dishes holding bland hospital food. Not to mention what she probably looked like.

"What are you doing here?"

"I told you to take care of yourself, remember?"

"Yeah," she said in a small, squeaky voice. "Guess I forgot."

He flattened his lips into a half smile. Then he grabbed an empty pitcher by the sink and filled it up, stuck the flowers in it, and set it on the counter. Made his way to the chair by Erin's side, flipped it around, and straddled it. When he sat, she noticed a gold band on his ring finger.

"You got married after all."

"I did what you told me to do, because you told me to."

"What are you doing here? Another bank merger in Portland?"

He smiled, looking sheepish. "Right, something like that. I suppose I could make up a lot of excuses about how I just happened to be stateside. But the truth is Jess called yesterday and told me what happened, I got on a plane this morning, and Bob's your uncle."

Erin looked into his bloodshot eyes. The collar of his stiff white shirt was rumpled, two buttons undone, a tuft of blond chest hair peeking out. He smelled vaguely of whiskey and transatlantic flight. Something inside her pulsed, a spark of life.

"Did you just get off the plane?"

"Pretty much."

"But why are you here?" This man confused her, and she was in no mood to play games. Twice now he'd flown from London to Oregon to visit her. What did he expect from her?

He took a deep breath. "I don't know. I guess I'm still trying to save you."

"But what about your wife? Your job?"

"Fixating on other people helps me forget my problems."

Erin leaned her head back and stared at the fluorescent tubes in the acoustic-tiled ceiling. She didn't know what to say to him. In another life, another world, she would've understood this situation. Known what to do. But all of her instincts were broken. Finally, she said, "You're married. I'm broken."

"Well, at least one of those problems I'm working on fixing." He picked up the spoon on the tray in front of Erin, slid a cube of red Jell-O onto it, and moved it toward her mouth. With a casted arm, she took the spoon and ate.

They sat a while, Jell-O dissolving on Erin's tongue, Alec's concerned eyes darting to her occasionally. On the small television mounted close to the ceiling, Oprah talked about living your best life.

Erin took a deep breath and closed her eyes, trying to connect to a soul she'd numbed and nullified for longer than she could remember. A feeling expanded in her chest, a desire to reach out and grab Alec's hand. With a sudden clarity, like a burst of flavor after you've lost taste, she realized that in another set of circumstances where her husband wasn't killed on the same day she met Alec, she could have loved this man. And it seemed he could have loved her. But it just wasn't possible to meet your next soul mate while you're losing your first one, was it? If there was universal order at all—and she had to believe there was at some level, since she existed to ponder it—this situation was fucked-up.

Erin had already decided to go back to New York, to cling to life by forgetting herself and helping other people. She was going to do it for Daniel, not Alec. Alec didn't fit into her plans. But still. He was here, and he wanted to fix her. Let him try.

During a commercial break, she poked at the mute button and turned to face him. She told him about getting kicked out by Laila after her dad froze her bank account, taking the car and driving, about the deer. About the feeling of freedom when she was flying through the air. About the Daniel vision and her decision to go back to New York. About the thin thread that tethered her to life.

Alec listened and nodded, fed her more Jell-O squares. They focused on the future. Brainstormed about funding for the charity, how to pull off the race. Alec had experience in volunteering for the London marathon and had some good ideas. He took notes as they talked and said he would email everything to her. Promised to help, maybe even get Barclays to sponsor.

For the next two days he brought her lunch—soup and crackers and cheese and sandwiches that she nibbled on. He didn't push her, or ask anything of her, or unload any of his own problems onto her. They discussed politics, the weather, what English people mean when they say *Bob's your uncle*. Erin didn't ask about his wife or how long he planned to stay. Alec didn't push Erin for answers to any life questions or ask about her feelings for him. Never asked for a commitment or probed her interest. Never offered anything but his support and his presence.

Chapter Twenty

March 24, 2003

The plane made its final approach low across the New York skyline, coming in from the south and then banking east to LaGuardia. Seeing it laid out beneath her, Erin's heart did a double pump. It was morning when she began the journey, but the plane crossed paths with the sun in midair and now it was leaving the day, thick swaths of orange and pink and blue painted along the horizon. Emerging from the puffy low-altitude clouds, Erin had a bird's-eye view of all her favorite landmarks: the Statue of Liberty, the Brooklyn Bridge, the Chrysler Building. And the big, gaping chasm where the towers once stood, their scorched-earth emptiness a stark reminder of what she lost.

Erin's breath became shallow and she closed her eyes. She hadn't taken any numbing agents since she was released from the hospital the day before, and she hadn't prepared herself for a sober aerial view of Daniel's grave. Her hands shook and warm, salty tears ran down her face. She wiped them away before her seatmate, a chatty mother with a now-sleeping toddler, noticed and took it as yet another opening for a conversation.

The plane pushed low over Flushing Bay, and Erin smiled. She and Daniel always laughed like fourth graders about the name *Flushing*. It looked as though they were going to touch down in the water, but then they hit ground just as it came into view. The landing was abrupt but confident. *Navy pilot.* The thought hit her consciousness almost as if Daniel himself were sitting there, saying it as he had so many times before, every time their plane landed with a jolt.

As she walked through the airport, memories of coming home to New York flooded over her. After traveling for work or visiting her parents, stepping off the airplane into this place—with its cramped airport and abrupt people and honking cab drivers—wasn't comforting. It was exhilarating. *Game on*—time to hit it hard again. It had always given her a proud thrill that she knew how to navigate the city and was making it in New York. That used to be important to her.

Now, walking through LaGuardia, she felt like an observer. Someone just traveling through. The thrill was still there but low-level and sprung from memory, like tingling sensations from a phantom limb. New York—the scene of Daniel's demise—was not the place it once was for Erin. She tamped down the remnant of traitorous excitement.

She planned to stay with Jess for a while. Jess insisted on sending a car for Erin—New Yorkers didn't meet people at the airport, but getting a car was the next best thing. The driver was there when Erin exited the secured area after getting her luggage. He was dressed all in black with a limo driver's hat on, holding a small whiteboard with *Ms. Erin O'Connor* written in black.

Outside the airport doors, it was a rainy and cold New York evening. Erin put on her coat and followed the driver to his black town car. She settled against the cool black leather and gazed out the windows while the driver whisked her into the city. It was almost full-on dark now, just a fog of twilight in the western sky obscured by buildings and billboards and bridges.

New York City. What it did to her, the excitement battling with her demons. She thought about everything she had to do here, and it felt overwhelming. There was much to make amends for. She'd basically disappeared from her friends' lives after she left, burrowed into her hole and tried to forget the world while others moved on. Hardy New Yorkers cleaned up and bounced back. Daniel always admired Erin for her strength, independence, ambition, tenacity. She felt she'd let him down.

And then there were her parents, her financial situation. They had come to see her after her accident and had put a small amount of money back into her bank account, hesitantly, to pay legitimate expenses. She had to convince them, and herself, that she'd changed and could take care of herself now, which in itself offended her. She was a grown woman and the money was hers. Why did she have to convince anyone of anything?

Then there were the O'Connors. She'd have to see them and talk to them if she wanted to get this charity event off the ground in Daniel's name. She didn't know how she'd face Aidan again.

And of course, the demon that would never go away. Daniel, and what happened to him. She still didn't know how he died, not for sure. He died while they were in a fight, and she'd never have closure. She was terrified at the thought of facing that head-on, every day, without numbing herself.

The driver flipped from station to station on the radio. "What kind of music do you like?"

What did she like? She'd been listening to Pearl Jam and

club music for the last year, and she couldn't remember what else was out there. "Anything is fine."

"So what are you in town for, business or pleasure?"

Erin stared out the window at passing Queens suburbia. They passed a Best Buy, Babies R Us, Target. She didn't fully know what she was doing here. Neither sounded right. "I'm actually moving back here."

"Oh, yeah? Welcome back. How long you been gone?"

She smiled through the tears that coursed down her cheeks. "A long, long time. Feels like a lifetime ago."

New York on the surface seemed the same—the natives still wore black, were still quick and busy, rudely efficient. They still moved past each other without acknowledgment, not even the hint of a smile on their collective face. Yellow cabs still honked their horns and sped impatiently past great clusters of pedestrians. Tourists wearing shorts and sneakers and brightly colored tops still looked up and down and all around, cameras at the ready around their necks.

But underneath something had shifted, and it was more than the gaping hole in the cityscape. It felt deflated, a two-day-old balloon. A loss of bravado. New York was no longer invincible. A chink in the armor, a bruise beneath the glossy skin of the Big Apple.

People called her, one by one. Friends she hadn't spoken to or heard from since they left messages on her voice mail in the days and weeks right after September 11. Someone, probably Jess, spread the word that Erin was back in town. Her first inclination was not to answer the phone. But she wasn't there for herself. She was there to orchestrate something big for Daniel, and she was going to need all the help she could get. So she answered the phone and talked to them. She told them where she'd been, leaving out the drugs and the alcohol and the accident. She told them she was back in New York not to resume her former life but to put together a charity event for Daniel. And she asked them for their help. She declined invitations for dinner and parties but agreed to lunch or coffee—time-bounded, socially polite meetings where no alcohol was expected.

But not for the first week. The first few days back, all she did was sleep and roam the city. Got her bearings, took stock of how things had changed. Reacclimated herself to the energy of the place. New York without an agenda, a luxury she'd never enjoyed when she lived there. But not like a tourist—no museums or Empire State Building or Broadway shows. She walked the streets, observed people coming and going, saw how New Yorkers really lived. She needed to just *be*, in this city where Daniel lived and died, without drugs or booze to numb her being.

Erin walked along the streets of the Upper West Side dressed in jeans and sneakers, a black shirt with the sleeve pushed up on the casted side, clutching a latte from Starbucks. Jess was already at work. She still worked for the software company she was with before, but it was struggling in the post-dot-com, post-9/11 era. The neighborhood hadn't changed—still former boho-rebel turned preppy and family friendly. Nail salons, neighborhood markets, nannies with their charges in double strollers. Movie theaters, chain boutiques like Zara and Banana Republic. Lots of bars and restaurants. Riverside Park, where the waters of the

Hudson flowed on. People jogged and rollerbladed along its paths. Dark town cars and cabs whizzed by, business as usual on the West Side Highway.

Erin followed the path along the river for a few miles, then wandered through Chelsea, where the sidewalks were populated by fortune-tellers and muscle-shirt-clad twenty-something men holding hands, the West Village with its cool intellectualism, the Meatpacking District where grisly, rib-laden dumpsters and men with blood-stained aprons existed on the same block as red-rope hot spots, Parisian restaurants, and celebrity sightings.

It took her a few hours of wandering, but she made her way, physically and emotionally, to Ground Zero. Farther and farther south, metal to a magnet. On the streets of Tribeca, which before was mostly warehouse and loft space, there were white vans with the names of paint and renovation companies along the side in capital letters. *R. A. Smith Painting, Rodriguez & Sons Renovations.* Men carrying lumber and paint cans and portable lathes went in and out of buildings with doormen. Apartment buildings. A nanny pushing a baby in a black stroller passed by, singing the ABC song. There were families in Tribeca now. If Daniel had lived, they might have moved here when they had a baby. The thought stopped Erin in the middle of the sidewalk. The nanny walked north and disappeared around a corner. The sun hit the street and bounced off the window of the lobby the nanny had come out of.

The sidewalk was lousy with black dots—old, tread-upon gum. The scourge of New York City. Rampant underfoot, every few inches, adhered with gummy tentacles onto the sparkling mica and there to stay, indefinitely. Most people barely noticed, and Erin never used to.

How did the gum fall to the sidewalk? Did people spit it out like chaw, like the southern boys she went to law school with who sat in the library at finals time spitting into their cups? Or were the gum-spitters of New York more surreptitious, spitting the spent wad into their hands first and then dropping it casually onto sidewalks? And why didn't anyone ever notice it, say anything about it, start a public-awareness campaign to end the blight?

Erin dug deep, analyzing the emotion as she'd learned to do sober. The dark wads of gum offended her because this ground was sacred now. People may as well have spit gum all over the stained glass images of St. Patrick's Cathedral.

She sat on a bench next to the bus stop for a northbound bus. She could get on it and go back to Jess's apartment, and nobody would care.

The sun cast a disinterested glow from its comfortable southern perch. It was there on September 11 too. Watched the whole thing unfold and did nothing. It has all the power, in perpetuity, but it never helps. It just observes, witnesses devastation, and takes a noninterventionist stance. Gives its denizens, good and bad, a dose of life-sustaining energy and moves on.

To Erin's left, just a few blocks south on Greenwich Street, was the site. There was no more smoke, no more burning metal or concrete effluvium. It'd been eighteen months. The fires went out within four, and the debris was cleared in nine. Designs for a new building, to be called the Freedom Tower, were in the works. The city always moves on.

Erin walked slowly, taking neither the head-down quick steps of a New Yorker nor the wide-eyed leisurely steps of a tourist. And tourists were everywhere, along with men in metal carts selling tragedy porn. Posters, teddy bears, thick programs, and NYPD hats, T-shirts, and badges for kids. People walked around with cameras around their necks and guidebooks in their hands, stumbling into other people. It twisted Erin's stomach to see hawkers profiteering and gawkers behaving as though Ground Zero were a sightseeing destination.

She put one foot in front of the other until she came to a tall steel mesh fence cordoning off a construction site. This was not the temporary makeshift barricade of sawhorses and sentries that kept her out after the attack. This fence was planned, installed, erected to stay a while. It was like a prison fence, except instead of barbed wire at the top there were fluorescent bulbs. Lighting was installed on the fence that kept people out of Ground Zero. So permanent, accommodating. Efficient and useful.

The site was a vast pit, wires and concrete in seeming disarray, men in yellow safety vests and hard hats moving this way and that like ants. It was no longer a war zone. Instead it was the orderly disorder of a construction site. Spaced around the perimeter in even intervals were huge floodlights—what in Texas would've been the telltale sign of a football stadium. Steps led down into platforms and scaffolding in the pit. Machines lifted and beeped as they backed up. The little ants were rebuilding the colony.

Was Daniel still here? Would he be forever?

People accumulated to her left, gazing up at something on the fence. Black plaques above eye level inscribed with names in gold. Above were the words *The Heroes of September 11, 2001.* The list was alphabetical. About two-thirds of the way to the right, close to the bottom of the plaque, there it was, in tiny letters—*Daniel F. O'Connor*. Small and inconsequential. Just one name among thousands.

What was it, really? In the big scheme of things, just a scrape along the sky. A sharp jab that left a smoldering scar in the forest that was New York City. It took out the two tallest trees and a lot of the leaves, but the roots were still there. Razed a wide swath through the city's emotions, leaving it traumatized and angry.

And the forest bounced back, carrying the memory of what it lost.

She stared at his name for a long time. People pushed in front of and behind her, stood next to her, but mostly they let her be. The sun was at a deeper angle now, bathing the scene in deep yellow light.

Erin reached up and caressed the letters of his name, then turned and made her way back to Jess's apartment.

Chapter Twenty-One

April 1, 2003

Zen music played, some sort of flute or other wind instrument. Trickling water dripped from the Buddha's pelvis onto a pile of rocks below. Eighty different teas to choose from. Erin's tea was served in a glass kettle raised on a stand over a flaming votive candle. Except for her, the tea shop was empty. At a table across the room, a woman was not sitting there, but her laptop, teacup, cell phone, and handbag were. The last swig of her tea sat in its glass pot.

Erin considered what to say to her mother-in-law. Former mother-in-law, no more law to hold them together now. That disappeared along with the *r* in *Mrs.* when the towers fell. She hadn't seen Helen since she left New York, in December of 2001. Over the phone, Erin told Helen she was coming back and wanted to see her in person, to catch up and discuss the race. Helen had been skeptical. Erin didn't blame her—she'd dropped off the face of the earth for a year and a half, after all. And who knows what Helen may have heard—the grapevine had branches even stretching to Oregon.

The missing woman finally walked in and joined her laptop, the first Erin had seen of her in the five minutes since she'd been there. Svelte and smartly dressed, dark hair and big sunglasses. She poured the remaining tea into her cup and used the metal lid of the teapot to snuff out the candle. There was elegance in her movements. She sat for a few minutes and then was gone again, taking her small purse and cell phone but leaving her laptop and teacup. After she left, the man tending the shop brought a fresh pot of tea and replaced the empty one, relit the candle. Erin felt as though she were observing a ritual.

Another woman came in, with dark blond hair and big sunglasses, and sat opposite the dark-haired woman's chair. This woman talked to the owner and called him Sam. Commented on the absence of spiced masala chai and asked when he would have it again. She carried an enormous Evian water bottle. She also sat for a few minutes, then answered a phone call and walked out, leaving her things on the table. Erin wondered who these women were, their empty chairs facing each other, an open laptop and a fresh pot of tea waiting, flitting in and out of the shop as if they owned it.

"I guess those women are regulars?" Erin tried to act casual as she refilled her kettle of tea.

"Sure." The man working the counter was big and gruff and Long Island-y, more like a mafioso than a purveyor of fine teas. "Yeah, they come in almost every day. It's like an office for them."

"You don't mind?"

"Nah, they're doing good things. And they buy my tea."

"What good things are they doing?"

"Charity stuff. They're September eleventh widows. There was an article in the paper. You can ask them about it." He handed Erin a fresh pot of hot water and turned away, ending the conversation.

Helen chose the location, so maybe she knew. To rub Erin's face in her failure? Other widows were bouncing back—drinking tea and obnoxiously big bottles of water instead of booze. Keeping themselves fit. Starting charities. Doing everything Erin should have been doing. Was it intended as judgment or inspiration? But no, Helen wouldn't have done that. It was probably just coincidence.

Helen walked in a few minutes after two o'clock. She was just as Erin remembered except a little bigger, a few more lines in her forehead, a few more gray hairs. Erin stood up, tentative. After a slight hesitation, Helen leaned forward and gave Erin a hug.

After pulling away, Erin asked her how she was.

"I'm holding up, dear." Helen eyed Erin warily. "From the looks of it, better than you are."

"Seems everyone is," Erin said. Erin's appearance probably was shocking. Hollow eye sockets, sagging skin. Bruises from the accident still covered much of her body, faint greenish-yellow streaks on her face, hands, and neck; her arm was still in a cast. She didn't wear makeup, instead carrying the grief of a widow in every line of her face.

Helen ordered tea at the counter, then sat down heavily across from Erin.

"Are you eating?"

"Not much of an appetite these days," Erin said.

"I wish I handled grief that way. Unfortunately, I just cook more and eat more."

The gruff tea man delivered Helen's pot of tea, and she emptied two sugar packets into it and stirred. Eyes glancing up at the bruises, Helen said, "We heard about your accident. I'm so relieved that you're OK."

"Thank you." Erin averted her eyes for a moment, then forced them back to Helen. "I've had a rough time."

Helen nodded and put her hand over Erin's. Erin studied her former mother-in-law. Daniel's eyes sparkled there, the likeness indescribable but acute. They were family eighteen months ago —reluctantly, maybe, but nevertheless intertwined. And just like that, in the space of 102 minutes, the time it took the towers to fall, the tie was severed. But now Erin felt closer to the old Irish woman than ever. Daniel's demise was their common burden, one that nobody else felt as keenly.

"Helen, you know about the money, right?"

"Of course, dear. I'm glad for you."

"I've talked to my father. He's helping me manage it. But I'm giving half of it to you, to do what you want with it. Pay off your house, fund your retirement, share it with Aidan and Cathleen and Robert. Whatever you decide." Erin's voice shook a little as she spoke.

"Erin, that's very generous of you. You don't have to do that."

"I want to. It would have made Daniel happy that you're taken care of."

Tears surged behind Erin's eyes when she said his name. He would have smiled his heartbreaking smile to know his mom wouldn't have to worry about money anymore. Erin stared at the ceiling to staunch the flow. The painted white metal tiles looked a hundred years old. She'd promised herself she wouldn't cry, but the tears came anyway. She pushed through what she really came to say. "I have to apologize to you, because I can't apologize to him. I'm sorry I didn't stay for your birthday party. I'm sorry for a lot of things I can't change."

Helen leaned forward and patted Erin's hand on the table. The large-boned, highly capable older woman choked back her own tears to get the words out. "You loved him, and that was enough."

They both were silent while tears slid down their cheeks. Erin wiped hers away with the back of her hand. After the worst of it had passed, she forged ahead with a question she hadn't planned to ask. "Can I ask you a question?"

Helen nodded her assent, wiping her tears with the square napkin intended to cushion her teacup.

"Do you ever think about his last minutes?"

Helen bobbed her head in an *of course* gesture. "They keep me up at night."

The tea man set a box of tissues down wordlessly. Apparently, his tea shop was where widows went not only to work, but also to cry. Erin choked down a sip of tea. Earl Grey, lemony and hard-edged. She should've chosen chamomile.

"How do you not . . . How do you keep yourself from . . . envisioning it?"

Tears trickled down Helen's cheek. She daubed a tissue on each side of her nose, shook her head, then looked into Erin's eyes. "Erin, honey, do you have a support group? You need people around you. People who have gone through the same thing you have. Other 9/11 families, maybe. There are women about town, other widows, who have been doing things. Perhaps you could ask around, find out who they are."

So maybe Helen had known about the other women here. Maybe this was a common spot for widows to hang out. But Erin wasn't ready for support groups. "What about you, Helen? How are you coping?"

"I have my friends, you know. So many of us lost people. Sons, daughters, husbands, nieces. And I have my church."

"I'm afraid to go to church."

"Why, dear?"

"I'm afraid they'll just gloss over the whole thing and tell me Daniel's in a better place. Or it was all part of God's plan. Or God doesn't give you anything you can't handle."

"Well, that's all true."

"Maybe, but I don't need to hear that. I need to hear why it happened, that Daniel wasn't scared. I need to hear that he was trying to get out, helping other people, that he didn't feel any fear or pain. I need to hear . . ." Erin stopped, uncertain how far to go. But Helen must've thought about it. "I need to hear that he didn't jump."

Helen sat back, wide-eyed, as though she hadn't thought of it. "What makes you think he jumped?"

Erin had never spoken of this before and was starting to regret bringing it up. It was shameful—a dark, buried secret. "There were so many, Helen. So many who jumped."

"How do you know that?" Helen seemed genuinely aghast, and now full regret set in. "I haven't seen anything about that. There would have been articles, news reports."

"There were a few."

"Daniel would have fought for his life, Erin. He didn't jump." Helen sounded so certain, so assured. As confident as a parishioner reciting the Lord's Prayer. "Daniel never would've jumped. Now, let's talk about getting you into a support group."

And like that, the matter was closed. *Daniel never would've jumped.* Erin tried to believe it. But she knew there were jumpers. There was an article about it, a photo. There were things on the

Internet. Those women talking about it as they walked away from the site, gazing over their shoulders with the fake horror of someone who liked to imagine they could imagine terrible things but couldn't actually imagine them.

Though it was impossible to conceive what could've led people to leap out of windows, Erin couldn't help but dwell on it. He was so close to the impact zone, where fires raged. The hellish circumstances he must have faced—death either way. By slow, agonizing fire, or by choice.

Julius Caesar said, *It is easier to find men who will volunteer to die than to find those who are willing to endure pain with patience.* Somehow, Erin knew what Daniel would've done. She'd felt it in her heart, in the wind, in the cold concrete where she'd lain that October afternoon, broken and cold. It comforted her to think Daniel exercised some version of free will when faced with grim death either way.

After tea with Helen, Erin made her way back to Jess's place on East 15th Street, where she'd been sleeping on the couch for the past week. Jess was in the kitchen unloading the dishwasher. Erin set her purse down and helped her.

Jess pulled clean plates from the bottom rack, stacking them in the crook of her left arm. "How'd the day go? Make any progress?"

"I saw Helen. Daniel's mom." Erin carried the silverware rack to the drawer and started unloading.

"And?"

"And we cried."

"Of course you did."

"Is that progress? I'm not sure. We didn't talk about the run. Listen, tomorrow I'm going to find a place to live."

"You're welcome to stay here as long as you need to, you know that."

Erin did know, but she also wanted to stay friends with Jess. "I'm going to be in New York at least a year and a half. I can't sleep on your couch that long."

"Why a year and a half?"

"Fall of 2004. That's when the run will be."

"You set a date?"

"September 11, 2004. It's a Saturday." Each time she thought of the fundraiser—the run she was planning in Daniel's honor—there was a pang of insecurity. Fear and trepidation, darkness squeezing out the hope. How was she going to pull this off?

Before-Erin was not someone who spent her time on charity work. Her life had been planned out, and volunteering came much later. After she honed her legal skills and made some money, raised her kids and got them out of the house. She watched her mother, a wealthy wife with just one child and a household staff, spend her time on nothing but decorating her house, volunteering with the Junior League, and trying to navigate her way through Dallas society, ending up with nothing but a nervous condition. Erin recoiled at the thought of that as her future. She never would've predicted she'd quit her job and take on a charity project full-time, from the trenches, in her late twenties, for zero compensation. But her world had a way of changing despite her expectations.

Jess closed the dishwasher and wiped her hands on a kitchen towel, folded it carefully and hung it on the oven bar. "I have some news."

"Yeah? What's that?"

"Nick and I are moving in together."

Erin's head spun, and the knife that lived just beneath her breastbone dug in. She walked into the living room and sat in a club chair, looking out the window. Jess's apartment faced north, hovering four stories over Gramercy Park. "I didn't realize you two were so serious."

"I wanted to tell you, but I didn't know how you would take it. It's such a strange thing, how the world works. If it hadn't been for, you know . . . the tragedy. Nick and I were both helping our companies through the aftermath, and we bonded over it. I thought it might be painful for you to know. So long story short, yes. It's serious."

"I'm happy for you," Erin said, but it sounded hollow to her own ears. A question popped into her head, one she'd had a while but didn't have the courage to ask. "Why wasn't Nick in the office that day?"

Jess sat down on the sofa next to Erin and crossed a leg underneath her, pulling her sleeves over her hands. "Are you sure you're ready to hear it?"

"Yeah. I need to hear it."

"I wish I could make this better, Erin. It's so arbitrary. But here it is. He was working out with a trainer for the first time, and his session ran late. He was on the subway, on his way to the office, when they shut it down. He had to get out at Chambers, and he stood there watching from the street. That's it." Jess picked at her cuticles, then bit a thumbnail. "He said the first thing he did was call Daniel. There was no answer."

Erin nodded, thinking about how thin the line, the difference between death and survival. It was as arbitrary as whether you made your training session that morning. The lucky ones were those who slept in, missed the train, had doctor appointments, got the flu, had a tee time or a breakfast meeting out of the office, or took their kids to school on their first day.

Schaeffer's CEO, Walter Riggs, was another one of the lucky ones. He'd recruited both Daniel and Nick, took them under his wing. He was filling an eyeglass prescription in the tunnels below the World Trade Center, about to go up the elevator, when the plane struck. One of the many headlines about Schaeffer in the weeks afterward called him "The Nearsighted CEO," a play on both his ocular prescription and his myopic focus on rebuilding the company. Like Daniel, Walter was from the Bronx and came from a hardworking middle-class background. Walter's mentorship and friendship had been one of the reasons that Daniel stayed at Schaeffer.

As one of Walter's handpicked favorites, Nick took on a lead role in the days and weeks after the tragedy, helping set up the temporary office in Midtown, hiring new employees, rebuilding the client list from collective memory. Jess had told Erin that he spent all day and all night at the temporary location, sleeping on the couch, eating takeout. He also took it upon himself to make sure that every single person was accounted for and to take care of the families of those who weren't. He'd been instrumental in determining that the firm would continue to pay salaries to victims' families for a full year and provide health-care benefits for five years. Because of the decisions that were made in those critical hours and days, many of them spearheaded by Nick, Schaeffer was thriving again.

Nick did all of that in the face of tragedy. A bright, shining beacon of American fortitude.

Erin became hooked on drugs and alcohol and almost killed herself twice.

"Erin, you really need to talk to Nick. About the race. I'm sure they'd be willing to help. Plus, you never really talked to anyone after. You just kind of disappeared."

"Aren't you the one who said I've already punished myself enough?"

"Talking with Nick isn't punishment. It's closure. And also, he might be able to help."

Erin sank back into her chair and closed her eyes. "I really am happy for you," she said, the temporary blindness allowing her to actually feel it. "It would make Daniel happy too. It would have been so great, the four of us doing things together." But that would never happen now. Erin felt the unfairness of it all and held back the tears.

A few days later, Erin sat in a metal-backed chair across from Nick at a Starbucks in Midtown. Coffee beans infused her sinuses, clothes, hair. Busy people streamed in and out. Outside the windows, New York happened fast, the air itself a jolt of caffeine.

Pleasantries and congratulations out of the way, Nick looked at Erin expectantly. "So what did you want to talk to me about?"

Erin tucked her shaking hands into her lap. "Did you know about Wheelchair Warriors?"

"Yeah, of course," Nick said. "I was helping him with it."

This gave Erin a fresh pang of guilt, but she pushed forward. "I'm going to do it. In his honor."

"That's ambitious." Nick leaned forward and blinked a few times, staring into his latte. Then he looked up at her again. "Don't take this the wrong way, but do you really think you can pull it off?"

A woman with a long blond ponytail walked in, pushing a stroller with a baby inside. Next to them, a guy with dark curly hair tapped away at his laptop. "I understand why you're asking me that. And the answer is yes, I know I can pull it off. And I'm going to, for Daniel."

Nick raised his eyebrows. "All right. Where are you going to find the kids?"

"I don't know. Ask schools in the area. Talk to people who work with disabled kids. It'll be an event just for them, raising money for a good cause, all in Daniel's name."

Nick fumbled with the cardboard holder on his coffee cup. "It's a good idea," he said, but he didn't sound convinced.

"You don't like it?"

"I do like it. I just want to make sure you've thought it through. I mean, what kind of kids in wheelchairs? It's a broad group. They could be suffering from everything from car accidents to genetic disorders. And which of their charities are you going to support?"

Erin handed him a draft business plan she'd typed up. "All of them. They can get pledges, run as a team, donate the money they raise to whatever charity they support. And then the money we get from sponsors we'll divide and give to the top ten biggest fundraisers. And of course, some September eleventh charities. I need to look at them all." The number of charities out there for victims of 9/11 was overwhelming, and an emotionally wrought subject to research. She'd have to ask around for advice on that.

Nick leaned back, crossed foot over leg, and inspected Erin's business plan for a few beats. "I like it," he finally said, pushing the paper back to her.

"You do? Really?"

"Yeah. It sounds like you've thought about it. But what I like most is how excited you seem about it. And that you're doing this for Daniel. I just hope . . ."

"You just hope what?"

"I hope you can sustain the momentum."

Erin nodded. "I've had some rough times. But this has given me a purpose."

"All right. Well, Jess believes in you. And of course, Schaeffer will back you, a hundred percent. We'll be the lead sponsor. Just let me know when you've got the charity set up, and I'll send the check."

Lead sponsor? Erin wasn't sure what that meant, exactly, but it sounded good. Her face crumpled. Nick handed her a rough brown Starbucks napkin, and she blew her nose and tears into it. "Thank you, Nick. I appreciate that."

"Anything for Daniel. You know that." Nick had changed. He was authoritative and confident, where before he'd been awkward and quiet.

Erin took the last sip of her latte. She was tempted to end it here, say thank you and move on. She had what she came for.

But there was more to discuss. Nick was in charge of the Schaeffer post-9/11 operations. She suddenly had so many questions. "Tell me, please, what happened to him?"

Nick looked hesitant. "I don't know for sure."

"You've investigated it, right? Pieced together all of the stories?"

He nodded slowly. "Erin, trust me. There's nothing good there."

She narrowed her eyes at him. Maybe she didn't want to know. Maybe she couldn't handle the truth. "Did people from Schaeffer jump? Do you think Daniel jumped?"

"Don't do that to yourself. I know enough to know that we will never know for sure. So just let that go."

She swallowed the lump in her throat. He was probably right. Nobody could tell her what really happened. She'd have to decide on her own where Daniel's story ended, the stepping-off point for her sorrow.

Nick shifted into professional mode again. "I'm glad you're back, Erin. There'll be a lot of support for you here. A lot of people doing great things to make it mean something. Trying to bring about accountability and change. Schaeffer participates in a lot of it. There are organizations set up to help the families of the people who died, design a memorial at Ground Zero, put victims' kids through college, take care of the rescue workers. There are all sorts of ways you can help. And of course, the firm will support you however we can."

Close to three thousand people died on the same day as Daniel, for the same awful reasons. Their only sin was showing up to work on time, getting on a plane, trying to rescue others. They left behind tens of thousands of other spouses, mothers, fathers, brothers, sisters, and children, each grieving their loved one. And then there were the survivors left injured and traumatized, the rescue and recovery workers who suffered long-term health issues from breathing in ash, the rest of the world who grieved and whose worlds were changed. The casualties of wars that sprang from the event.

Erin was just one spouse, one mourner. She was humbled and motivated by the fact that most survivors didn't bury their sorrows in a pit of pills and vodka. Humbled because she tried to take the easy way out, selfish even in her grief. But motivated because the burden she bore was not hers alone. Each person's story was one piece that fit into the mosaic of September 11. She had only her own jagged shard, turned over and over in her hands, slicing her fresh each time. It was time to place it alongside the other parts of the bigger picture it fit into.

Chapter Twenty-Two

September 11, 2004

Mid-morning sun shone at her back, flinging her shadow in front of her. A sea of smiling faces, people eating bagels and drinking coffee on a cloudy and mild day. The forecasts all predicted a high of 72 degrees and no rain. A great day for running a race.

Erin was a buzzing bundle of nerves. She didn't sleep all night, wondering how she got to this moment, feeling like an impostor. Only whole, complete persons could stand in front of a crowd this big and say something coherent, like how nice it was that so many people showed up to support Daniel's cause, how overwhelmed she was by the support and participation, and how this process helped her heal the pain of Daniel's death. She didn't know if she could say any of that, because she wasn't sure she was a whole, complete person. But she was getting there.

Over two thousand people signed up for the inaugural Wheelchair Warriors 5K in memory of Daniel O'Connor. Many of them were just running or walking in support, but over three hundred would be pushing children in wheelchairs the entire way. Wheelchair Warriors was now a bona fide charity. And setting it up wasn't that difficult, once she was focused and sober. She received a letter from the IRS in July of 2003, and things began to fall into place. By putting the word out to schools around town, they received 347 requests from kids in wheelchairs who wanted to be in the race.

Almost everyone she knew had come out to make it happen—Jess, of course, wearing bright-white running shoes, even though she was a newly addicted yogi and didn't run, ever. A teary-eyed Helen, looking like a tourist with her khaki shorts and camera around her neck. Cathleen with her husband and teenagers. Robert—bright and happy Robert, still single and supportive. Then there were the people from Erin's former life. Lawyers from her old firm where she'd worked, partners and former associates who were now partners, a handful of secretaries. Shelley, who told Erin with tears in her eyes that she'd graduated from chef school and was now a pastry chef. Even Judy was there to cheer on her two grown sons, both wheelchair pushers. When Erin thanked them for coming, Judy brushed her off. "I mean, come on, look at them. They need the exercise." She play-punched one of them in the gut. "Are you kidding me?"

Aidan stood in the crowd, quiet and smiling. It was the first time she'd seen him since she left. He didn't say much to Erin, but he gave her a hug that lasted a little too long.

A Lee Ann Womack song crooned from raised speakers at the starting line. Aidan had filled an iPod with music from artists Daniel liked, the songs he listened to when Erin wasn't around. All the country music Erin used to hate but now found sentimental, though she still cringed. Aidan had also included Faith Hill, Brooks & Dunn, Tim McGraw. Erin mixed in some of her music too, so that people would want to come back next year.

When Chris Martin began to sing "Viva la Vida," it was time. Erin climbed two steps to the platform to take the stage. Number-clad runners and wheelchairs cut a wide arc, extending at least a football field deep to the end of Pier 26. From Erin's vantage point it appeared as though the pier of runners reached all the way to New Jersey, forming a triangular bridge across the Hudson.

It was impossible to describe how she felt seeing all of them, there in memory of Daniel. Young and old, men and women. Families and children, babies in strollers. Policemen, firefighters, Port Authority. All of them sporting a bib with a black number pinned onto the Wheelchair Warriors T-shirt that Jess designed, a Picasso-esque line drawing of a wheelchair propelled by a winged runner, the twin towers looming in the background.

Silence fell over the crowd as Erin took the mic.

She spoke about Daniel, Nate, and the race that started it all. About September 11, of course, and the darkness that descended on her. She said things she didn't know she could articulate, like "Everyone here today is a continuation of Daniel's legacy, the legacy of selfless giving he stood for all his life. It's a legacy that cannot be killed or snuffed out by radical terrorists intent on destroying the American way of life, because no matter how hard they try, we will not let them succeed."

The roar of the crowd took her by surprise. She imagined Daniel there, seeing all of it. Tears sprung to her eyes, and she gritted her teeth. "Daniel would be amazed and inspired by you. Now let's run!" She raised the starting pistol. "Ready, set, go!" She pulled the trigger, and runners raced by in a happy stream of colors. She watched, smiling and laughing through tears, as Daniel's dream was fulfilled.

Within twenty minutes, the first runners pushing wheelchairs—the lean ones with striated leg muscles and aerodynamic sunglasses—trickled across the finish line. Where did all of these people come from? She didn't know most of them. Maybe in a previous life she did. Hordes of volunteers cheered the runners on, stationed at the finish line with reward bags full of PowerBars and water bottles and coupons from local stores. Jess, one of the early finishers, came to stand with Erin at the podium.

"Where's Nick?"

"He was too slow. I left him behind halfway through. He kept talking to people from the firm."

"Thanks for being here. It means a lot to me."

"News flash! I wouldn't have missed it for the world." Kids in wheelchairs streamed by, decorated with race bling and grinning ear to ear.

"What are you going to do once this is over?" Jess asked. "You're going to have a lot of time on your hands."

"I don't know." Erin surveyed the crowd, all the happy people. "This feels pretty good. Maybe I'll work in nonprofit law. I do have a law degree, after all."

Across the pier, twangy music rang out. *It's a great day to be alive.*

"Look over there." Jess pointed across West Street at a man wearing a race number jogging toward them. "He looks familiar."

Erin's breath caught in her throat. He was tall and fit, maybe thirty, with floppy blond hair. It looked like Alec Carlisle jogging toward the finish line. She felt for her wedding rings as she did a hundred times a day, snug and secure on her ring finger. "Did you call him?" Erin asked.

Jess played dumb. "Call who?"

Anxiety mounted as the man came closer. Erin didn't fully believe it was him until he was close enough that she could see his smile, teeth slightly crossed in front. He took her breath away. She stood trying to breathe as Jess gave him a big hug. When it was Erin's turn, she collapsed into him. He was warm and sticky with sweat. It was like seeing a long-lost best friend. She held on to him for a long time, tears dripping down her face.

After a long moment, Erin pulled back to arm's length and shook her head at him. "I can't believe you came." Barclays was a sponsor, and Erin and Alec had talked on the phone about the race, but he had given her no inkling he was thinking of showing up. "Why didn't you tell me?"

Alec looked at Jess, and Jess winked at Erin. "I might have had something to do with it," she said.

"Wait, you knew?" Erin looked at Jess, happy but a little annoyed.

"We wanted it to be a surprise."

They had dinner that night, the three of them, in a small Italian restaurant in Little Italy off the beaten path. Alec filled them in on what had been going on with him for the past year and a half, since the last time Erin saw him. He was married but didn't seem happy, and he didn't even mention his wife's name. Erin knew her name only because he'd said it as they were walking through the park that sunny Portland afternoon. Poppy. He probably married her because of Erin's encouragement. Or discouragement, viewed from another angle. Undercurrents darted beneath the surface of their conversation, but she wouldn't acknowledge them. Erin still blamed herself for Daniel's death, and felt she didn't deserve to be happy. But Alec still had a shot at happiness.

Jess told Alec about Nick and their engagement. And then she broke the news to both of them: she was expecting a baby. April 12, 2005 was the due date. Daniel's birthday. Erin didn't know if Jess realized that, but surely Nick had. Erin felt a swell of happiness that life moves on.

There was a sense in New York now that time was fleeting. People seemed more eager to commit, get married earlier, have babies sooner than before. There was a baby boom after it happened, not just in New York but everywhere. For a moment, instead of talking about the weather or their workout regimens, people were deeper, kinder. Focused more on what mattered. Erin noticed it among her friends but also on the subway, in line at Duane Reade, infused into magazine and newspaper articles.

She assumed this too would change, the same way cabbies started honking their horns again and people on planes quit clapping for a smooth, safe landing. The world would go back to normal; people would forget to remember. But for now, the things that mattered were felt more keenly, for everyone.

After dinner they went their separate ways, promising to meet again every September 11 for dinner in the same place, at the same table. Just the three of them.

Chapter Twenty-Three

September 11, 2011

Silence. That's what she would remember most about the ceremony—rich silence. Thousands of people and several children were in the crowd, but the quiet that occupied downtown New York City, just before the ceremony and then twice more, at 8:46 a.m. and 9:03 a.m., was full and earnest. Profound.

Erin was in a crowd she never wanted to be a part of, at a private memorial she didn't want to be invited to. She wore a black blouse, gray pants, black flats, dark sunglasses. Only her wedding rings for jewelry, hair in a ponytail, no makeup. Aidan, Robert, and Cathleen stood with her. The gamut of human phenotypic possibility was apparent in the heads and bodies around them—tall, short, old, young, a spectrum of skin colors, hair colors, eye colors. Short, long, curly, and straight hair, bald heads and those covered with red, white, and blue ball caps plastered with *FDNY* and American flags. Eyeglasses, sunglasses, no glasses. Thin and overweight. As many ways of appearing as there were of dealing with grief.

Two presidents, one current and one former, stood at the front next to their wives behind a clear, bulletproof-glass barrier.

Another glass barrier covered the speaker's podium a few steps up. All four of them wore somber blue or gray. Their consultants did their job well, avoiding the color red.

Military personnel up front, the sharp white hats of naval officers. In the background behind the stage and beyond the fence, candy-striped cranes reached toward the sky, straining but paralyzed. The work of rebuilding—a museum, a new skyscraper—was paused for this Sunday, Patriot Day. The flat spot of ground where the ceremony was held was surrounded by New York structures of various eras. Shiny, sharp, and ambitious juxtaposed with stout and comfortable, decorative edges, natural cream-colored facades. The new crowding out the old.

A girls' choir occupied the middle of the stage, about fifty of them wearing black pants and shirts with royal blue vests belted with black. A few boys too—in all black with royal blue ties. They sang the national anthem, voices clear and pure offered up to the cloudy skies above. After the choir left, kilted men in bagpipes played and marched across the stage. Military officers performed a ritualistic folding of the American flag, each step executed with precision until it was in the tight formation of a triangle, four white stars showing. In the crowd, people held up signs with photos on them, names. Blown-up and laminated versions of the flyers plastered across New York for so many months and years, ten years ago, except taking the place of *Missing* were new words—*RIP*, *Never Forget*, *Forever Young*.

The mayor of New York took the podium, spoke in his nasally voice. "Ten years have passed since a perfect blue-sky morning turned into the blackest of nights. Since then we've lived in sunshine and in shadow . . ." He spoke of children who lost their parents growing into young adults, of grandchildren being born, and again there was the familiar hollow ache of not having Daniel's children. The mayor talked about the healing power of good works and public service, and how those things were supposed to honor those we loved and lost.

And then, at 8:46 a.m., a moment of silence. Exactly ten years ago that minute, the plane hit Daniel's building, and Erin's journey through darkness began. Church bells pealed in the distance, two flags on the podium swayed gently in the breeze that brushed past her face.

A speech about God by Obama, then Bloomberg took the podium again. The victims of that day were "2,983 innocent men, women, and children," and each of their names would be read. The mayor quoted Shakespeare, and the words rang in Erin's thoughts: "Let us not measure our sorrow by their worth, for then it will have no end."

Erin had been doing that for ten years. *How to measure our sorrow, then, Mayor?* she wanted to ask him. *How to express our grief, shed our guilt, make our reparations? Where's the handbook for that, the rules of the game?* But there was no time set aside for questions and answers.

A recitation of all the names, alphabetical order. Erin stood through them all, sandwiched in among thousands of waving flags, people hoisting framed photos and video cameras. Close to three thousand names, two or three words each. About two seconds each. Six thousand seconds, one hundred minutes to read them all. *Will they really read them all?* She felt disrespectful as she thought it. *O'Connor* would be in the middle, about halfway through. She couldn't leave and didn't want to, but it was a long time to stand. Maybe that was the point.

By two and taking turns, other victims' family members read the names. *Daniel Franklin O'Connor* was read after several *O'Briens* and an *O'Callaghan* and before four other *O'Connors*. When she heard his full name spoken ceremonially for the first time since his funeral, she breathed in deep, tucked her lips into her teeth, and pushed down until it hurt. She listened to every name. Imagined their lives, their stories, their abandoned hopes and thwarted dreams.

After the ceremony was over, everyone was herded to the memorial, one block west along Liberty Street. Erin walked with Daniel's siblings. There was some talk about the ceremony—how well done, the respect shown to the victims and the families, the generosity of time taken to read each name—but the group was mostly quiet and somber.

When they got to the memorial, everyone but Erin stopped to use the restroom. She squeezed Cathleen's hand, gave them all a kiss, and took her leave. She needed to do this on her own.

The cloudy, quiet day added to the severity of the moment. Here was the footprint of the 110-story north tower, Daniel's building, nothing now but a square waterfall with another square in the middle. It was beautiful, well-done. There was a thick bronze surround with names five deep engraved in strong capital letters. Heart beating rapidly, she scanned each name.

Erin had been told where Daniel's name was placed, alongside other victims from Schaeffer. Around the corner, on the top row. It took up about a foot and a half of width, three inches high. The name no more than a hollow in bronze, the person now nothing but shadow and memory. Shards of DNA in a storeroom somewhere, waiting to be identified.

She pulled a single long-stemmed red rose from her bag, slid it into the upper corner of the bronze *D*. Closed her eyes, rubbed her fingers across the letters like a blind woman reading braille. Water crashed down in an infinite loop around the square. Birds chirped. Wind rustled the branches of the small trees planted in even rows around the footprint of the north tower. Clouds rolled across the sun and cast the whole scene in shade. Erin tried to conjure Daniel's face. In her alternate universe, he was standing next to her and holding her hand. Both of them quiet, contemplative, imagining the what-if. Thinking but not talking about how close he came to dying that day.

The image of his face wouldn't come. Instead, she squeezed his imaginary hand, told him she was sorry for leaving that day. She told him she had always loved him and loved him still, and she would never forget him.

They were building a museum too, right by the memorial, which would open in two years. They let the families take a tour of the construction site and give feedback on the design. After Erin left the rose, she joined a group of people converging beneath the unfinished asymmetrical glass box that blended in with the new One World Trade next door. Inside, they descended a spiral walkway until they were level with the massive concrete footprints of the buildings. On the outside, these were the waterfalls that formed the memorial.

There weren't many artifacts yet, but in the various spaces that would be the rooms of the museum there were flyers and brochures describing what the displays would look like. Artists' renderings of the photos of everyone who died, firemen's helmets, women's dirty and bloodied shoes, twisted steel beams with white letters and numbers painted on them. Concrete stairs that survivors used to evacuate. A shredded red fire engine. There were two pages with photos of the flyers so ubiquitous in the days after. Erin skipped over them, not wanting to see Daniel's flyer.

On the next page, her breath faltered. It was a photo of a glass-covered shadow box containing a relic found on the streets during the recovery effort. A paper airplane, singed and dirtied and crumpled, but intact. The airplane was pictured on the top half of the page, and below was what must have been a photocopy of the words that were written on the paper.

E—
I'm sorry.
I wish I could fly.
I love you.
Love, D

The words were rushed and messy, barely legible, but it was unmistakably Daniel's handwriting. Erin's hands began to shake. She dropped the brochure, knelt to grab it, and rushed out of the site. She ran down sidewalks, dodging people and strollers and cars, until she could go no farther because she met the West Side Highway, cars streaming by fast. She stood staring past the cars out onto the shimmering waters of the Hudson. Next to her was a street café, steps leading down to the noisy basement kitchen. A man carrying a box of tomatoes on his shoulder was going down.

Erin looked down at the brochure that she still held in her hand, opening it gingerly. There it was, Daniel's paper airplane. There was a description underneath it: *Paper airplane found near the entrance to a parking garage on West Broadway, two blocks north of World Trade Center site. Believed to be written by someone trapped in the north tower of the World Trade Center.*

Erin sat on the number 4 train, Lexington Avenue express to Woodlawn Heights. It was about forty-five minutes from her brownstone on Henry Street to Helen's house in the Bronx. A car might have been quicker on a Sunday afternoon, but she preferred the low profile and reliability of the subway. She stared out the window as the dark subterranean tunnels whipped past, the rhythmic sequence of the seams in the concrete.

The brochure with Daniel's paper airplane message was clutched in her hands. She hadn't let it out of her sight since that morning.

He forgave her. He released her in the same way he caught her.

Ten years of wondering. How he died, whether he'd forgiven her, if he knew he was dying. What he might have said if they could've talked. Now she knew he thought of her in his final moments and that he knew they were his final moments. For his final message, he chose to channel the way they met, the way they'd gotten engaged. He said he was sorry, but she had forgiven him before he wrote the words.

All that time, the paper airplane was out there. Someone found it and gave it to someone who knew it was important but had no idea who it was from. Or to.

She'd call them, probably. Tell them who wrote it. For posterity's sake.

In the meantime, there was more exhuming to do, and more laying to rest.

The call had come from Aidan three weeks ago, while Erin was walking her dog past Cobble Hill Park. As she pulled out her buzzing phone, Franklin spotted a squirrel darting across the sidewalk and let out a high-pitched, squealing bark, straining at the leash. The gray-tailed squirrel flew through the metal railings of the fence and paused halfway up a tree trunk, head cocked to the left, black almond eyes trained on the spaniel. Daring him. Taunting him.

While Franklin struggled and yipped, Erin yanked back firmly on the leash, twisted it around her wrist, and sat down on a bench. The screen said "Aidan O'Connor." She always hesitated before answering a call from him. Not just because of her lapse of judgment, but because there'd been other phone calls through the years that made her hesitate. The ones reporting grizzly discoveries—a bone fragment, a sliver of skin—identified in later years using ever-advancing technologies. The caller ID always said, innocently, *City of New York*, but she knew who was really calling—*Department of Forensic Biology, Office of Chief Medical Examiner.*

The first time, it'd been a relief. To know, finally, with certainty. Even if she still didn't know how, at least she knew the outcome.

With each additional phone call, though, she descended into the comfortable darkness, the space she inhabited in Portland. But now she knew there was as much a place for darkness as the light. So she'd learned to accept it, preparing for its visit as she would for an old, familiar houseguest, bound by duty, not choice. She notified the people in her office that she'd be out for a few days, retreated to her bedroom, pulled the shades as Eleanor did when she was suffering from a case of nerves.

Eventually she took her phone number off the city's list and replaced it with Aidan's as the contact person. He didn't call unless it was significant, something he thought she needed to know about. It didn't happen often; usually the calls from him were invitations to dinner with the O'Connor family or questions about Wheelchair Warriors or planning the annual race. Regardless, though, when his name showed up on her screen, her heart sank and she couldn't breathe.

After she answered, he said, "I'm afraid I have some bad news."

His voice was so much like Daniel's, the tone and cadence. She saw Aidan occasionally now, over dinner or coffee, and always there was one thing—an expression, a smile, a crinkle of the brow—that brought Daniel back to life, simultaneously making her cringe and breaking her heart.

This time, though, the call wasn't about Daniel's death. It was about Helen's.

"I'm so sorry, Aidan. How did it happen?"

"Heart attack, they say. Yesterday evening. She'd been to church that morning, worked in the garden. Ate corned beef and cabbage for dinner. She died eating a bowl of pistachio ice cream, kicked back in her recliner, watching *The Bachelor*. They say it was immediate, no suffering. All in all, not a bad way to go."

"I know how much you loved her."

"She was an amazing woman. But you know, after Daniel died, death didn't scare her anymore. I think she was ready." His voice cracked with emotion. "She grew to love you as a daughter, you know."

Erin yanked at the leash, shifted her cell phone, wiped away tears. "I appreciate that."

✧

In the three weeks since Helen's death, the O'Connor siblings had been going through the things in Helen's house in preparation for selling it. Helen became a pack rat in the years after Daniel died, and it was a big job. Erin had been too occupied with planning the eighth annual Wheelchair Warriors 5K in Memory of Daniel O'Connor, which had taken place yesterday, to help out much. She attended the funeral in late August at St. Barnabas Church, which she hadn't been back to since Daniel's memorial service. She was at the visitation at Helen's house the night before, took the family a casserole, cried and laughed through tears at stories about Helen and stories about Daniel. Childhood antics, pranks, sibling tattles. Stories she wasn't ready to hear before.

Cathleen had approached Erin yesterday, after the race was over. The stage was packed up, the Hudson wind sweeping party confetti off an abandoned Pier 26. The siblings had finished clearing out most of Helen's house, but they needed Erin's help with Daniel's room. After he died, Helen had preserved it as it was. She kept all the things she took when Erin left New York a few months after September 11, down to the last pair of underwear. When Cathleen asked Erin if she wanted to look through it all, she of course said yes.

She was prepared for the darkness to descend. She wouldn't be able to escape it after the memorial service and the paper airplane and being face-to-face with the possessions of a young Daniel O'Connor.

At Woodlawn, the end of the line, Erin got out and walked the six blocks to the O'Connor house. Clouds closed in, threatening rain. She walked like a prisoner to the gallows, steeling herself for an onslaught of Daniel memories. September 11 had always been a difficult day. It was impossible to make plans. Even watching television was rife with hazards. She avoided the news channels, but still it was easy to catch an image. A plane veering into a building, an explosion, a smoldering tower. People staring up, crying, at the carnage in the sky, huddled gray masses in the streets, reenactments of the Pentagon crash, Shanksville. Each year in the days leading up to it, she would think, *I'm better this year. Maybe I can watch it, view it as a normal American might. Tears and emotions, yes, but not devastating ones.* And then each year proved the same—debilitating grief sandwiched between numbness and regret.

But there was a tradition she was looking forward to—the annual dinner with Alec and Jess. It had happened every year without fail since 2004. They reserved the same dimly lit table in the back of the same Italian restaurant in Little Italy, the place they went on the night of the first race. They drank wine and ate pasta, assessed how they did the year before, and plotted out the following year. It had become their version of a New Year's gathering.

For five years, Alec came into town specifically for this dinner. He tried to make it seem coincidental for the first few years, until Jess and Erin called him out and he fessed up. In 2010, he didn't have to travel anymore, because he finally threw in the towel on his marriage to Poppy and moved to New York for a fresh start. It had been a mistake from the beginning, he said, and he was tired of throwing good years after bad. The prospect of seeing Alec tonight for their annual dinner was the only thing keeping Erin together today.

But there was one more thing she had to do first.

The O'Connor house was a narrow, three-story white clapboard on a street lined with other narrow, three-story houses separated by the thinnest expanses of driveway. Cathleen answered Erin's knock and welcomed her in, through the entryway, past the living room and into the small kitchen. The house was cramped and warm and smelled of decades of bad coffee. Boxes were stacked up along walls, spilling into open spaces. Daniel's siblings had been busy packing up the detritus of Helen O'Connor's life.

Cathleen waved toward the worn wooden table in the small kitchen. "Sit down, please. Coffee?"

"Sure. Thank you." Other than the cleaned-off counters and mostly bare cupboards, the kitchen looked the same as it did the few times Erin had accompanied Daniel to his mother's house. Probably the same as it did when the O'Connors first bought the house in 1974, when Daniel was a baby. From Erin's chair, she had a narrow view into the living room. The cherrywood urn from Ground Zero, the one she didn't want, sat on the mantel.

"Are you the only one here?" Erin asked Cathleen.

"Yeah, I've been doing most of the work around here. Aidan had to go home and rest after the ceremony. It was his weekend with the kids. My kids are adults now, and they don't want me around anymore."

Cathleen opened a cupboard and pulled out a white coffee cup, filled it from the Mr. Coffee carafe and handed it to Erin as she sat down, along with a bowl of sugar and a spoon.

"I'm sorry to pile all this on you. The annual race yesterday, the memorial this morning, and now you have to come to my dead mother's house to clean out Daniel's things." The skin beneath Cathleen's eyes crinkled like papier-mâché when she spoke. Deep creases lined her forehead. She didn't resemble

Daniel; she looked more like their father. It made it easier to talk to her.

"It's OK. I think I can handle it now."

"That's good to hear."

"You doing OK? I know you were very close to your mom."

"Yeah, I'm OK. She had a good life. For the most part." Cathleen ran her hands through her hair, looking as though she were about to cry. "Ma used to say that once you lose a child, you've looked death in the face, and it holds no more power over you. So I know she was ready."

Erin nodded. "I understand the feeling. I've been to the precipice and back a few times myself."

"What's going on with you now?"

"I'm fine."

Cathleen shifted forward in her chair. "I mean, are you seeing anyone?"

Erin bit her bottom lip. "You mean a relationship? No, nothing serious." There'd been a few dates, but as soon as they got serious, she got out.

Cathleen's right hand grabbed Erin's left and squeezed. "Erin, don't you think it's time?"

Erin shook her head. "It still feels like a betrayal."

"He's been gone ten years. He would want you to live your life."

Goosebumps dappled Erin's flesh as she pulled out the brochure and pushed it across the table to Cathleen. She didn't say anything, just opened it to the page showing the paper airplane display.

Cathleen gasped. "That's Daniel's handwriting."

Erin nodded.

Cathleen pursed her lips while she read the description that Erin had already memorized. They sat quietly for a moment, staring at the photo, tears spilling down both their cheeks.

"He always loved making paper airplanes. Since he was a kid." Cathleen shook her head as she stared at the photo. "Sweet Daniel. He was just too good for this world."

"We can agree on that," Erin said.

Finally, Cathleen squeezed Erin's hand, then stood up and put her cup in the sink. "Well, are you ready?"

"Now or never." Erin tucked the brochure back into her purse, put her cup in the sink, and followed Cathleen out of the kitchen.

The stairs were narrow, covered with matted cream carpet. They creaked on the way up. Cathleen opened the door to the bedroom at the end of the hall, on the front side of the house. "We want you to have anything you'd like out of here before we pack up the rest. I'll let you go through it on your own. Take your time. I'll be downstairs packing boxes if you need me."

Daniel's room was a shrine to the boy Daniel, mostly unchanged since high school. Pennants lined the walls—Princeton, Mets, Knicks, Giants. A *Top Gun* poster. A green and maroon quilt covered the bed, betraying a concave mattress. To the right of the bed were shelves made of two-by-fours held up by cinder blocks holding an Onkyo stereo system and an impressive collection of cassette tapes and CDs. On the far wall, a dresser with an oval mirror, a few photos tucked into the crevice where mirror met frame. Photos of a young, grinning Daniel with various friends; number 44 posing knee-down, football in hand, on the fifty-yard line; number 10 in a baseball uniform armed with a bat and smiling at the camera. The two of them at their wedding. Erin cringed at how different they looked. The hair, the makeup. The look of unmarred confidence in life.

On top of the dresser were two bottles of cologne, Polo and Drakkar Noir. She sniffed them both, breathing in hazy memories. She opened drawers, rough wood scraping against wood. Socks and boxers and underwear all neatly folded, patiently waiting to be worn. Athletic shorts and sports jerseys and T-shirts that Daniel used to wear on weekends. Erin pulled one out and pressed it to her nose, but it didn't smell like him anymore. It smelled of old person and burned coffee, worn linens and dust-lined drawers.

The mirrored sliding closet doors held Daniel's wardrobe, transplanted from their Manhattan apartment. White and light blue button-down shirts, navy blue and charcoal suits, a hanger holding several ties, most given to him by Erin. She had assumed all of this stuff had been sold, given to Goodwill, thrown away. Apparently what she couldn't bear to keep, Helen couldn't bear to give away.

Erin ran her hands over the clothes numbly, wishing as she had a million times before that she could bring him back, somehow. See his smile just one last time.

A stack of jeans was folded neatly on a shelf. She pushed her fingers into the pockets, searching for remnants of Daniel's life. A receipt from Patsy's Pizza, an old Metro card, some loose change. Encouraged, she rummaged through all the pockets. More receipts—Duane Reade for toothpaste and mouthwash, a latte at Starbucks.

Something hard and metal in one front pocket of Levi's. Erin dug in, turned it to vertical, slid it out.

It was a gold tube of Estée Lauder Rich Red lipstick.

Erin pulled off the top and set it carefully on the dresser. Twisted the bottom to make it rise. Its angles were clean, not yet flattened by use. It'd been a new tube when Daniel picked it up from the street and tucked it into his pocket that warm September afternoon before the world changed.

In the mirror, her face was tired and haunted, but strong. A few lines and creases with age, but good bone structure, defined angles. She still had something to work with.

She applied the lipstick slowly, breathing in the crayon scent of old wax. The right half of the top lip first, then left. A swoosh along the bottom. As she rubbed her lips together, something shifted. A hint of energy she hadn't felt in a very long time.

She'd given ten years to that one September day, the best sacrifice she had to make. Given herself over to Daniel's life and goodness completely. Done her penance. As Cathleen said, it was time to move on.

In his room, Erin felt forgiveness and permission envelop her like a lover's embrace. Chills began deep and radiated out, like being warmed by the fire after a walk in the snow. She twisted her wedding rings around a few times. Slowly and gently removed them. Tucked them into the front pocket of her pants.

In the mirror, surrounded by photos of a smiling Daniel, she mouthed, *Thank you.* Then she walked out of his room, taking nothing but her lipstick.

Acknowledgments

This book began its journey in September of 2015, when I toured the September 11 Museum for the first time. My husband Billy and I lived in New York City from 2000 to 2003, but we had since moved back to Texas to raise a family. On September 11, 2001, he was at work on the 85th floor of the north tower of the World Trade Center when the first plane hit, and like most people on the 91st floor and below, he was able to escape the building and get out safely, helping save people along the way.

After that day, we tried to move on. We had kids and jobs and busy lives and we tried not to dwell on the "what if" scenarios that inevitably snaked their way into our thoughts.

But when we visited the museum, it all came back. I was emotionally overwhelmed by the intensity of the displays at the museum, especially the artifacts found and excavated from the site, the speakers overhead playing clips of news footage from that day, and, tucked away in an alcove with warning signs to those who dared enter, images of the victims who'd fallen to their deaths. The line between my husband and those images, between life and death, was disturbingly close. I studied their faces, scrutinized their stories, wondered how their wives and husbands and parents and children moved on.

After the tour, I went straight to the airport, and at the gate I opened my laptop and began to write Daniel's story. I am lost for words to describe what the victims and their loved ones must have experienced that day, but I did my best to acknowledge them, remember them, honor them.

Thank you to Chris Cander, my best friend and walking partner, for the writing wisdom, inspiration, reminders, and support she gives me daily. We have resolved so many plot issues and life problems while trekking through the neighborhood. Thanks as well to all my other Fun Friday friends who support me, make me laugh, and are there for me when I need them—Sarah Blutt, Simmi Jaggi, Kat Tramonte, Lee Ann Grimes, Theresa Paradise, Holly Wimberley, Sabrina Brannen, and Paige Dominey.

I'm in three fantastic writing groups—Sushi Monarchs, the Salon of Literary Forensics, and the Best Damn Fuckahs—with immensely talented writers and friends who inspire me and challenge me to be better at telling stories; in addition to Chris and Sarah, they include David Eagleman, Mark Haber, Cameron Hammon, Melissa Olson, Kim Tidwell, Sheri Boggs, Nina Barufaldi, and Sarah Orman.

I'm so thankful for feedback from friends and early draft readers Anissa Paddock, Katie Forney, Carolyn Forney, Cindy Burnett, Tami Kazdal, Allison Cunningham, Susan Dison, and Terri Lewis. Special thanks to John Lightsey, FDNY Dispatcher, who was working on 9/11 and graciously gave me his perspective to help ensure authenticity. A huge thanks to another amazing writer, Laura Heffernan, who loved the book so much that she chose me as her Pitch Wars mentee.

Thanks to the She Writes Press team, especially Brooke Warner, for believing in me and creating such a vibrant community of writers, and Shannon Green, who kept this project on the rails. Gratitude to all the other authors in the cohort who taught me, showed me the way, helped me, lifted me up, and inspired me. And thanks to the BookSparks team and Crystal Patriarche, who helped me to fearlessly launch this baby into the world.

To Billy, for always supporting me and taking the kids to Chick-fil-A more times than I can count. And of course to Bella, Luke, and Lexie, for putting up with my laptop always being in front of me and for being the funniest and most amazing kids in the world, and who wouldn't be here if their dad had been on the other side of that line.

ABOUT THE AUTHOR

photo credit: Chris Cander

TABITHA FORNEY writes books to appease the voices in her head. She's a mom, attorney, and yoga devotee who lives in Houston with her three kids and a husband who was on the 85th floor of the north tower on 9/11 and lived to tell about it.

SELECTED TITLES FROM SHE WRITES PRESS

She Writes Press is an independent publishing company
founded to serve women writers everywhere.
Visit us at www.shewritespress.com.

Center Ring by Nicole Waggoner. $17.95, 978-1-63152-034-1. When a startling confession rattles a group of tightly knit women to its core, the friends are left analyzing their own roads not taken and the vastly different choices they've made in life and love.

Stella Rose by Tammy Flanders Hetrick. $16.95, 978-1-63152-921-4. When her dying best friend asks her to take care of her sixteen-year-old daughter, Abby says yes—but as she grapples with raising a grieving teenager, she realizes she didn't know her best friend as well as she thought she did.

The Trumpet Lesson by Dianne Romain. $16.95, 978-1-63152-598-8. Fascinated by a young woman's performance of "The Lost Child" in Guanajuato's central plaza, painfully shy expat Callie Quinn asks the woman for a trumpet lesson—and ends up confronting her longing to know her own lost child, the biracial daughter she gave up for adoption more than thirty years ago.

Profound and Perfect Things by Maribel Garcia. $16.95, 978-1-63152-541-4. When Isa, a closeted lesbian with conservative Mexican parents, has a one-night stand that results in an unwanted pregnancy, her sister, Cristina adopts the baby—but twelve years later, Isa, who regrets giving up her child, threatens to spill the secret of her daughter's true parentage.

Shelter Us by Laura Diamond. $16.95, 978-1-63152-970-2. Lawyer-turned-stay-at-home-mom Sarah Shaw is still struggling to find a steady happiness after the death of her infant daughter when she meets a young homeless mother and toddler she can't get out of her mind—and becomes determined to rescue them.